UNRIVALED

UNRIVALED

Jerica MacMillan

Marycliff Press

Unrivaled
Jerica MacMillan
Copyright © 2021 by Jerica MacMillan

ISBN-13: 978-1-956937-00-8

PROLOGUE

Tiffany

A familiar voice calls my name, but I ignore it. It's Carter. My ex as of two days ago when I went to his house to surprise him with his favorite ice cream only to find him balls deep in Jenny McKnight, one of the sophomore cheerleaders.

She's here tonight. Why isn't he bothering her and leaving me alone?

Ignoring Carter, I move closer to Ethan, the guy I'm dancing with, and place his hands on my hips, moving with the thrumming beat that reverberates through my body.

Ethan's fingers tighten, giving me a quick squeeze, and then let go. "I like you, Tiff," he says in my ear, "but not enough to be on Carter's shit list. Sorry."

Then he backs away, leaving me dancing on my own

in the middle of Dax Bowman's crowded basement.

Frustrated, I spin around and look for Carter. I catch sight of his perfectly gelled, dirty blond hair at the foot of the stairs, following it down to find an angry glare on his face and his hands on his hips. Ugh. And to think I thought he was cute for actual years. We've been together since halfway through freshman year. Everyone always said how adorable we were together. The classic All-American power couple—blond, attractive, and athletic. This was supposed to be our year—the quarterback and the cheer captain, high school royalty.

But that's all over now, and having him standing there glaring at me like *I'm* the one who did something wrong is too much. *He's* the one who fucked up and shit all over everything we've had. We were supposed to go to college together. It was just a question of where. Since all the big football programs recruiting him also have great cheer programs, I was going to follow him wherever gave him the best deal.

Not now, though. Now I'm going to reevaluate everywhere that we've applied and weigh where I want to go for myself.

"What do you want, Carter?" I demand, arms spread wide. "You don't get to tell me what to do anymore, remember? Isn't Jenny here? You said she didn't stress you out as much. Go find her and chill out. Leave me alone."

Pushing past him, I start up the stairs, but he grabs my arm and spins me to face him. "Look, Tiffany," he says, remorse replacing his glare. "I'm sorry, okay? I screwed up. I know I did. Please give me another chance."

I yank my arm away. "No. You were pretty clear the other day that I'm too much for you to handle. So I'll just take all my too much and find someone who can. Leave me alone."

"Tiffany, please," he calls after me, but I don't even acknowledge him as I stomp up the stairs.

This was supposed to be fun. A party to relax and celebrate how far we made it in the postseason, even if the football team lost tonight to our crosstown rivals in the semifinals for state. It's not quite the state championship season we were hoping for, but considering I won't have to keep cheering in the frigid November evenings anymore, I'm not too torn up about it. And the fact that it pisses Carter off makes the loss even more bearable. Not that I'm saying that out loud to anyone other than my best friends, Maddy and Heidi.

Maddy sidles up to me when I exit the door at the top of the basement stairs, a cup in each hand. She hands one to me and taps her cup against it. "I saw Carter go downstairs and figured you could use a drink when you came up."

I give her a grateful smile and take a sip of some kind of spiked punch—fruity with a kick. They don't call it punch for nothing. After another sip, I shake my head. "I'm gonna have to take it easy. Dad'll be grumpy tomorrow because of the loss. No need to add a hangover to the misery."

My dad's the football coach, and he's the only reason I'm actually a little sad that we lost. I know about football from him and from dating a football player for the last four years, which makes following the games from the sidelines easier. But I'd be lying if I said I cared very much about the sport in general. I'm far more interested in my own sport and crafting routines to wow the crowds at halftime. There's not much of a budget for competitions, but we've done well at the few we've managed to go to.

Maddy grins back, her hips swiveling to the music that makes its way up the stairs. It's quieter up here, with fewer people, making it easier to talk and move around.

There's a shift in the air, and everyone's gaze swivels toward the door. A group of guys comes in, bringing a gust of chilly November air with them, though in the confines of the house, the fresh air is welcome. Fresh air and fresh faces.

They're cute in their letter jackets, even if the maroon and silver mark them as Ridgeview students—the school that just tanked our chance at the state football championship.

There's some grumbling as people take in their appearance, but then one of the younger cheerleaders hops up from her spot on the couch and throws her arms around one of the guys. He kisses her and follows her back to the couch, settling in with her on his lap.

My eyebrows climb my forehead. I guess that explains why Ridgeview students are at an Eastwood party. But the part of me that's been inundated with school spirit for years can't help feeling like she's a traitor.

The other four step into the room, talking and laughing as they remove their jackets and toss them on the chair where everyone's coats are piled.

"Good thing Carter's still downstairs," Maddy mutters next to me. "Because I don't think he'd much like Grayson Kilpatrick being here to rub Ridgeview's victory in his face."

As though he can hear us talking about him from across the room—though of course he can't—Grayson Kilpatrick lifts his head and looks right at us as he runs a hand through his short, dark hair. His eyes move up and down, taking in the crop top and denim mini I put on after the game to come to the party tonight, and a slow smile comes over his face.

"Oohhh, looks like someone's caught his eye," Maddy says, nudging me forward with her elbow. "Go have fun. Do you want me to send Carter up for an eyeful or distract him so he doesn't interrupt?"

Before I can answer, Grayson approaches me, and something flutters in my belly at his approach. I honestly haven't felt this way about a guy in a really long time. I've been with Carter for so long that I'd forgotten what the first thrill of attraction feels like.

Maddy slips away as I smile up at Grayson. "Congratulations on your win."

His plush lips pull even wider, and he places a hand on his chest. "The head cheerleader for the rival team congratulating me on my win? I'm shocked."

I shrug one shoulder, tilting my head and dragging my fingers across the low scoop neck of my top, drawing his eyes to the movement. "Good sportsmanship was drummed into me from a young age. You played well. It was a hard-won victory. You deserve the win. Good luck with the championship."

His brown eyes light up when they come back to mine, his smile turning more sincere and losing some of its arrogance. "Thank you. Your team played well too. And I saw some of those tricks your squad pulled off. You guys are really good."

My cheeks warm from the compliment. "Thanks."

We stare at each other for a long moment, apparently having exhausted the available topics of conversation. But since I haven't really flirted with a guy in so long, I'm not about to let this opportunity slip through my fingers.

I wonder what Maddy decided between making sure Carter sees me with Grayson Kilpatrick or keeping him away ...

Because I honestly wouldn't mind if Carter saw me making out with his biggest rival. No one else is willing to step on his toes, but Grayson clearly doesn't care a bit about Carter's feelings.

Perfect.

Finishing my drink, I set it down and reach for Grayson's hand. "Come on. Let's go downstairs and dance."

He drags his gaze over me again and bites his lower lip. "Sounds good."

Tangling my fingers with his, I tow him to the staircase. When I glance at him over my shoulder, he gives me a sexy, heavy lidded smile.

Yeah, Grayson's presence is offsetting my irritation with Carter nicely.

The music grows louder as we descend the stairs, the low pulse turning into a booming thump. I pull Grayson to the middle of the basement where there's a clear space full of couples and groups dancing.

Without an ounce of shyness, he hooks an arm around my waist and pulls me close as we begin moving together to the music. We dance through two song changes without speaking—and without interruption from a certain jealous ex. When the next song starts, he leans in close, and I think he might kiss me, but instead his warm breath fans over my ear, making me shiver.

"Weren't you dating Carter Vandermeer?"

Ah. Right. Apparently our reputation as the golden couple extends beyond the halls of Eastwood High School. With a shrug and what I hope is a convincing laugh, I wave that away. "Oh, yeah. Him. We were. We broke up. And what about you? Isn't there a hot girlfriend waiting to celebrate with you?"

Grayson's eyebrows jump up his forehead, a smile stretching his lips as he shakes his head in a quick negative. "Who broke up with who?"

"Can we not talk about Carter and me? It's not exactly a fun story."

He examines me, and understanding slowly dawns on his face. It makes me really uncomfortable, because I don't know what he could possibly have put together from such innocuous statements. People break up all the time, especially in high school. It really shouldn't be that big of a deal.

"Gotcha," he says at last, pulling me close again, his

hands moving my hips against his, letting me feel the effect my proximity is having on him.

And wow. Is this an offer? Is he wanting to hook up? Do I want that? I was just thinking dancing and making out, but …

Biting my lip, I look up into his face. His eyelids lower to half mast as he stares at my mouth and licks his lips.

He lifts one hand, smoothing his thumb over my lip and freeing it from between my teeth, then lowers his head and brushes his lips across mine. At my gasp, he does it again, this time sliding his tongue into my mouth.

Are we still dancing? I'm not sure, because all my attention is on kissing this guy. His fingers flex on my hips, moving farther back like he wants to grab my ass but doesn't. I rub against him as much as I can, grateful when he shoves his thigh between mine, giving me something more to rub against.

When I groan softly into his mouth, he tears his lips from mine, his eyes intent and searching as he looks at me. "You want to find somewhere more private to continue this? Or do you like putting on a show?"

My cheeks heat at the idea of putting on a show. "Somewhere more private," I answer quietly.

Lifting his head, he looks around, and apparently finds exactly what he's looking for, because seconds later he spins me in front of him and guides me through the crowd toward a door in the back corner of the basement.

He closes the door behind him and flips on the light, revealing a small bedroom with a window high on the wall covered by light blue curtains and only a full size bed, a dresser, and a side table inside it. It doesn't look like it's used regularly judging by the nearly empty closet standing open next to the dresser.

Grayson sits on the foot of the bed and pulls me close by our joined hands, urging me into his lap. I follow his lead, straddling him and resting my weight on his muscular thighs.

When he spreads his legs, mine go wider too, my skirt hiking up indecently high.

He makes a sound of satisfaction, his hand cupping my head under the fall of my curls and bringing my mouth to his again.

I'm not sure how long we make out, but it's long enough for me to relax into him and enjoy his touch, the way his hands grip and squeeze and explore over my clothes until I'm grinding against the bulge in his jeans.

Wrapping his arms around me, he pulls me down onto the bed with him, rolling over so I'm next to him.

He props himself over me on one arm, his other hand growing bolder as I sift my fingers through his short, dark brown hair. He smooths his hand down my side, then back up, his fingers sliding under my top, curling around my rib cage, his thumb stroking back and forth along the bottom of my breast. When I don't object to that touch and instead push my chest against his in search of more sensation, his thumb moves higher, finding my nipple through the thin padding of my bra and teasing it to a hard peak.

He dips his head and claims my mouth in another deep kiss, all lips and tongue, his hand growing bolder, dipping into the cup of my bra, his skin shocking and hot against my bare breast. But he's paying attention to my reactions, because when I suck in a breath, he slows, letting me get comfortable with his touch there before brushing my nipple with his thumb again, varying his touch until I'm arching and rubbing against him.

It's different. The way he touches me is somehow both rougher and more gentle than the way Carter handled my boobs. He'd pinch and twist right off the bat, regardless of my reactions. And if I ever said I liked something, he'd dive right into doing that the next time with no warm up, no awareness that sometimes I'm more sensitive or that I don't want the exact same move every time. Just straight to pinching and pulling, and if I asked him in the gentlest way possible to go easy or warm up to that or anything at all, he'd pout about me being critical of him in bed.

Somehow Gray doesn't even need verbal directions— not that I could give them with his tongue wrapped around mine. He follows my body's lead instead, which makes me bolder, letting my natural reactions take over rather than trying to suppress them so I don't embarrass myself or hurt his feelings.

Nudging my knees apart with his knee, Gray settles between my thighs, hips pressed against mine, the hard ridge of his erection once again right. There.

He grinds himself into me, and our kiss gets more frenzied, more intense. When he pulls away, panting, his lips look as red and swollen as mine feel. With his eyes on mine, he reaches between us and pulls my skirt up, running his fingers over my panties. "This okay?"

Swallowing hard, I nod.

His eyes narrow a fraction like he's not convinced, though his fingers keep caressing the cotton between my thighs. "You sure?"

"Yes," I breathe, and that seems to be enough, because his fingers slip beneath the elastic, and he starts to pull my panties down.

"Lift up for me," he murmurs, and I do. Dear god, I do.

He runs his hands up my thighs, the air cool on my wetness as he spreads me wider. "Look at you," he says in that same quiet voice. "So wet for me already."

My cheeks heat as a fiery blush races up my chest and over my face.

His eyes meet mine, and he chuckles softly, his fingers sliding through my wetness and gliding up and over my clit in a way that makes me gasp. Leaning over, he kisses me, his tongue diving into my mouth again as his fingers continue to work me slowly.

When I start pushing my hips against his hand, he slips one finger inside me, then two, moving them in and out of me a few times before sitting back on his heels again. He pulls his shirt off, and I can't help enjoying the sight of his body. He's leaner than Carter, but if anything I think he's sexier. Or maybe that's just because I don't like anything about Carter anymore. I should probably stop comparing him and Gray, but it's hard since that's my only frame of reference.

Gray jerks his chin at me. "You wanna take your top off?"

My cheeks heat up again, but I jerk my chin down in a nod, planting my arms behind me and pushing myself back so I can sit up. I pull my shirt up and over my head, then reach behind me to unhook my bra, but stop when he gets a big grin on his face and shakes his head.

"Let me."

Another furious blush, and there's no denying the amusement in his eyes as he watches it wash over my skin. But he doesn't comment on it, instead tipping my chin up with two fingers and kissing me briefly.

"Babe, these tits are amazing," he says when he pulls back, cupping my boobs in his hands and holding them up as he stares down at them. Circling the nipples with his thumbs, he leans down and sucks on one, biting down gently before pulling away.

Reaching into his pocket, he pulls out his wallet and retrieves a condom, holding it up with a raised eyebrow.

At my nod, he grins again, standing to shuck off his pants and underwear, and then he's totally naked before me and rolling a condom down his dick.

I know I already decided to stop comparing him to Carter, but I really, really can't help it. Because he's packing a lot more heat than Carter.

He lets out another chuckle when my eyes go wide, his fingers wrapping around his dick and stroking himself. "You ready for me, sweetheart?" he asks.

Another jerky nod from me, another smile from him, his eyes hooded as he looks me over and bites his lower lip. "Lay back."

I lower myself to my elbows as he climbs over me,

resituating himself between my thighs, and I lie back against the pillows as he lowers himself to his elbows.

He claims my mouth in another kiss, this one surprisingly gentle, and then I feel the broad head of his dick pressing against my entrance. He withdraws, then presses forward again, sliding in just a little before pulling back, repeating this, going incrementally deeper on each thrust, until he moves my leg over, spreading me wider, and sinks all the way in.

With him inside me, it's even more obvious how much bigger he is than Carter. I feel so full, stretched, stuffed.

I must let out some kind of sound, because he stays still, raising his head to look down at me, his eyes searching my face as he brushes a strand of hair off my neck. "You alright, baby?"

Breathless, I nod. "Yeah. Yeah. Fine. You're just …"

His lips curl up in a satisfied smile. "Bigger than you're used to?"

Another hot blush covers my face as I nod again, which only makes his grin go wider.

He drops a sweet kiss on my lips. "Don't worry, baby. I'll make it good for you," he whispers.

I gasp when he starts moving, because it's so intense. But he goes slow, giving me time to get used to him, and soon I'm pressing up to meet him. When I plant my feet on the bed to get more leverage, he lifts up and looks down. I follow his gaze to where he's moving in and out of me.

His hand cups my face, his thumb over my lips.

"Open up for me," he says, soft and rough.

I do as he asks, accepting his thumb into my mouth, sucking and swirling my tongue around the tip. His eyes meet mine, bright with lust, and he groans as he pulls his thumb from between my lips. "Fuck, babe, that'd feel amazing on my cock."

The smug smile I give him in response melts away when his now-wet thumb slides over and around my clit. His eyes find mine again, watching my response as he starts out light, varying how and where he rubs until I give a favorable reaction.

When I do, he grins, and gives a hard thrust. "There we go. Told you I'd take care of you."

He picks up his pace, continuing to rub circles around my clit with his thumb while I writhe against him. When he stops, I whimper, but he just gives me another one of those boyish grins.

Pulling out, he taps the outside of my thigh. "Flip over for me. I can get you better this way."

I do as he asks, rolling onto my belly and letting him pull my hips into the air. He drags the head of his cock all over my soaked pussy, rubbing it on my clit before moving to my opening and sinking in with a groan of satisfaction.

From this angle he feels even bigger, and his heat washes over my back as he leans over me, planting one hand next to my elbow, his other hand snaking over my hips and between my legs.

"Fuck, baby, you're so tight like this," he says as he gathers my wetness with his fingers and paints my clit with it, strumming it as he gets into a rhythm, the only sounds in the room the slap of his skin on mine and our growls and sighs of pleasure.

When he starts moving faster, I worry I'm going to be left wet and aching without the satisfaction of an orgasm. Squeezing around him, I close my eyes and focus on the sensation of him in and around me.

"I feel you squeezing," he mutters. "You close? Please, please be close. I'm almost there, and I want you with me."

His fingers move faster, and he slams into me harder, his cock dragging over that spot inside me that makes everything feel even better.

"Let me feel you," he growls. "Let me feel that tight pussy squeezing my cock. Come on, baby. I got you. Give it to me."

And like he's actually capable of commanding my orgasm, I fall apart under him. His steady rhythm falters as he fucks me through my orgasm and his own.

His hand falls away, and I feel his weight sagging against me for a second before he places a kiss between my shoulder blades and pulls out.

I roll onto my side, looking up at him as he deals with the condom and cleans himself off. Once that's taken care of, he crawls over me and peppers kisses over my shoulder before kissing my lips once more. "Thanks, babe. As tempting as round two is with you lying here all sexy and satisfied, we better get dressed and head back out there before anyone barges in on us."

Sighing, I flop onto my back as he climbs back off the

bed. He lets out a chuckle as he pulls his jeans back on and tosses my bra at me.

I pull it off my face and sit up, giving him a mock glare as I put it on. He just grins back. "Aw, baby, don't be mad. I'm just trying to help you out."

"Uh-huh. Sure, sure. 'Helping.'" I make air quotes with my fingers around the word.

He lets out a low, sexy grunt. "You liked my help a few minutes ago." Another chuckle as a wave of heat washes over me from chest to scalp. "And *now* you're embarrassed. That's cute."

Pulling on his shirt, he runs his hands through his hair and leans over the bed in front of me as I sit on the edge, preparing to pull my skirt on. With his fists propped on either side of me, he gives me another kiss. "Don't leave without giving me your number. And if something happens, be sure to find me at the next party. I'm happy to help you get revenge on your ex as many times as you like."

"Noted." I can't help chuckling, not sure if I'll bother giving him my number. Yeah, in this case, revenge was pretty sweet. But I'm not sure I want to make a habit of hooking up with the rival team's quarterback on the regular. My dad would probably kill me, for one. And having just gotten out of a several year high school relationship, I don't know if I want another one. I want some time to just be me, enjoy my senior year with my friends, maybe date, maybe don't, but nothing serious for sure.

Like a gentleman, he waits for me to finish dressing

before slipping out of the room. I wait a few more minutes before following him out.

As soon as I've returned to the party, Maddy grabs my arm. "There you are! Did you get what you came for? Because I am beyond ready to leave. Let's go." Before I can even answer, she starts tugging me toward the stairs.

"Wait, what about Heidi? Are we just leaving her."

Maddy makes a disgruntled sound. "Yes. We absolutely are. She can find her own way home."

Before I can register another protest, we're out the front door and into the night. I manage to shake off Maddy and shoot a text to Heidi letting her know we're leaving and asking what happened. She responds that it's fine and she'll talk to me later.

Rolling my eyes, I follow Maddy to the car.

I guess that's my decision made for me, though. I won't be giving my number to Grayson Kilpatrick. And I'm definitely not planning on finding a Ridgeview party to crash for another hookup. This was fun for sure. But not a habit I'm trying to form.

* * *

About six weeks later

Another wave of nausea overwhelms me as I sit on the closed toilet lid, watching the seconds on my phone timer count down one by one. I hit stop just before the timer goes off, picking up the pregnancy test with shaking hands.

Two lines.

I double check the box to make sure it means what I think it means, then look at the test again to make sure I'm not hallucinating, swallowing down the bile threatening to rise up at the confirmation of what I suspected.

It's positive.

I'm pregnant.

Dropping the test in the trash, I scramble off the toilet, throw open the lid, and throw up the little bit of water that's all I've had this morning.

How is this possible? Carter and I were always careful. And the one other person I've slept with in my life used a condom.

Sinking to the ground, I rest my head on my arm propped on the edge of the toilet.

"Fuck," I whisper quietly.

No matter who the father is, I'm screwed.

CHAPTER ONE

Four years later

Gray

Raising a hand, I wave at my buddy Jackson who's waiting for me under a grouping of trees. He lifts his chin in acknowledgment, but doesn't otherwise respond to my confused look. We normally meet outside the athletics center for our workouts. Why would he text me to meet him here?

My eyes stray to the girl standing with him.

That's a potentially interesting development. Jackson isn't known for his prowess with the ladies. Too shy and too oblivious. I've heard rumors that he might be gay, but given how he blushes any time someone mentions a girl liking him, I don't get that vibe.

Perhaps there's something going on with the two of them? Especially if he's delaying meeting up with me for our workout.

As I get closer, my confusion turns to speculation. She looks familiar, but I can't quite place why. I give her profile another scan—blond hair piled on top of her head in a messy bun, cute little nose, layers of sweater and jacket obscure her figure, though when she turns I catch a glimpse of cleavage above the V-neck of the shirt she has on beneath all those layers. Purple joggers, sneakers, and a tote bag slung over one shoulder round out the look. It's the same outfit every other college chick puts on who doesn't feel like making an effort when they roll out of bed for class in the morning, but somehow she makes it look cute and sexy. I can see why Jackson would find her attractive. Hell, *I* find her attractive.

Following Jackson's line of sight, she turns her head, looks at me, and freezes. Her soft, pink lips parted in shock, her eyes widening as she takes me in. Then her mouth snaps shut and her gaze turns distinctly chilly. I swear ice forms over the blue pools of her irises, at odds with the rare sunny and above-freezing early January day.

She makes a show of checking her phone, then turning to Jackson. "Well, I gotta go. See you next class."

Clutching the strap of her bag tightly, she pivots and brushes past me, leaving a hint of some flowery girly scent in her wake.

I watch her march away until she turns the corner and disappears from sight.

Huh.

That was a weird reaction. It's almost like she knew who I was and ... didn't like me.

But why?

I mean, she's not the first person to dislike me on sight, but there's usually a reason for it. My sister's boyfriend, for example. He despised me the moment he laid eyes on me. But I never really held it against him— well, until he decided to use my sister against me a few months ago. But apparently that's not something I'm allowed to be upset about anymore according to my sister. I'm the transfer student who stole his starting quarterback spot, though. I can't say I wouldn't hate him if the situation were reversed. Still. I wouldn't go after his sister. That's fucked up.

But what's the deal with this chick? Is she a McAdam fangirl? If so, she should know he's quite happily taken these days. By my sister. So maybe it's spillover hatred for her?

Turning to Jackson, I nod my head in the direction we need to head and he falls in step beside me. "So who was that?"

Jackson glances back over his shoulder. "Oh, that was Tiffany."

I wait a beat to see if he elaborates, but he doesn't. Typical Jackson. "And? What's the story there?"

He gives me a surprised look. "We have theatre together, and the professor assigned us to do a scene?"

"Oooh." I grin at him and nudge him in the side with my elbow. "Is it a romantic scene? Do you have to kiss her? How're you gonna handle working with a hot chick one-on-one like that?"

His normally tan cheeks turn red, the blush climbing all the way to the tips of his ears. At my snort, he gives me a hard shove. It doesn't do much, though. I'm used to getting pushed around in the pocket, and even though Jackson isn't much shorter than me, I outweigh him by a good fifty pounds. He's bulked up some since August, but the coaches want to keep him light and lean to replace Martinez as the first string wide receiver next year.

Cackling, I shove him back, but not hard enough to make him stumble.

"No," he eventually answers, his voice all exasperated sullenness. "It's not a romantic scene, no I won't be kissing her, and no, she's not interested in me. I promise."

Raising my eyebrows, I look at him. "And how would you know? I've seen chicks throw themselves at you all year long, and you've never paid any attention."

He sighs heavily. "You guys all say that, but you're reading way too much into it. Autumn—you know, the chick with purpley hair that's around a lot?" At my nod, he continues. "She's in our group too, but had to run off to class on the other side of campus. She tasked Tiffany with organizing our rehearsal times, so I was giving her my number and schedule so we can figure it out."

"Ohhh, right. Okay. Just giving a hot chick your number. No big deal."

Ears pink again, he shakes his head. "Shut the fuck up, man."

With a laugh, I pull open the door to the athletics center and we walk in companionable silence to the locker room, where we part ways to change for our workout.

And that's where it hits me—why I recognize Tiffany.

She was a cheerleader. Not for my school, but for our biggest rivals, Eastwood High. I think her dad was also the football coach?

Visions of her with her blonde hair in a high ponytail, curls spilling down to the nape of her neck, a white ribbon tied around it, wearing her navy, silver, and white Eastwood cheerleading uniform as she bounces around on the side of the football field, yelling out cheers.

I'd always thought she was hot in that untouchable, distant way. Firmly off limits, though, with her long-term boyfriend and all.

But then …

Then I'd crashed that Eastwood party with my friends because one of them was dating an Eastwood cheerleader. And there she'd been, standing in front of me like all my dreams come true, no boyfriend in sight.

My buddy Kurt saw me looking. "Heard she broke up with Vandermeer," he muttered. "You gonna hit that?"

Instead of answering, I approached her. And yeah, yeah I did hit that. And I'd wanted more than a quick tumble in a back bedroom at a party. I asked for her number, but she left without giving it to me. And I never saw her at another party again.

I was bummed for a while. I kept an eye out for her for months. But then with prom and graduation and getting ready to go to Ohio, I decided it was probably for the best. I'd broken up with my last girlfriend over the summer, and it was better to leave entanglement free.

I wonder what she's been up to the last few years … What's she getting a degree in that she's just now fulfilling her arts credit as a senior?

Why didn't she give me her number that night all those years ago?

And why does she seem to hate me now?

CHAPTER TWO

Tiffany

I step into the classroom to the sound of my favorite guy's little voice shouting, "Mommy!"

He runs for me, and I squat down, scooping Ben up into a big hug. "Hey, Benny Boo! How was your day?"

Throwing his arms around my neck, he squeezes me again, then he puts his hands on my cheeks and gives me a big smacking kiss on the nose.

Laughing, I give him a squeeze, my heart still racing and my eyes falling closed as I think how close I came to Ben's father just a few minutes ago. The father who abandoned us years ago. Who would've thought that standing around and getting Jackson's contact information to schedule time to rehearse our scene for theatre class would lead to *that*.

Luckily, I didn't actually talk to him. He didn't seem

to know me, his gaze flitting over my body before returning to my face, no flicker of recognition in his expression.

I can't decide whether to be relieved or fucking furious about the fact that he didn't even recognize me, the mother of his child.

But from the way he ignored my attempts to contact him and then took the coward's way out by having his high school football coach tell my dad that he couldn't possibly be my baby's father and that he has no memory of ever meeting me, well ...

If he had recognized me, the ensuing scene wouldn't have been pretty.

After that—after my dad came home from meeting with the coach at Ridgeview who'd said that Grayson didn't even remember meeting me—I vowed to never have any contact with Grayson Kilpatrick ever again.

It should've been easy. He was supposed to leave, go on to play football somewhere far away, and I was never supposed to have to hear his name again. Unless he became famous, of course. But, seriously, what are the chances of a kid from Spokane becoming the next famous quarterback? I mean, I guess someone has to, but it never struck me as likely.

But now ...

Now he's back in town, and his name has been on everyone's lips the last few months as the football team did better in their first Division I season than anyone could've expected.

Why did he come back here? Why would he want to

come back here?

Why didn't I leave?

Well, the answer to that question is right here in my arms. We're still living with my parents, and they help with childcare while I'm in school. They're the reason I don't have to split my time between work and school.

In two years I'll finish my degree in accounting, get a good job with a solid paycheck, and we'll move into a place, just Benny and me. But for now, our current arrangement works well.

Accounting wasn't necessarily my first choice when I was originally planning to go to college—before I got pregnant. I was going to major in Finance and cheer and I'd hoped to one day cheer for a professional team while supporting myself with my degree.

But Ben changed everything. No more cheerleading. And I needed to pick a major that would lead directly and easily into a job.

When I finally accepted the reality that I was pregnant—which took peeing on a half dozen pregnancy tests to confirm what my missed period and puking every day for a week already told me—I was terrified to tell my parents. I didn't know what to do, so I just pretended like everything was normal, like I wasn't pregnant. I'd heard about how such a high percentage of pregnancies miscarry in the first trimester in health class, and maybe that would happen to me, and I could just … not have to do anything. The problem would take care of itself.

But it didn't, of course. I'm not sure how long it took for my mom to catch on that my persistent nausea was morning sickness—probably not long, but she let me carry on in my delusion for at least a couple of weeks before confronting me about it. I'm sure she was waiting for me to come to her with the information, but when I didn't, she finally took the reins and started the conversation herself, finding me in my room one night after dinner while I forced myself to get through my reading for Economics.

She sat on my bed and cleared her throat, gently asking how I was feeling and telling me she'd noticed that I'd been nauseous for two weeks and that she thought I should take a pregnancy test. In fact, she brought one with her, offering it to me.

That's when I broke down and confessed that I'd already taken six and that they were all positive. She held me and stroked my hair while I sobbed out my fears, grateful that she offered nothing but support.

After the paternity test confirmed what I suspected—that Carter wasn't the father—my dad wanted me to get an abortion, especially after the conversation with the coach at Ridgeview. But Mom said it was up to me, and that they'd support me no matter what I decided. I waffled for a while and let Mom make a doctor's appointment for me. When they offered to let me hear the heartbeat, I nodded, and after that my decision was made. I wanted to keep my baby.

And true to their promise, Mom and Dad have supported me every step of the way. I finished the first semester of my senior year in-person, but switched to online when I started to show and had to quit cheerleading, news of my pregnancy spreading through the school. Everyone at school assumed Carter was the father, and he was nice enough to let the rumors go. Of course my parents hate Grayson as much as I do. Who can blame them? If anyone screwed over my kid like that, I'd be making sure I knew all the places to dump a body too.

Shaking off thoughts of Ben's sperm donor, I turn to his teacher Miss Kate with a smile. "How was he today?"

She continues moving through the room, picking up the slips of paper the kids use to practice tracing their names, snapping caps all the way onto markers, and stacking chairs on top of the small tables. "We had a good day today, didn't we, Ben?"

"Yes!" he shouts.

"Do you want to tell your mom what we did today?"

His hands back on my cheeks, Ben turns my face to his. "We learned the letter E! I drew it all by myself." He points to a group of papers on the wall featuring vertical lines with varying numbers of horizontal lines coming off of them. "And we learned words that start wif E, like ephelant and excellent and egg!"

"Wow!" I exclaim, moving closer to the wall of papers so he can point out his purple E with five lines coming off it. "What an excellent E you've drawn." I give him another squeeze. "I'm super proud of you. I'm gonna put you down now so I can sign you out, okay?"

"Kay!"

He slithers down my body and races to his cubby to gather his backpack and jacket while I sign the notebook saying I picked him up, passing off the pen to another parent when I'm done.

"Come on, Ben. Say bye to Miss Kate."

He races over and gives her a high five. "Bye, Miss Kate!"

"Bye, Ben!" she says with a smile, offering me a wave as we head out.

I slow as we approach the outside door, wondering if Jackson and Grayson will still be outside. Will Jackson want to meet Ben if he is? Will Grayson recognize me if he glances at me for more than just a quick once over? Will he acknowledge that Ben is his?

My breath freezes in my chest at the thought, and Ben lets out a squawk of protest as my hold on his hand tightens involuntarily. That bastard doesn't deserve access to a child he abandoned before he was even born. Even if he realizes Ben's his, as far as I'm concerned, he gave up any rights to claim paternity way back then.

"Sorry, Benny," I apologize hastily. "Mommy just remembered something."

He yanks his hand out of mine and races for the door, and I swear I'm going to have a heart attack from this kid.

"Ben, wait for Mommy," I call to my son. "Only grownups are supposed to open doors, remember?"

He waits patiently, little hands wrapped around the bar, ready to push it open as soon as I reach him. "Hurry up, Mommy! I wanna see Gramma!"

Smiling, I pick up my dragging feet and suck in a breath. There's no reason to think that Grayson will recognize me this time, if he's even still outside. And in the future, I'll just need to not let Jackson walk me to pick up Ben. If Jackson's not with me, then there's no chance of Grayson stopping to talk to him, and he definitely won't stop to talk to me. I've successfully avoided him for more than five months. I only need to avoid him for a few more.

When we get outside, it's clear that all my worrying was for nothing. Grayson is nowhere to be seen, and neither is Jackson, both of them obviously off living their own lives, not giving me a second thought.

Thank god.

* * *

"This was fun!" Autumn chirps as we finish rehearsing our scene. "Let's all try to be off book by next time. When are we meeting next, Tiffany?" She turns to me, her eyes wide, a smile stretching across her face.

I roll my lips between my teeth, biting back my smile. This chick cracks me up, and it's totally not on purpose. She's got this boho-chic thing going on with her flowy tops and crystal pendants and pinky purple wavy hair. Tonight she has part of it French braided back over one ear, the tail of the braid hanging down her back. She's all sunshine and charm but she's also very take charge, directing the rehearsal and assigning parts—though with only three of us, there's not a lot of options. The only real choice is deciding which of the female parts she and I get, though she did check with Jackson to make sure he didn't want one of those. He'd blushed to his ears and shaken his head, saying he was fine with the male part.

Something about this trim, muscular football player getting embarrassed about being offered a female role only served to endear him to me even more. I'd already decided that Jackson's a sweetheart with his quiet friendliness. And that moment had just cemented it.

"Okay," she'd said. "It might be fun to do a gender-bending twist, but I'm good with playing it straight too."

Which is why her deciding that I'm in charge of the schedule is hilarious. She's literally running everything else—which is fine with me because I have plenty else to be in charge of, so not having to take charge of this project is a relief—but apparently she doesn't want to handle deciding the schedule.

I'm the master of calendars, though, juggling my class schedule, Ben's preschool schedule, plus keeping track of my parents' work schedules so I know when they're available to help out with Ben. Since football season is over, Dad's more free, which makes having these types of non-class time meetings easier for me. As the football coach at Eastwood High School, his free time is severely limited from August through November or so, depending on how far the team makes it in the postseason.

In the spring he just has to worry about his school day schedule of PE classes, so he's home in mid afternoon and entertains Ben so I can get homework done, including meeting up with study groups or to work on group projects like this one.

Picking up my phone, I look at my calendar. "I could do this time again on Thursday. Would that work for you two?"

They both nod when I glance up, so I type the event into my calendar.

"And Tiffany," Autumn says as she puts her jacket on and picks up her bag, "Jackson and his roommate Eli are having a thing at their place on Thursday evening. You should come. We can go over as soon as we're done rehearsing. If we all have our parts memorized by then, I don't think we'll even need much more rehearsal."

I glance at Jackson to see what he thinks of Autumn's invitation on his behalf. I'm not quite sure how I feel about him anymore since discovering he's friends with Grayson Kilpatrick. But maybe they're not actually friends. Maybe they're just acquaintances. And it's not like Grayson would go around bragging about how he abandoned the girl he got pregnant with his child his senior year of high school …

I probably shouldn't hold Grayson's bad choices against Jackson. Not yet, anyway.

The tips of Jackson's ears are pink, but he nods and clears his throat. "It's nothing fancy. We get together and play video games once a week. It's really relaxed, so you don't have to stay out late or anything."

"Oh, do you have early classes?" Autumn asks.

"Something like that," I offer, not feeling the need to share all the details of my life with everyone. Jackson knows about Ben because he walked me to the on-campus preschool the other day.

I don't hide Ben's existence. But I don't necessarily volunteer it either. Being my age with a three-year-old gets varying reactions, from pity to disapproval and everything in between. I learned a long time ago that navigating that minefield is more trouble than it's usually worth, so I avoid it when possible.

Ben's preschool starts at 9:15, so while I don't have to be up super early, getting him up and ready to go is a lot more work than just getting myself out the door. But Jackson knows the real reason I wouldn't want to stay too late is so I can get home and put my kid to bed.

"Well, it'll be super fun," Autumn says. "I'll be there, my roommate and her boyfriend usually go, and there are a few other girls who show up as well. Plus Jackson, of course, his roommate Eli, and various other football players."

"Oh, yeah?" I ask, trying to be as casual as possible. Because if a certain football player goes, I will definitely not. "Like who?"

Autumn waves a hand airily. "I dunno. It varies, doesn't it, Jackson?"

He nods. "Yeah. Just Eli and me are the only fixtures. And Dani, Eli's friend. Sometimes she brings her roommate, who's lately been bringing her boyfriend, McAdam." He gestures at Autumn. "If her roommate's coming, Hindley will be there too."

I have no idea who any of these people are, but I'm not sure it matters. I doubt I'll be going. "I'll see what I can do."

CHAPTER THREE

Gray

I let myself into Jackson and Eli's place, giving the door a courtesy knock as I open it. Eli waves from the kitchen where he's dumping chips in a bowl. There's more junk food at these things now that the season is over. Not that I can afford to indulge.

Returning Eli's greeting with a jerk of my chin, I nod at a few other people as I make my way to the kitchen to deposit my offering of flavored sparkling water to use as mixers.

"Hey, man. Thanks," Eli says, tearing open the plastic and displaying a few of the bottles on the counter near the alcohol while sticking the rest in the fridge.

"No problem." I grab a cup from the stack on the counter and pour myself a drink. No alcohol for me tonight, though. Not during the week, and not with drills in the morning. Even if I don't drink a lot, the next day's workout always feels like a slog. I wouldn't care if I were in the off-season like these guys, but with the combines coming up in just over two months, I'm not taking any chances. I have to be at the top of my game to make sure I secure my future.

"There's a veggie tray on the coffee table," Eli offers as he pours himself a drink as well, his with a generous helping of vodka added to it.

"Sounds good. What's everyone playing tonight?" Eli and Jackson's video game nights have become something of a tradition since last semester. They started inviting a friend or two over—at first just my sister Piper and her roommate Dani, because Dani and Eli are friends. But somehow it's expanded, one time turning into a full-blown team-wide single elimination tournament. Tonight the crew includes Piper and McAdam—I mean Cal, the second-string quarterback—plus Simon Hindley, the left tackle, and his girlfriend, Ellie, who's apparently now friends with Piper as well. There are a couple other chicks I recognize, plus a few more sophomores and juniors from the football team.

"We're going old school with the original *Super Mario Brothers* tonight. Head over if you want to play. The usual rules apply."

Since the crowd has expanded, the game picks tend to be things that can cycle through everyone who wants to play pretty quickly. It's still fun, but it doesn't have quite the same energy as when there were only a few of us actually playing. We could spend longer on each turn, so we had a wider selection of game choices.

I guess the point is more social now than gaming. Sipping my drink, I head for the living room, parking my ass on the edge of the couch near my sister. I flip her ponytail, and she looks up, the consternation on her face smoothing into a polite smile when she sees it's me.

"Hey, Gray. How's it going?" It sounds like a normal greeting, and it shouldn't make me grit my teeth, but things between us still feel strained, and I really hate it. A couple months ago, she'd reach up and pinch my side and call me buttface instead of Gray. The fact that she's still using my first name means she hasn't forgiven me for trying to protect her from Cal McAdam.

The fact that I was actually right about him using her to try to get in my head and make me fuck up on the football field so he could regain his starting spot doesn't seem to matter. According to her, 'He's not like that anymore,' and that makes everything okay between them I guess.

And to be fair, their relationship does seem like something deeper than what she told me it was multiple times last semester—fucking, and lots of it. Which ... *shudder*. I've never needed to know that about my sister.

The fact is that he's part of her life, and will be for as long as she decides to let him. It's up to me to make peace with that, and I have. Mostly. What I haven't made peace with is her insistence on still holding me at a distance. We've always been close, and since Thanksgiving, we've barely spoken. And when we have, it's been these stilted, polite, perfunctory exchanges.

"Good," I answer, needing to keep up my end of the show. I can't just demand that she go back to treating me like she always used to. For one, Piper's never responded well to being bossed around. And for two ... well, who would that work on anyway? "How's your semester?"

She makes a face. "Busy. Another full schedule."

"You know you don't have to punish yourself by grinding yourself to death, right?" I ask before I can think better of it.

Her eyes flash, her mouth flattening into a thin line as she burrows closer into McAdam's side. His hand tightens on her shoulder in a gesture of support. "Thanks, Gray. I'm well aware of what I do and do not have to do without you explaining it to me. I'm *choosing* to work hard so I can finish sooner rather than later. I'm aware of my limits and capabilities, thanks."

"That's not ..." Trailing off on a sigh, I happen to catch McAdam's eye.

He gives me a sympathetic look. "I think your brother just wants to make sure you're not overloading yourself. But he's well aware that you're smart and capable and wouldn't take on more than you can handle. Right, Gray?" He gives me a significant look, and I dip my head in a nod.

"Yeah," I croak. "Yeah, that's all I meant." It's weird having McAdam call me by my first name when he's called me by my last in varying tones of irritation and disdain for months.

Piper narrows her eyes at me. "Then maybe try saying that next time instead?"

"Sure. Of course. Sorry, Pipes." I touch her shoulder, but she's still stiff. Still mad at me.

Will she ever not be mad at me?

With another sigh, I straighten and look around for another spot to park myself. Somewhere shielded from my sister's irritation.

Should I stop coming to these things and give her some space? Fuck. Maybe. But I don't want to. Jackson and Eli were my friends before they were hers. And it's partly because of me that she even started coming around at all. After I found out Dani was her roommate, I encouraged Dani to help Piper get out more since all she was doing was isolating herself from the world and working herself to death after what happened in California. I hated seeing my formerly daring, fun-loving sister imprisoning herself in a cell of classes and homework, too afraid of repeating past mistakes to even try again.

What I didn't count on was her running headlong toward what looked like the same type of bad situation all over again—a douchey guy just wanting to use her for his own douchey games.

In California it was a frat guy taking nonconsensual nudes and posting them online. Here it was the guy who's had it in for me all year using her to knock me off my game enough to replace me. While it didn't work—I remained the starting quarterback through the Poppy Bowl—he did manage to worm his way into Piper's life and apparently her heart no matter what I or anyone else said to try to change her mind.

I do have to give McAdam credit for the way he handled things with Piper's ex, though. And as far as I know, he and Piper weren't even together at that point. We bumped into the ex and his frat brothers while we were in California for the Poppy Bowl, and I managed to goad the guy into taking a swing at me. Even though I didn't start the fight, Coach Reese was still prepared to suspend me from the game for violating the no fighting clause in the team code of conduct, but McAdam took the fall for me instead, much to everyone's astonishment.

He could've had exactly what he wanted—the chance to carry Marycliff University to victory in their first Division I bowl game. But instead he took the suspension, watching his only chance at a bowl game from the sidelines while helping the offensive coaching staff.

Maybe Piper's right that he's not such a bad guy after all, and I have to admit our interactions since then have been better even if we're not what anyone would call friends.

The seats are all taken, so I plant my ass on the floor next to someone's legs, leaning back against the old brown loveseat.

"Oh, hi," says a friendly voice behind me, and I crane my neck around to see the girl I don't really know but have seen around. "You're Gray, right?" At my nod, she gives me a sunny smile, pushing her wavy light purple hair over her shoulder. "I've seen you around a lot, but I don't think we've met. I'm Autumn."

I take her proffered hand and give her a weird, over the shoulder handshake. She's pretty, and she gives off some of the same flirty vibes as the groupies that come to the larger football team get togethers. But if she's here, she's clearly entwined in the lives of more than one teammate and/or teammate's girlfriend, which means I'm automatically not interested.

My focus is all on going pro, not on relationships. I'm honestly surprised that McAdam and Hindley have gotten entangled in what appear to be serious relationships so close to the draft, even if I'm glad for Piper that McAdam isn't as awful as I thought in the beginning.

Still. How's that going to work when they're gone?

Not that it's my problem. But also why I keep myself entanglement free. I'm happy to have a distraction for a night, but not for the long haul. I don't need anything stealing my focus.

My attention strays to the other girl on the couch with Autumn. Her long blond hair is swept up high on the crown of her head, the tip of her ponytail brushes her shoulders. Pretty pouty lips. Cute little nose. Thin brown eyebrows, darker than I'd expect given the honey-blond color of her hair, arch over her blue eyes.

Holy shit. It's that chick I saw with Jackson, the one I hooked up with in high school. She looks hot tonight, all dolled up. Not that she didn't look hot in her casual clothes, but this is another level.

Interest piqued, I lean in her direction. Maybe I can figure out why she snubbed me all those years ago and see if it has anything to do with the chilly reception she gave me the other day.

"Have you met Tiffany?" Autumn asks, her eyes darting between us. "This is her first time coming to a game night. She's in drama with Jackson and me, and we're doing a scene together."

Tiffany stiffens at being discussed, giving Autumn and me a forced smile before returning her attention to the TV. I glance at the TV as well to see what has her so enthralled. It can be fun to watch someone get through a particularly harrowing part of a game successfully with everyone shouting directions and encouragement. But Jackson's just starting his turn and is only on the first level. Given that he's played half a million times at least, this is no problem for him. Maybe she's never played before?

"We've met," I drawl slowly. Does she remember that night? I mean, I should think so, because otherwise, why get all stiff and prickly around me? I know I didn't leave her hanging then—I relived that night in detail for a long time—so it can't be that I sucked in bed. But why?

"Enjoying the game?" I ask her, trying to be friendly and see if I can get some kind of in.

She purses her lips and jerks her chin down in a perfunctory nod.

Ooookay.

"Did I do something to upset you?" I ask, because if everything I say is going to piss her off, I might as well see if I can figure out why.

She freezes, her eyes darting to me and back to the screen. Then her lips purse, and she nods. "Yes, actually. You did."

My eyebrows jump up my forehead in surprise. I glance at Autumn, but she looks just as mystified as me. Refocusing on Tiffany, who's once again studiously ignoring me, I clear my throat. "Care to fill me in?"

Scoffing, she gives me a glare so full of venom I almost shrink back. But I'm made of sterner stuff than that. I've withstood months of my sister's disdain, after all.

I give her a grin and hold up my hands in surrender, hoping to lighten the mood. "What's the matter? You still mad about an old high school rivalry? That your school lost its shot at the state championship our senior year? We're on the same team now."

At my words, she jumps to her feet. "Yes. That's exactly it. I'm *furious* about an old high school rivalry. Bravo. You've figured me out."

And with that, she stomps to the door, slamming it closed behind her, leaving everyone staring after her.

Well, shit. That didn't work at all.

CHAPTER FOUR

Tiffany

"Mommy," Ben whines, clinging to me and sniffling. "Don't leeeeaave. I want snuggles."

Trying to extricate myself from my sick son's embrace is killing me, but I'm supposed to meet with Jackson and Autumn for our last rehearsal. Which, given the way I stormed out of Jackson's house last week, could be awkward. Neither of them said anything about it during class yesterday, but since we all have places to be afterward, there's not a lot of time for standing around and chatting about why I hate the star quarterback. Or maybe, like Grayson, they think it's all due to an old high school rivalry. While letting everyone continue to think that is easiest, I'm not a fan of how petty it makes me look.

Of course the alternative is telling Jackson and Autumn the truth. Though why shouldn't I? I'm not the bad guy in this situation. Grayson is. *He's* the one who pretended not to know me when informed he'd gotten me pregnant. And while he at least seemed to recognize me this time, he either doesn't give a shit that he got me pregnant and has a kid he's never met running around or he's still pretending he doesn't know.

And accusing me of hanging onto a high school rivalry, as though that would be something to arrange my life around? Ugh. Not even. I didn't care that much about it at the time. Sure, I pretended to, because that's what was expected. But who actually gives a crap about that in real life?

Ben whimpers again, cinching his arms tighter around my neck and bringing me back to the present. I'll worry about his sperm donor later.

My mom gives me a sympathetic look. "Could you reschedule?"

I shake my head. "Our performance is tomorrow. We need to run our scene a few more times to make sure all the kinks are worked out. This is a major part of our grade."

With her focus on Ben and a soft look on her face, she suggests, "Could you meet here instead?"

Sucking in an audible breath, I consider the idea.

"I know it's probably not cool to still live with your parents at your age and you feel like a high school kid inviting your friends to your parents' house. But I'll keep Ben company on the couch. We'll be your dress rehearsal audience. That's a thing that happens, right?"

Chuckling, I shake my head. "I'm not exactly some

insider person in the theatre world, so I have no idea."

Ben sniffs loudly, and I look down to see a snot bubble over one nostril. Grabbing a tissue, I hold it over his nose. "Blow," I command.

He whines and makes a pitiful effort. He hates blowing his nose. He hates being sick. And he hates being with anyone other than me when he feels this way.

And while I couldn't snuggle him while performing the scene, I could still give him attention if we meet here. Plus Mom would make snacks, and the lighting is nicer here than in the library study room we usually book. Someday, when I've graduated and I'm working for an accounting firm and living on my own, I won't have the luxury of doing this. Of course, Ben will be older then and maybe he won't want me as much when he's sick. But I still like it when my mom takes care of me when I don't feel good, and I'm twenty-two. I might as well take advantage of the opportunity while I have it.

"I'll text them and see what they say."

Thirty minutes later, Autumn and Jackson show up at my door. I answer it with Ben clinging to me like a snotty monkey and give them a grateful smile as they file in. "Hey, guys. Thanks so much for accommodating my last minute venue change."

Autumn gives me a sunny smile, her gaze settling on Ben as Jackson closes the door behind him. "No problem. And who's this little guy?"

I hitch Ben up my hip. "This is Benjamin. He's not feeling too good today." I kiss his forehead, and he buries his face in my shoulder, nothing like his usual friendly self since he's feeling crummy. He doesn't have a fever, at least, but when I picked him up from preschool, he was dragging and complaining, and it's gone downhill since then.

"Awww, poor guy," Autumn says, her face a mask of sympathy. "Chamomile tea with honey is good for colds if you can get him to drink it. If he has a sore throat, it'll help with that too."

"Thanks for the tip," I tell her, leading her and Jackson to the living room where Mom has already pushed the coffee table out of the way.

She comes out of the kitchen carrying chips and salsa that she sets on the coffee table next to the paper plates and napkins she's already set out. "Hey, guys. I'm Dana, Tiffany's mom. Help yourselves to some snacks if you like. I'll be keeping Ben company while you rehearse. Otherwise, just pretend I'm not here."

I hide my smile against Ben's head. I love my mom, but ignoring her is basically impossible.

Mom sits on the couch and holds her arms out for Ben, but he just clings onto me even tighter.

"It's alright, Mom. We're not quite ready to start yet." I sit next to her and wait while Jackson and Autumn take off their jackets and get themselves settled, which includes Jackson helping himself to the chips and salsa and folding himself up to sit on the floor. He's not the tallest guy on the football team, which I discovered when I was surrounded by giants at his house on Thursday, but he's not exactly short either. Certainly taller than anyone here.

I manage to sit next to my mom and scootch Ben so he's between us. When it's time for me to stand and perform the scene, he protests with a little whimper, but then snuggles into his gramma, yawning widely as he blinks up at us.

When we finish, Mom claps, provoking laughter from me, but Autumn does a bow like it's a real curtain call. Jackson looks away, his cheeks flushing.

"Alright," Autumn says. "That was really good. Let's run it one more time, and then I think we can get out of your hair and let you get back to taking care of your son, Tiffany."

"Take all the time you need," Mom chimes in, proving my thought that pretending she's not here is impossible.

Autumn gives her a smile as we all resume our places and run it again. This time, Jackson trips over a few of his lines, blushing every time, so we have to do a third run through to be sure we all have our lines and blocking solidified.

When we're finally done, Autumn pulls me into a hug before leaving. "This was fun. We should do it again sometime, maybe without the rehearsal. Or we can hang out somewhere else, and you can bring Ben too if you want. Either way, let's hang out again. I don't know what happened at Jackson's, and I'm sorry for making you go. I won't suggest that again, alright?"

Blinking at her unexpected offer, I just stammer out an, "Oh, uh, alright."

She beams at me and puts her jacket on.

Jackson raises a hand and gives me a small smile, his

hazel eyes warm. "See you in class tomorrow, Tiffany."

"See you tomorrow."

Once the door is closed and locked behind them, I flop down on the couch next to Ben and my mom. He climbs into my lap, and Mom stands to gather up the remains of the snacks she put out. "They seem nice," she says in that tone of voice that's too casual to be real.

"Uh-huh," I agree warily. "They are."

"They're the friends who invited you to their get-together the other night?"

"Yeah. What's your point, Mom?"

She shrugs, setting the dishes in the kitchen, then standing in the doorway, her shoulder propped against it as she studies me. "Just that it's good for you to have friends again. It's okay for you to go out and have fun, even as a mom. What's that boy Jackson's story? Are he and Autumn an item?"

Holding back my chuckle, because I can see where she's going with this a mile away, I shake my head. "I don't think so. Doesn't mean he wants to date me, though."

Shrugging again, she straightens. "Doesn't meant he doesn't, either. You're young. He's cute. It's okay to date, too."

"Thanks for the advice."

She holds up her hands and steps back into the kitchen. "I'm just saying. I want you to be happy, baby girl."

I soften at that, dropping a kiss on Ben's head, noticing that his eyes are nearly closed. Standing, I heft him into my arms. "I appreciate that. I want to be happy, too. But for right now, I think I need to get this one to bed."

Mom crosses to me and rubs Ben's back, giving him a kiss on the head too. "I'll take the morning off so you can go to your classes. Your dad will be home in time to watch him for your late afternoon class."

"Thanks, Mom." I give her a kiss on the cheek, grateful for her support, even if it does include trying to meddle in my love life.

She's a good mom, and, like she said, she wants me to be happy.

As a mom myself, I can understand that.

CHAPTER FIVE

Gray

"Thanks again for hiring me, Mrs. Kilpatrick," Jackson says as we head into the kitchen, just getting back to my parents' house from helping Mom move furniture around one of the houses she's designing. The furniture was delivered yesterday, but apparently Mom can't figure out where she wants everything until it's all actually in the house. We carried one couch to four different spots in each of three different rooms before finally carrying it back where we started.

Mom sets her purse on the counter and levels a glare at Jackson. "How many times have I told you to call me Melissa? Mrs. Kilpatrick is my mother-in-law, and I won't be as old as her for many, many years."

Jackson shrugs, and I chuckle as I grab a couple of

glasses out of the cabinet and fill them from the fridge dispenser. "I'm not sure you're going to get your way on that one, Mom."

Another shrug from Jackson. "My mom raised me to show respect to my friends' parents. It's a hard habit to break."

"Be that as it may," she says as she pulls an envelope out of her purse, "I would prefer to be called Melissa." She sets the envelope on the counter in front of him but doesn't lift her hand, staring him down.

"Yes, ma'am," he says, sounding agreeable, but I can't help grinning, because we all know he's not actually agreeing.

"Say it," Mom commands. "Call me Melissa, and you can have your money."

Jackson's eyes dart to me, and I just shrug and finish my water to hide my smile. He licks his lips, looking all around as the red rises up his cheeks. "Melissa," he says at last, quietly.

Mom gives him a smug smile, releasing the envelope and turning away. "There now. That wasn't so hard, was it?"

"No, Mrs. Kilpatrick."

When she whips her head around, Jackson gives her a cheeky grin of his own, and she mock scowls at him. Then she turns to me, patting my cheek with one hand. "What am I gonna do with you and your friends? Better yet"—she continues, lips pursed—"what am I going to do without you when you're gone? I won't have anyone to move furniture around for me."

I pat her shoulder. "I'm sure you'll figure something out, Mom. You survived for three years with me away."

"Barely."

"I'll still be around," Jackson pipes up, and Mom swivels slowly to face him again, eyebrows raised.

"Oh? And what will you be calling me if you wish to continue working for me?"

His blush is fainter this time, but still there. "Melissa," he grumbles.

"Perfect," Mom beams. "You have friends who can help, I assume? I always need at least two people." At Jackson's nod, Mom lets out a sigh of contentment. "Oh, good. This might be just the in I need. Each of you can bring in an underclassman to help, and I can keep sourcing college football players to help me until I retire." Turning back to me, she pats my cheek again. "Like I said, what would I do without you?"

Laughing, I press a kiss to her cheek. "I'm sure you'd manage somehow, Mom. You always do."

"True, true. Now, boys. Are you staying for dinner? Or do you have somewhere to be?"

"We've got plans, actually," I put in, saving Jackson from having to figure out an excuse. We don't, but my mom makes him nervous as hell anyway, even if she does pay well. This interaction isn't helping with that at all.

Jackson's on the shy side anyway, but when he's comfortable, he'll relax and contribute to the conversation if he has something he thinks is worth sharing. Right now he's got his hands stuffed in the pockets of his joggers, his shoulders up around his ears, and a blush on a hair trigger. This guy needs out of here, pronto.

"Well, I won't keep you, then," Mom says, leading the way into the living room.

I follow, fishing my keys out of the pocket of my track pants and hooking my finger through the ring. Mom pulls me into a hug once we're in the living room and kisses my cheek, wiping the lipstick smudge away with her thumb before releasing me. "Do try calling your sister again."

Letting out a sigh, I take a step toward the door. If this is what conversation's going to be like, I'm glad to be escaping with Jackson. "I have, Mom. Lots of times. The ball's in her court. She's made it clear she doesn't want me around much, so I'm leaving her alone."

She purses her lips and crosses her arms, and I recognize Mom about to launch into a lecture, but I'm saved by Jackson's surprised comment of, "Hey, you know that kid?"

Distracted, Mom turns to see what Jackson's talking about, and her face softens as she takes in the family pictures on the wall. Crossing over to him, she lets out a laugh. "Of course I know that kid. That's Grayson." She points at the framed photo of me when I was four, dressed in brown corduroy overalls and perched on the edge of a large red block at some mall portrait studio, a big grin on my face. "And this is Piper." She indicates the photo next to it taken at the same studio with the same red block, but Piper's pouting.

Mom lets out an indulgent chuckle. "Piper looked so cute in that dress, but she was so mad that we wouldn't let her wear overalls like Gray. So she refused to smile for the photographer, and now her pouty little face is preserved in film."

That about sums up Piper to a T. She might be twenty now instead of two, but she still knows how to hold a grudge, that's for sure.

Jackson lets out a soft grunt, his brows furrowed as he studies the photos. Mom takes him on a tour of our wall of family photos, showing off family and school pictures of Piper and me through the years, but Jackson's attention keeps straying back to those photos from when we were little.

Weird. But if looking at family photos makes him more comfortable around my mom, who am I to judge? She has a big personality and can be too much for some people. I never had a choice but to get used to her.

After their stroll down memory lane, Mom squeezes Jackson's arm and gives me one last hug. "Thanks again for your help, boys. I won't keep you any longer since I'm sure you both want showers before whatever else you have planned tonight. Jackson, I'll be sure to get your number from Gray so that when he's not available, I can call you for backup, alright?"

"Sounds good, Mrs."—at her stern look, he blushes but course corrects—"I mean, Melissa. See you next time."

Jackson follows me to my car, but is quiet the whole way to his place. While that's not unusual, he seems more distracted than like he just doesn't have anything to say right now.

"Everything okay?" I ask as we turn onto his street.

He seems to startle out of his thoughts and looks at me. "Huh? Oh. Yeah. Everything's fine. Just tired. Lots of homework. You know how it goes."

"Yeah. Same."

He opens his mouth like he wants to say something as I stop in front of his house, but then shakes his head and doesn't say anything.

"You sure there's nothing bothering you?" I ask before he can get out.

"Nah." He clears his throat. "Nah, it's fine. See ya later." And with that, he's gone.

CHAPTER SIX

Tiffany

Relief washes through me as the class applauds for our scene. Jackson, Autumn, and I link hands and take our bow like this was a real performance and not just an assignment for our drama class. But according to our professor, giving and receiving applause is a life lesson as well. Something about learning to show appreciation where appropriate and also how to graciously accept compliments even if you think they're undeserved.

Either way, I'm just happy this scene is done and that it went well. I've never thought of myself as someone who could get stage fright—I mean, I performed countless cheerleading routines at packed football and basketball games, including halftime performances and pep rallies. I performed in front of people all the time for three and a half years.

But dancing and doing flips in front of cheering sports fans is a far cry from reciting carefully memorized dialogue—not catchy, rhyming cheers—and having to portray a range of emotions that don't include peppy and cheerful. Nervous butterflies swooped and dove in my belly as we waited our turn, but once we got in front of the class and the rhythm of the scene we rehearsed so many times already took over, it wasn't so bad. And now it's over. I can relax.

The professor rattles off the names of the groups who'll perform next time and dismisses us.

Standing, I put on my jacket and sling my bag over my shoulder, my thoughts already moving to the available snack options for Ben when we get home this afternoon.

"We should celebrate," Jackson says. "Grab a drink or a coffee or something."

"Oh, uh …" I hesitate, caught off guard by his suggestion.

Autumn makes a disappointed face as she pulls her hair out from under her jacket. "I have a class right after this."

"And I have to get home to Ben."

Jackson shrugs, unconcerned. "We can pick something up and bring him a treat. Even if it's just hot chocolate from the coffee shop by the student center. How's he doing?"

While Autumn digs a piece of paper out of her bag, I cross my arms and study Jackson. "He's alright. Clingy and sniffly, but no fever. He'll be bouncing off the walls again in no time."

"Fine. You win, Jackson," Autumn says in a put-upon sounding voice that's contradicted by her wide smile. "How can I resist hot chocolate with the most adorable kid I've ever seen? Come on, guys. I had a high paying gig over the weekend. My treat."

Jackson raises his eyebrows. "What kind of gig?"

"Don't worry about it." She waves a hand dismissively in Jackson's direction and looks at me expectantly. "What do you say, Tiffany?"

"Fine," I relent. "I'll let my mom know you're coming over again. If you really want to celebrate with a three-year-old mucous factory, who am I to say no?"

"That's the spirit," Autumn says, chuckling and leading the way out of the room.

Loaded down with drinks and pastries, Jackson and Autumn follow me to my parents' house, and it feels ... good. Maybe Mom's right, and I have been cutting myself off from trying to make new friends.

When I shared that I was pregnant with my best friends in high school, they were shocked and horrified, even more so when I announced my decision to keep the baby. They promised their support, but once I started online school, their texts and phone calls and time together grew less and less, stopping altogether when they left for college.

Apparently me discussing birth plans and baby gear was a drag. And while I made a few acquaintances at the mommy groups I went to when Ben was a baby, none of them became good enough friends to hang out with outside of that setting. Most of them were older, in their twenties or thirties and married, most already done with college and trying to decide whether to go back to work once their maternity leave was up. And there I was trying to decide how many classes to take, calculating how long it would take to get through my gen eds before I could get to the accounting classes I was really interested in, and deciding whether I should start in the fall or wait until spring.

At least I've always had the support of my parents to help with Ben and encourage me to go to college anyway, even if my experience would be different from the majority of my peers—no going away to some new and exciting place, no dorm living, and no rushing and pledging like I'd always planned. Definitely no college cheerleading. Even though I could probably get back into shape for it, I just don't have the time or the drive anymore.

But I knew and accepted those consequences when I decided to have Ben, and even though sometimes I'm jealous of the carefree existence of most of my classmates, I wouldn't trade him for anything.

Jackson and Autumn park on the street on either side of the driveway as I let myself in the house, only closing the storm door but leaving the main door open so they can come on in.

"I'm ho-ome," I call as I step inside, my coffee in one hand and Ben's small hot chocolate in the other.

"Mama," comes his congested voice as he pops up

from his blanket nest on the couch where he's been watching *Daniel Tiger*. "You're home."

I give him a wide smile. "And I brought you a surprise."

His face brightens even more. "What is it? What is it? Did you get me a toy?"

Laughing, I set the drinks on the coffee table so I can put down my bag and jacket. "No, baby, it's super yummy hot chocolate. You can drink it on the couch, but you have to be really careful not to spill, okay?"

He nods eagerly, and I hand him the cup with a straw sticking out of the lid.

"Remember Mommy's friends from last night? They're here too, and they have some snacks."

His dark eyes get round with excitement, but he's too busy sucking down his hot chocolate to respond.

There's a quick knock on the storm door, then Autumn pokes her head in. "Hey, is it okay if we just wander in?"

"Of course, come on in." I wave a hand from my spot on the couch, beckoning them inside.

Jackson follows Autumn through the door, and they set the bags of pastries and their respective cups on the coffee table. Autumn sits on the floor and starts unpacking the bags while Jackson claims my dad's armchair.

Mom comes in and kisses Ben on the head. "I'm off to work. Your dad should be home about three." Waving at Jackson and Autumn, she says, "It's nice to see you two again. Make yourselves at home and feel free to get refills from the kitchen." She drops another kiss on Ben's head and one on mine before leaving.

"Your mom's so sweet," Autumn says, brushing crumbs from her hands onto a napkin on the coffee table. "That's great she's here to help with Ben. I bet that makes a world of difference."

"It really does. I don't know how I'd manage without them. I know not everyone who finds themselves pregnant in high school has as much family support as I do."

Ben hands me his empty cup and snuggles into me.

"Where's his dad?" Jackson asks from his spot, his voice lacking the light chit-chatty quality that Autumn and I just had.

Freezing, I glance between him and Autumn. Her brows pull together as she glances at Jackson, like she can detect the tension coming off him too. Jackson's usually pretty quiet and easygoing, though he's gotten a little more talkative since we've spent time together working on our scene. But the dark, serious edge to his question has me narrowing my eyes.

"Oh, he's not in the picture." I try to play it off like it's no big deal that the boy wonder quarterback that everyone loves abandoned us. Like acid doesn't burn its way up my throat just at the mention of his name. "We're fine just Ben and me and Gramma and Grampa, right, Benny?" Because we are. Grayson made his choice. And I made mine. I want nothing from him anymore.

Ben nods against me, his head burrowing into my armpit. I jiggle him. "Hey, let's try and go potty alright?"

Without waiting for his answer, I stand and carry him to the bathroom, needing a second away from Jackson's probing stares. I get Ben situated in the bathroom—thankfully he actually needs to go and doesn't object—and with a murmured, "Be right back," I head for the living room, ready to tell Jackson that he needs to save those questions for when Ben's not around at least.

But it seems like Autumn's doing it for me, because when I'm almost back to the living room, I hear her hissing, "Dude. What the hell? You sound like her dad, and I'm pretty sure she already has one of those. She doesn't need you interrogating her about her life and reproductive choices."

From my spot just inside the hallway, I can see the stubborn tilt of Jackson's chin. Neither of them has noticed me. "My sister's a single mom," he says, "but my niece's dad is very involved. I'm just wondering why it's up to Tiffany to take care of her son all by herself."

"She's not all by herself. She has her parents. And again, it's not your business. Unless you think that kid is yours, you should stay out of it."

His lips press together, like he wants to say something but is stopping himself.

Stepping into the room, I hold up a hand. "I got this, Autumn. But thank you." Hands on my hips, I face Jackson. "Ben's dad is not in the picture. And that's all you need to know. Please don't bring that up again in front of my son."

Before Jackson can respond, Ben calls me from the bathroom.

I hit Jackson with another patented mom-glare. "Drop it, Jackson. I know you think you understand because of your sister, but like Autumn said, it's not your business."

After helping Ben finish in the bathroom, we resettle on the couch, but conversation never resumes the light and easy quality it had before Jackson ruined it. I'd thought he was a pretty good guy, sweet and kinda shy. But him pushing like this, stepping out of line, reminds me that he is friends with Grayson. What's that old saying? Birds of a feather flock together? Grayson's a douche. It's not a big stretch that Jackson would be too beneath the shy exterior.

After a few minutes, Autumn checks the time and stands, gathering her things. "Well, this was fun, guys. I'm glad we did it. But I have yet another class, so I need to head back to campus."

She puts on her jacket and waves at Ben, giving him a big sunny smile. "Bye-bye, Ben! It was great to see you again!"

He lifts his chin from the blankets and says, "Bye," in his sweet little voice.

Autumn starts gathering up her trash, but I wave my free hand. "I'll get it. Don't worry about it."

"If you insist," she says, still stuffing everything into one of the paper bags so it's easier to take to the trash can later. With one last, "Bye!" for everyone, she leaves.

Jackson and I sit in relative silence until Ben says, "Mommy, can I keep watching *Daniel Tiger*?"

Smiling, I ruffle his hair. "Of course. Hang on, let me find the remotes, and I'll get it started." Once the show is going again, I take advantage of the fact that I'm already standing to gather up the trash from our impromptu celebratory coffee and pastries.

Jackson stands and moves to help me, despite my murmured protest that he doesn't have to. He follows me to the kitchen, and once there stops me with a touch to my elbow. "Sorry about earlier. I didn't even think that Ben might not know who his dad is." His expression sombers. "Was it ... did he ... were you hurt? By Ben's dad?"

Crossing my arms, I let out a defensive chuckle and shake my head. "No, not like that. I wasn't raped or abused or anything. It was just ... an accident. A random hook up at a party my senior year. Never saw the guy again." Despite my attempts to contact him. He never wanted to see me again, it turns out, even though he'd said he did. Guess when you contact a hookup and say you're pregnant, that changes things.

And while I've technically seen him again, since he's still pretending to be clueless, there's no point in bringing it up.

A range of expressions cross Jackson's face—relief, understanding, ending with a deep thoughtfulness, his mouth turned down in a frown. "You grew up here? Graduated from high school here?"

Now I'm frowning. "Yeah. Why?"

He looks away, shaking his head. "No reason. Just ... no reason." Stuffing his hands in his pockets, he takes a step back. "Hey, this was good. Thanks for indulging my need to celebrate. Comes from being a football player, I think. We always celebrate the wins. I need to get going, though. Homework and …"

"Yeah, no problem," I put in when it seems like he's struggling to come up with another reason to leave. "And don't worry about …" I wave a hand toward the living room to encompass the entire awkward conversation we've had about Ben's dad. Maybe Jackson's not so bad after all. "We're cool, okay?"

He gives me a brief smile. "Good. I'm glad. I do need to go, though."

"Of course. See you later."

He holds up a hand in a wave, and I stay rooted to the spot in the kitchen as he gathers his things from the living room, murmurs a goodbye to Ben, and leaves.

His reaction to my statement that Ben is the result of a random hookup seems … strange. Most people are either disgusted or stumbling over themselves to display their lack of disgust when I share that tidbit. But Jackson seemed like … I don't know. Autumn's words about him thinking he might be the father ring through my head.

Is that it? Is he worried I might've been a hookup from years ago he doesn't remember?

But I know that's impossible, because I absolutely know who Ben's father is. Shaking my head, I let it go. Jackson's worries aren't my problem. And unless he comes around demanding a paternity test, there's no reason to make them mine.

CHAPTER SEVEN

Gray

Jackson's quieter than normal during our workout. And acting weird. He keeps staring at the wall silently, his brow furrowed, punctuated by brief periods where he studies my face like there's a clue to some mystery I know nothing about lurking there.

"Everything alright, man?" I ask after the third or fourth time I catch him studying me while we swap places on the leg press.

He grunts, settling into position on the machine, and without giving me a real answer, proceeds to unlock the safeties and knock out his reps.

When he stops, I prop my arm on the top of the footplate, making it difficult for him to get up unless he wants to push me out of the way. "Dude. Seriously. You've been staring at me off and on all day. What's going on? Did I piss you off by missing yesterday's workout or something?"

With another grunt, he wraps his hands around the top of the footplate and pulls himself to standing, forcing me back unless I want his head clocking me in the face. "You know Tiffany?"

My brows pull together. "The chick from your theatre class? I mean, I wouldn't say I *know* her. I knew who she was in high school because she was the cheerleader who dated the quarterback at our rival high school pretty much the whole time. I met her maybe once before, though. And apparently she's still carrying a grudge from that old rivalry." I shrug, trying to figure out where he's going with this.

"Where did you meet her?"

"Huh?" I'm really thrown by this conversation, and also thinking back over our encounter at Jackson's place last week. She looked really pretty, just like I always thought back in high school, but she's more filled out now, like a woman instead of a girl, her tits bigger than I remember, and they were a lovely handful before.

"Where did you meet her?" he repeats. "You said you met her in high school. Where?"

This is a really weird conversation. And I've never known Jackson to pry like this. "Dude. Why does it matter?"

"It just does," he insists. "Was it at a party?"

Nodding, I remember that night, the way she looked standing with her friends when I walked in, the way she danced with me, grinding against me, letting me take her to a bedroom, all hot and ready for a hookup to get back at her boyfriend.

"She has a kid," Jackson says, jarring me out of the memory.

"Huh?"

"Tiffany," he repeats, sounding pissy at having to repeat himself so many times. "She has a kid. Little boy, three years old. Looks a lot like you in those pictures your mom has up in her living room. When did you say that party was?"

"Whoa, whoa, whoa." I hold up my hands. "Hold up just a second. What are you saying?"

He stares at me, his mouth flat. "When was the party? What month?"

"I dunno," I mumble. "It was just before the state championship, so like November?"

Ducking his head, he counts something on his fingers. "Nine months after that is August. A kid born in August the year you graduated would be three now."

"Dude," I say, feeling all the blood draining from my face, my lips going numb. "What are you saying?"

He levels me with a hard stare. "I'm saying that I think you got Tiffany pregnant that night."

"But I used a condom," I protest weakly.

"Didn't you take health class? Only abstinence has a one hundred percent pregnancy prevention rate."

Swallowing thickly, I shake my head. "No. That's … that can't be possible."

Jackson raises an eyebrow and doesn't say anything.

Heat floods through me, taking the place of the cold

numbness. "Fuck you, man. What the hell? It's not. I used a condom. It's probably her high school boyfriend's. I'd … I'd know. Right? If I got some chick pregnant? I-I'd know. Somehow."

Hands on his hips, Jackson waits patiently for me to finish verbally flailing. But wouldn't I know?

"How?" he asks, giving voice to the question I don't want to acknowledge. "How would you know? You weren't the one pregnant. Nothing about your body would've changed. If she didn't tell you, how would you know?"

"Why wouldn't she tell me?" If Jackson's right, then why not find me? I told her to give me her number before she left, and she never did. But still, she found me once. She could've found me again. If I got her pregnant, why wouldn't she find me and tell me?

Jackson shrugs. "Dunno, man. She didn't say anything about that. She just said the dad wasn't in the picture. To me it sounded like he didn't want anything to do with them. Like maybe *you* didn't want anything to do with them. You really didn't know?"

Shaking my head, my feet start taking me toward the locker room before I even realize I'm moving. "I gotta go." I don't bother to shower, I just grab my bag and keys, not even bothering to change out of my lifting shoes or put on a sweatshirt. I just have to get out of here, get away from Jackson, away from the accusation—revelation—idea—that I might have a kid out in the world that I don't know about. That I've never met.

That looks like me.

I get in the car and start driving, intending to go back to my apartment, but when I actually become aware of my surroundings, I realize I'm almost to my parents' house. Slowing, I pull into the driveway and put the car in park, sitting and staring at the house for a long time.

Eventually I turn off the car and climb out, noticing the chill in the air as I head up the steps and try the handle. It's locked, so both my parents must be out, which is a relief. I don't know what I'd tell my mom if she asked what was wrong right now.

I think I might have a kid?

Jackson says his friend has a kid who looks just like me. She's the daughter of the Edgewood High football coach. And she used me for revenge sex when we were teenagers.

Yeah, definitely not that last one. I do not need to discuss my teenaged sex life with my mother.

Letting myself in with my key, I push the door closed behind me, then go stare at the wall of photos in the living room that caught Jackson's attention when we were here last, staring at the picture of me he was most focused on.

But ... how is it possible? How could I have a kid and not know? Why wouldn't she tell me?

Maybe it's not yours, whispers the voice of denial in my head. She had that boyfriend. The one she wanted revenge on. Though he didn't look anything like me with his dirty blond hair. And Tiffany's blond, so she wouldn't have a kid with dark hair and eyes like me unless the dad had my coloring.

But if she were mad enough at her ex-boyfriend to have revenge sex with me, there's no telling how many other parties she went to and hooked up at during that time. There are a million guys with brown hair and brown eyes. And little kids all have the same round, cherubic faces. I remember my high school art teacher talking about how drawing kids was more difficult than adults because they don't sit still but also because their bones aren't fully formed yet, so their faces lack the definition of adults or something like that.

I never tried drawing kids, and those comments never made me want to try.

But I don't think Jackson would say something to me if he weren't convinced.

Does Tiffany know I'm the father?

I think over the two times I've seen her this semester—when she barely looked at me and scurried away when I saw her with Jackson near the communications building and the game night at Jackson's where she got pissed at me and left.

Holding onto a high school rivalry doesn't seem like a reason to act like that, especially not for the queen bee of Edgewood High School, the head cheerleader with her high school movie stereotype of dating the star quarterback.

But if she knows it's me and doesn't want me in her life, I could just … stay away. Take the easy out. Pretend Jackson didn't say anything, that I'm still blissfully ignorant, focus on my career and go wherever the draft takes me in a few months.

Even as I think of the possibility, my gut twists with anger and disgust. I'd be off making bank as a professional football player, while my kid and his mom struggle? What kind of miserable asshole would that make me, knowing they're out there, knowing they're entitled to my help, and me just ... pretending not to know?

The worst. That would make me the worst kind of asshole.

Savage determination takes over, and I swivel and head for the door, taking purposeful strides toward my car after locking the house behind me.

I'm going to find out the truth. And since Jackson's so eager to stick his nose in our business, he'll be the first one to help me.

* * *

"I need Tiffany's number," I bark as I enter Jackson's house without knocking.

Eli sits up straighter on the couch, pausing whatever he's watching. "Huh? Who's Tiffany?"

"Where's Jackson?"

Brows pulling together in confusion, Eli shrugs. "Dunno, man. I thought you guys were working out together. You should've seen him more recently than me."

Growling deep in my throat, I pull my phone out of my shorts pocket and fire off a text to Jackson.

"You alright, Gray?" Eli asks carefully.

I shake my head in a firm negative. I am absolutely not alright. An H-bomb just dropped in my lap, and I'm surprised I haven't vaporized already.

No, instead I'm going to have to disable the damn thing and figure out how to deal with the new version of reality I'm facing. But to do that, I need to get ahold of Tiffany and find out if her kid is mine.

My phone vibrates in my hand.

Jackson: Be there in 10

"Do you need something?" Eli asks. "We've got snacks and drinks in the kitchen. Help yourself if you need anything."

Sighing, I drop my head back, trying to rein myself in. Eli doesn't deserve my freak out. And if I'm planning on confronting Tiffany, I need to calm down so she doesn't feel threatened or something.

If she's been deliberately keeping him from me all this time, then … just showing up will probably send her running.

But where would she go? She's from here. If she never left, it's likely because her support system is here. I imagine she'd need help raising a kid on her own, especially if she's going to school. Does she work too? How does she get money?

A vision of her living in a squalid shoebox apartment flits through my head, making my stomach turn.

I mean, my place is little more than a shoebox. But it's just for me, and I barely spend any time there. It's a place to sleep and change clothes and do homework. And if I get sick of it, I can go to the library or come here to do homework. Or go to my parents' house. I'm not raising a kid.

Conscious of Eli's gaze following me, I stumble into Jackson and Eli's kitchen. He's probably wondering what the fuck is wrong with me, but I can't handle my own issues right now. I definitely don't have the mental space to make him feel better.

Grabbing a glass out of the cupboard, I fill it with water from the sink and suck it down, hoping it'll calm the roiling nausea in my gut. It doesn't really, but it does force me to regulate my breathing so I don't choke.

And I do need a snack. I'd normally have the chicken I made for this purpose at the beginning of the week, but I'm not at home, so I'll find something here.

Opening the closet door on their pantry, I settle on a chocolate peanut butter protein bar, tearing open the package and taking a huge bite.

That was a mistake. My mouth is dry despite the water I just drank, and chewing is nearly impossible. Refilling the glass, I take a little sip, which makes it a big, slimy mass in my mouth, but I manage to choke the thing down.

The front door opens and closes, and I hear Jackson and Eli exchange a few hushed words, then Jackson finds me staring at the protein bar, trying to decide if I can manage another bite. My body needs the protein, but I'm not sure my gut can handle it right now.

"Hey," Jackson says softly.

With a sigh, I pull the wrapper back over the protein bar and set it on the counter behind me. "Hey."

He stares at me, arm crossed, hazel eyes laced with concern. I stare back, certain I look like absolute shit. Maybe I should've waited for my mom to get home and told her about Jackson's suspicions. My mom's got her shit together. She'd know what to do.

But the thought of telling my parents anything before I know for sure one way or another has my stomach rebelling against the little I just put in it.

Swallowing down the bile, I inhale deeply, trying to get ahold of myself and ignore the echoing, *I have a kid. Do I really have a kid? What if he's not mine? What if he is?* going through my head.

"Can I get Tiffany's number?" I ask, my voice hoarse. I'd clear my throat, but I'm not sure it would make any difference.

Jackson looks me over. "What're you gonna do?"

I shrug, holding out my hands. "Get in touch with her, obviously. What d'you expect me to do? You just drop this bomb in my lap and think I'm gonna ignore it?"

Now it's Jackson sighing, pinching the bridge of his nose between his fingers and shaking his head. "No. No, of course not. But she's touchy, especially where her kid is concerned. I don't want you railroading her either."

A laugh splutters out of me, my hands going to the counter behind me, the edges digging into my palms as I squeeze. "Tell me, Jackson, what's the right course of action here? Do you have experience confronting a chick who you might've gotten pregnant like four years ago? Is there some protocol for confronting a woman you suspect is hiding your child from you that you're aware of?

Because I sure as fuck have never been in this situation before. I don't know what the hell I'm supposed to do. I just know that if I have a kid out there, I want to know for sure one way or the other and then do the right thing."

Jackson sucks in a deep breath, his nostrils flaring, and I half expect him to lecture me or yell at me or ... I'm not sure. But instead he nods once and pulls out his phone. My phone vibrates in my pocket a second later, and he puts his away. "Good luck, man. I have a feeling you'll need it."

CHAPTER EIGHT

Tiffany

I pull my phone out of my bag at the end of my biology class to make sure I don't have any notifications from my parents about Ben. Anything urgent would've rung through if they'd called twice in a row, of course. But sometimes they text me updates about cute or funny things he's done or little videos that he makes for me.

I absolutely have the cutest kid in the world, no contest. Anyone who thinks different can fight me.

But instead of texts from my mom or dad with updates about my adorable son, there are three in a row that make my blood run cold.

Unknown number: This is Gray Kilpatrick
Unknown number: We need to talk
Unknown number: Where are you? I'll meet you

My throat works, but I'm suddenly incapable of swallowing properly, and the only thing keeping me from choking on my own spit is the fact that my mouth has gone completely dry.

How did he get my number? And why does he want to talk to me?

Scalding rage melts the ice in my veins, and I squeeze my phone in my hand, tempted to chuck it at the wall. But I can't afford to replace it, and my whole life is held together by this device.

But I'd throw it in the Mariana Trench if it meant I never had to see Grayson Kilpatrick's name on my phone ever again.

He doesn't deserve my time.

"Tiffany? Are you alright?" says a voice from behind me.

I whip around, but it's just Bonnie. She went to high school at Edgewood too, but she's a couple years younger than me, so our paths didn't cross very often back then. I knew her older sister, though. This is what happens when you only go very part time for your first two years of college. You're still taking sophomore level gen eds when everyone else your age is a senior and getting ready to graduate.

But it was worth it to be able to spend those first two years with Ben. Which drags my thoughts back to Grayson's infuriating text messages.

I paste a smile on my face and nod far too enthusiastically in response to obvious concern. "Yup!

Great! Fine. Everything's fine. I'm fine."

That was not at all convincing.

Bonnie's definitely not convinced, because the concern on her face deepens. "Did something happen?"

Stuffing my notebook and pen into my bag, I make an effort to squash my rage until I can handle it appropriately and far away from people and hope my smile looks a little less forced when I stand and face Bonnie. "I appreciate the concern, but I promise I'm okay."

The fact that I sound more sane probably helps me sell this story, because I am in no way fine at this moment, but I haven't decided what to do yet.

I just know that Bonnie, sweet as she may be, absolutely cannot help me. In fact, no one can help me.

I can't tell my parents. They'll lose their shit, and my dad will start googling the statutes for assault and battery to determine if it's worth the potential sentence of trying to castrate Grayson. And then they'd start contacting attorneys to sue him for child support.

And tempting as those ideas might be, what I want more than anything is for him to leave me alone. Ben and I are good on our own. We don't need Grayson Kilpatrick or whatever amount of money we could bleed from a college student—even if he is apparently on track to go pro if the rumors are to be believed. And I certainly don't need his testicles in a jar.

Leaving the classroom, I look at the texts again, then tap the info symbol, scroll down, and select Block.

He had his chance to do the right thing. Whether he's

in some kind of twelve step program or just suddenly sprouted a conscience, I don't care.

He gave up his right to have access to me or my son four years ago. It's too late to come crawling back now.

* * *

The next theatre class, I avoid sitting near Jackson or Autumn. Autumn gives me a confused look from across the room that I pretend not to see. I'm not sure who gave Grayson Kilpatrick my phone number, but I know it has to be one of them. They're my only connection to him.

Though if I were a betting woman, my money would be on Jackson. Not just because he seems closer to Grayson than Autumn does, but also because Jackson won't even look at me today.

Fine by me. Maybe I'll be able to resume my relationship with Autumn after this.

At the end of class, she gives me a half-hearted smile and a little wave before heading for the door. Her next class is on the other side of campus, and there's no way for her to make it on time unless she leaves immediately. In this case, it's a relief, because it saves me from having to explain why I refused to sit in the chair that she'd so obviously saved for me.

Jackson, on the other hand, lingers, darting glances my way out of the corner of his eyes, taking his sweet time gathering his things, clearly hoping for an opening to talk to me.

Too bad for him that I have no more desire to talk to

him than I do his friend. For all his boyish cuteness with his dark hair and lighter eyes and cheeks that still hold a hint of roundness combined with that quiet reserve that invites confidence, he's clearly not to be trusted. He set me up. I introduced him to my child, invited him into my home, and he fucking set me up. I'm sure my lack of response to his friend's text messages has been a subject of conversation, and he probably wants to convince me to talk to Grayson. But that is a hard fucking no.

Absolutely not.

So I ignore Jackson, pack up my things, and head for the door. I need to pick up Ben. Ben is my focus, and has been since the day he was born. Before then, even. All of my decisions have been about what's best for Ben, and an asshole sperm donor who only wants in our lives now that the sleepless nights are over isn't best for him at all.

But I stop short when I get out the door. Because there standing in my path, arms crossed, looking every bit the athlete who dominates on the football field, is the asshole sperm donor in question.

Grayson Kilpatrick.

CHAPTER NINE

Gray

I hold up my hands in a gesture of surrender at the look of panic that crosses Tiffany's pretty features, quickly replaced by rage. "I just wanna talk," I say quietly. "That's all."

She covers it all with disdain, sneering as she moves to pass me, but I step in front of her and block her way. Looking me up and down, her upper lip curling with contempt, she scoffs, "Oh, really? That's all, huh?" Crossing her arms, she clutches a notebook to her chest and cocks her hip, fixing me with a glare that I'm sure makes lesser men quail. "Fine. Talk."

Spreading my hands, I glance around at the people slipping past us. "Maybe we can take this somewhere a little more private?"

She narrows her eyes, and I can't help thinking about

the last time she and I were somewhere private. The way she looked up at me, her lips parted, the way she tasted, the way she felt ...

But that's not important right now. What matters is that she got pregnant that night and didn't bother to tell me.

Instead of capitulating, she pulls her notebook even tighter against her, and it strikes me just how young she looks right now. When I've seen her before, I thought she looked so mature. Like an adult who's got her shit together, albeit one who hates my guts. But right now she looks young—young and terrified—her mask of disdain slipping the longer we stand here.

And I'm the reason she's afraid.

Rubbing my hand over my face, I try to formulate a new plan. She didn't respond to my original texts, and when I tried again, it didn't show delivered, making me think she blocked me, reducing me to waiting outside the one class I know she has. Because Jackson is in the same class.

I gesture toward the building's exit. "Can I walk with you, at least? I just wanna ask you a couple of questions."

She glares at me for another moment, but then she checks the time on her phone and seems to deflate. "I have somewhere to be," she says, her voice clipped, and then she maneuvers around me—I let her this time—and heads for the door.

I catch up to her and push the door open before she can reach it, holding it for her.

She gives me another narrow-eyed glare. "Holding a

door for me doesn't score you any points, for the record."

"Noted."

When she sweeps past me, walking quickly away from the building, I let the door go on whoever's following her and catch up again.

"You have a kid," I state without preamble. She's not giving me an inch here, so I'm going to have to just claw my way onto some kind of footing.

She glances at me out of the corner of her eye, but doesn't otherwise acknowledge that I spoke.

Sighing, I rub a hand over my face, jogging a couple steps so I can get in front of her and walk backwards. "Jackson saw him. And he's been to my parents' house, so he's seen the pictures they still have up from when I was a little kid. He says your son is the spitting image of me."

She stops in her tracks, her face blank except for the curl of her lip that communicates her loathing for me as clearly as when she stormed out of game night.

I hold up my hands. "Look. I just want to know. Is he mine?"

Her face goes slack with surprise for a second, and she looks away. When her gaze returns to mine, even that lip curl is gone. Her face is completely devoid of emotion. But her voice is full of fire when she shakes her head and says, "No. He's *mine*."

"Then who's the father? That's all I want to know."

Once again, she sidesteps to get around me, a woman on a mission, head down, arms still clutching that notebook to her chest like a shield, her tote bag banging against her side with her jarring pace.

"Tiffany," I call, but she doesn't slow, doesn't give any indication of hearing me. "Tiffany," I call again, louder. Then I curse quietly to myself, jogging to catch up yet again, this time making an effort to pitch my voice low. "I could get a court order," I say. "For a paternity test."

She stops again, her shoulders hunching up around her. But when she meets my eyes, hers are blazing. "Why?" she demands. "Why would you do that? Why do you suddenly care? You didn't four years ago when you had your *coach* tell my dad you didn't even know me. You didn't give a single solitary shit about me or my baby then. Why in god's name do you care now?"

My mouth hangs open, and all I can do is blink at her. My coach? Her dad? Her baby? Four years ago?

Before my brain can catch up, she squares her shoulders and faces me down. "You have zero obligation right now. You're not listed on the birth certificate. No one's coming after you for child support. Don't you want it to stay that way? Especially with you poised to start a career as a professional athlete? Don't you want to keep all that money for yourself? Save it up so you can retire once you're in your thirties and all beat to hell from getting tackled constantly for over a decade?"

But I'm still stuck on what she said about four years ago. I hold up my hands. "Wait wait wait. Back up just a second. What are you talking about?"

Looking at her phone, she shakes her head. "I really don't have time for this right now."

But I catch her arm before she can walk away. "*Make time.*" It's a menacing growl, and I release her, clearing my throat and stuffing my hands in my pockets. "Please."

She's uncowed by my reaction, simply staring up at me, her eyes narrowed once more.

"I'm not sure what part of this is unclear to you. The condom broke or leaked or had a hole in it from being stored in your wallet—which I hope you've stopped doing, by the way—and I got pregnant. After I ruled out my ex as the father via a paternity test while I was pregnant, I knew it had to be you. I *tried* to contact you. I sent you messages on Facebook and Instagram, all of which sat unread."

I take in her nearly emotionless recitation of events in silence, unwilling to interrupt for fear she'll stop talking, even though I definitely have questions. Namely, what the fuck does my coach have to do with this?

Her emotionless facade is starting to crumble, though, and her voice cracks on the next part. "So I asked my dad to reach out to your coach. Get the team roster so I could get your phone number and call you. When your coach got back to my dad, he said that you'd never met me and told me to leave you alone. That it was up to me to take care of my—" She stops, shaking her head, blinking rapidly. Sucking in a deep breath, she checks her phone again. "I have to go or I'm going to be late to pick up my son. Don't ever stalk my classes again."

"I want to meet him," I blurt out as she passes me.

She freezes, her back straight and stiff. "No," she says, the single word brooking no argument.

And while I get that she thinks I'm an asshole who abandoned them … "I didn't know," I say quietly, taking advantage of her momentary frozenness to give her my part of the story. "My coach didn't tell me. I never saw your messages, and my coach never said a word. I swear on everything I hold dear that I had no idea you were pregnant, no idea I had a kid out there wandering around with my face until Jackson put it together and told me. I thought you just didn't bother to let me know."

She whirls around, her cheeks red, eyes blazing. "I would *never* do that!" she spits, incensed. "Never!"

Stepping closer, I almost reach for her, but think better of it. Instead, I curl my hand into a fist at my side and look into her eyes. "And I would never abandon my child or his mother. *Never.*"

She stares up at me for a moment, her lips parted, her blue eyes wide and fathomless. Then she steps back, dropping her gaze and breaking that brief breathless moment where I thought she might believe me.

"I have to go," she mutters. "Miss Kate hates it when parents are late. And Ben will be worried. I have to go."

Stepping around me once more, she practically jogs away. I jog after her, catching up easily and keeping up with my distance-eating stride. She didn't tell me I couldn't come. And she's going to pick up Ben.

I have a son, and his name is Ben. What's his middle name?

I'm going to get to see my son for the first time in just a few minutes.

Holy shit.

I follow her inside a building I've never paid much attention to before. Never had a class here, and I guess I wouldn't because it's apparently dedicated to the preschool. Maybe if I were in Early Childhood Education I'd know about it, or if I had a kid ... that I knew about before now.

I wait in the hall while Tiffany unlatches the lower half of the Dutch door and enters the classroom, watching as she bends to scoop up a kid with dark hair that's getting long, curling at the ends. Reaching up, I run a hand through my hair, tugging on the ends where it curls above the collar of my jacket.

His piping voice comes out in a rapid tumble as he tells his mother about his day. She briefly speaks to a woman in a blue apron who's apparently the teacher, sets the little boy down, and bends to write something in a binder on the low table.

I tear my eyes away from the fabric of her leggings stretching across her round, squeezable ass, focusing instead on the child who runs to the other side of the room and gathers a coat and a tiny *Toy Story* backpack from a cubby on the wall. I watch as he carefully spreads his coat out on the ground so the hood points at him.

Over his shoulder, he calls, "Mommy, watch!" When he's certain she's looking at him, he sticks his arms in the sleeves and flips the coat over his head, turning to face Tiffany with a giant smile on his face.

And my breath freezes in my chest. Because Jackson's absolutely right. That face is identical to the one that smiles out of a photo frame on my parents' living room wall.

That kid is definitely mine. If there was any doubt, it just got erased.

And while Tiffany clearly isn't thrilled about me showing up and butting in now, she's going to have to get over that. Because I'm not going anywhere.

CHAPTER TEN

Tiffany

I keep the smile glued to my face throughout my interactions with Ben and his teacher, clapping for him when he does the trick that Miss Amber taught him to get his coat on.

Tongue caught between his teeth in concentration, he squints his eyes and tries to get the zipper started himself. He gets the open side inside the zipper, but can't manage to hold it there while he pulls it closed. After a few tries, he stomps his foot in frustration, his mouth puckered in a pout.

"Can I help you?" I ask, crossing the room to him.

He nods, his lower lip still stuck out. "It's so so frustrating!" he says as I kneel in front of him.

"It's tricky, huh? Let's do it together. Here, you put it in, and I'll hold it while you pull on the zipper, okay?"

He nods, then gives me a smile when he pulls the zipper up to where he wants it, wiping his wrist across his face to get rid of a stray tear.

Pulling him close, I give him a hug. "Thank you for telling me how you're feeling. And thanks for letting me help. You're getting so big that pretty soon you'll be zipping your coat all by yourself. We just gotta keep practicing, okay?"

"Okay, Mama," he says, his arms wrapped around my neck.

"Do you want to carry your backpack or do you want me to do it?" I ask as I stand.

"You do it," he says, then takes off running for the door.

My steps slow as I follow Ben to the door, dread pooling in my gut at the prospect of facing Grayson Kilpatrick again. I can just see his profile as he lingers outside the door while other parents go in and out, waiting patiently.

His vehement words echo in my brain. *I would never abandon my child or his mother. Never.*

Is that really true? Did he really not know?

Part of me wants to believe him. The foolish, hopeful, naive part of me that has secretly always wished he would've stuck around and been supportive and part of Ben's life, and deep, deep even farther down, that maybe we would've had some kind of fairy tale ending.

But I learned the harsh reality that fairy tales don't come true. Not the Disney versions, anyway. The Brothers Grimm might've gotten it right with their gruesome morality tales. I'm not so sure any of those characters could've gotten a successful happily ever after.

So maybe fairy tales are more true than I realized, because look at what fate has dragged back to my door?

My son's wayward sperm donor, claiming ignorance, and a newfound desire to be involved with his son's life.

I honestly don't know how to feel right now. Or what to think.

What does he even want from this? From me?

When Ben and I come through the door, I catch a glimpse of Grayson's face. He wears a mixture of pleasure and astonishment that just confirms that Ben looks exactly like his father did at that age.

No surprise to me. When Carter was ruled out, Grayson was the only other option. And while I've seen certain mannerisms of mine in my son, he looks nothing like me. To the point that people don't always think he belongs to me when we're out in public. But with Grayson at my side, no one would doubt that they're related.

My breath hitches at the thought of Grayson being at my side. I've long since given up on the idea of a traditional nuclear family—or so I thought.

Teen motherhood doesn't exactly lend itself to normal dating. Especially after learning that one-night stands are far more dangerous than movies and TV shows lead you to believe. One bum condom, and suddenly you're a mom at eighteen. But I haven't been a nun. I've gone on some dates, even had a steady thing for a while last year. He got fed up when I wouldn't prioritize him over my son or school, though, so that inevitably fizzled out.

So I've told myself again and again that my dad would be enough of a father figure for Ben.

But now? Seeing Grayson's face lit up with delight at the sight of his son?

Who wouldn't want to believe that he'd been clueless before now?

Swallowing down all my confusion and fear and residual anger, I give him a brief nod before turning my attention to Ben. Grayson will just have to wait.

"You need to go potty before we go?"

"Nope!" And he's off, running down the hall to the door outside.

Grayson chuckles next to me, the sound low and smooth, full of indulgent amusement. "He's energetic, isn't he?"

"Yup." We take a few steps in silence, my mind whirling with questions. So he's here. Let's say I buy his story that he never found out about Ben, that his coach didn't bother to tell him and fobbed my dad off with a story designed to make me leave him alone. It sounds like something out of a prime time drama or a daytime soap opera, but let's just pretend, for the sake of argument, that it's the truth.

What does he want now? What's his plan?

I spread my hands in front of me. "So you've seen him. What now? You gonna walk us to my car?"

He stops, blinking at me with those chocolate brown eyes that I can't deny are so similar to Ben's, down to the gold flecks that you can only see up close. With a glance at Ben waiting by the door, he clears his throat. "I mean, if that's my only option, then yes. I'd hoped we could maybe go somewhere. Get some ice cream or ... I dunno what little kids like to do. It's kinda cold for a park today. We could go to the toy section at a store. I could maybe buy him something."

Oh god. He really wants to be involved. And I've been on my own for so long, expected to be on my own forever, really, that I don't even know how to react to that like a normal human. Though really, what would a normal human reaction be here? I haven't had time to look, but I somehow doubt there's an eHow article about how to respond when the sperm donor you believe abandoned you and your son shows up saying he never knew about his son's existence and now wants to be part of his life.

Puking all over Grayson Kilpatrick's broad, muscular chest seems like one on a long list of potential responses. Not that I should be noticing his broad, muscular chest. Or how sweet it is that he wants to buy Ben a toy or ice cream or both.

Because it's not sweet that he's trying to buy my kid's affections right off the bat.

Nope. That's not the way we're going to play this out. Not today, at least.

"Walking us to the car is fine," I croak out. I need some time and space to consider what amount of involvement I'm okay with. Figure out some ground rules. Tell my parents.

Oh god. My hand flies to my forehead involuntarily. My parents are going to lose their shit.

His face falls, but I don't have the bandwidth to do much more than register his disappointment, certainly not any extra space to care about it. "Alright," he says quietly. "But unblock my number so I can get in touch with you. We should get a DNA test, just so there's an official record that I'm the father in case anyone questions it. I absolutely believe you, but …"

"Yeah. Sure. Fine. That's fine. I get it."

His lips press together like he's annoyed at my response, but I'm not sure what else anyone can expect from me here. *He* blindsided *me*, after all. Sure, maybe this is all super surprising for him too, but as far as I knew, he decided he wanted nothing to do with us years ago. To have him suddenly show up demanding to meet his son and asking for a paternity test …

No matter how reasonable that might look on the surface, it's thrown me for a huge loop, and I need time to sort out my feelings. And Grayson Kilpatrick's handsome face watching me do that will not help at all.

I stride ahead, catching up to Ben, who glances behind me at Grayson bringing up the rear. "Do you know him, Mommy?"

"Um, yeah. He's friends with one of my classmates." No way am I calling Jackson a friend after this. "Remember Jackson? He came over to rehearse with Mommy for a class project and brought you those pastries?" Ben nods.

Before I can finish, Grayson interrupts. "I'm good friends with Jackson. And Jackson introduced me to your mom."

"Oh, okay," Ben says, unconcerned with the fact that I'm basically pretending Grayson doesn't exist, minus the minor concession of not talking over him.

Ben helps me open the door, even though he knows only grown ups are supposed to open doors here. Constantly pushing the edges of any boundaries, this one. Guess he gets that from his dad, from the looks of things.

Grayson follows behind us, catching up once we're on the sidewalk. He glances at me before focusing on Ben and holding out a hand. "I'm Gray. What's your name?"

"Ben!" He slaps Grayson's hand and runs ahead, giggling.

"Don't go too far ahead," I call after him. He runs a bit farther, but stops at the corner of the building where we need to turn. We've done this enough times that he knows not to leave my sight.

Grayson chuckles. "Should've known better than to expect a little kid to have a whole conversation with me."

I bite back my smile at the idea of Ben being still for any length of time when he's not sick or asleep. "You spend much time around kids?"

Adjusting his backpack on his shoulder, he shakes his head. "Nope. Not much opportunity. I only have one sister, and she's only two years younger than me. She's here too. At Marycliff. But she doesn't have any kids."

I hum in acknowledgment but don't volunteer any information as I dig my keys out of my tote bag. Grayson sighs.

Yeah, man. I know the feeling behind that sigh too. But what do you expect, dude? You abandoned me years ago, and then show up out of the blue demanding to meet my son. You think I'm just going to welcome you with open arms, thrilled for whatever crumbs you decide to throw our way?

Not fucking likely.

Sure, yeah, he says he didn't know. And it's not that I *don't* believe him. I'm just not sure I *do* believe him either.

Ben stops on the curb of the parking lot and walks along it while he waits for me to catch up, his arms outstretched for balance. When I reach him, I hold out a hand. "Hold hands in the parking lot, please."

He gamely grabs my hand and uses his hold on me to jump off the curb higher than he'd be able to do on his own. I help him out, swinging my arm up, and he hangs onto me with both hands, squealing and giggling.

"Hey," Grayson says. "If you let me hold your other hand, your mom and I can swing you between us."

I hold my breath, hoping that Ben will turn him down. We've been abandoned once already. I don't want Ben getting used to this kind of treatment, only to have it taken away again. But what kid in his right mind would say no to that offer?

"Okay!" he shrieks, getting his feet under him and tugging me closer to Grayson, his arm outstretched.

Grayson gives me a hopeful smile but quickly looks away when he sees my expression. With Ben's hand firmly in his, he counts, "One, two, three, jump!"

Ben jumps, and Grayson and I lift him into the air, swinging him up and out in front of us. Giggling and squealing, Ben shouts, "Again!" as soon as his feet hit the ground.

"Hope you realize this will never end now," I mutter.

Shrugging, Grayson gives me a crooked smile. "I don't mind."

And that's how I transport Ben to my car today, laughing and happy, jumping higher than he could imagine over and over again, because Grayson gets him even higher than my dad and I do together.

If all I had to worry about was Ben having fun, I wouldn't have any qualms about Grayson's sudden appearance in our life.

But no matter how much fun Ben has, my goal is what's best for him no matter what. And swinging him through the parking lot is not enough evidence to conclude that Grayson is what's best for him at all.

CHAPTER ELEVEN

Gray

I open the door to my apartment and step inside, the gloom a stark contrast to the cold, sunny day outside. Dropping my things next to the door, I toe off my shoes, not bothering to turn on a light. Instead, I flop down on my couch and sit in the semi darkness, slants of sunlight filtering in through the crappy white blinds that came with the place.

My mother is disgusted that I didn't let her help decorate this place. But I don't care that I have a secondhand couch and no throw pillows or artfully arranged lap blankets or that my mattress sits on the cheap metal frame I got with it from the mattress store. It's just me here in this one bedroom, and I don't need anything fancy.

What's Tiffany's house like? Does Ben have his own

room there, overflowing with toys?

My mind is still blown over the fact that I have a son. An actual living, breathing child running around wearing a face that looks just like mine. It's ... amazing, shocking ... infuriating.

But I don't even know where to direct my rage. Not at Tiffany. I already confirmed the truth of her story. The messages she said she sent me were still there in my Others folders, and I finally found them four years too late. She gave me her number—the same number she still has—telling me to get in touch, that it was really important that we speak. And finally, in an obvious last ditch effort, the bald truth: *I'm pregnant. You're the father.*

Five little life changing words.

She did everything she could to get in touch, to give me the chance to be involved, only to get no response, and then to be told by my coach that I said I don't even know her.

That fucker.

Standing, I pace my living room—three steps one way, turn, three steps back—my hands on my head, my muscles taut and flexing as I try to channel my anger somewhere. Coach Lawson retired a couple years ago. Even if I wanted to get in touch with him, to confront him for fucking around in my life, I wouldn't even know where to find him.

And if I did, what then? He'd probably just tell me he did me a favor and that I should stay away from her.

I can almost hear the words in his gruff, no-nonsense voice.

Grabbing my keys, I slam the door behind me and head out for a jog. My training is scheduled to a T, and my body doesn't need the additional wear and tear of an unplanned jog, but if I sit in my apartment with no outlet, I'm going to start punching holes in my walls.

Jogging is definitely the better option.

Flashes of today keep playing in my head—Tiffany confronting me, ready to bust my balls about abandoning her, and I can't help but feel a surge of attraction. Her fire is intoxicating. Her fierceness. Her unwillingness to be cowed. Mama bear in action. And I can't help wondering what it would be like to have all that fire on my side instead of turned against me.

I got to experience it once. A little. That night we were together and she was all flirty and forward, wrapping herself around me, kissing me like that. Sure, she just wanted to get back at her boyfriend for dumping her or something, but she knew what she wanted and she went after it without any second thoughts.

I can already tell she's brought the same spirit to motherhood, raising him herself and going to school at the same time. The way she gives him her full attention when he talks. The way she takes care of him.

She's a good mom. It's obvious they love each other. I don't want to do anything to mess that up.

I just want to get to know my kid.

* * *

Going to the pharmacy to get a home paternity test

feels strange. Worse than the potentially awkward exchanges when buying condoms. Because this means I might've knocked up some chick but I'm not sure it's actually mine.

It sounds like something out of a crappy reality TV show. And this is my life now.

W. T. F.

Fortunately, the cashier doesn't bat an eye as she scans the box and drops it in a bag, delivering the total in a bored voice. After paying, I give her a tight smile as I take the bag and head out.

Yesterday's sunshine is a distant memory, and January has decided to get back to normal with a low sky full of drifting snowflakes and wind that finds any opening in your outerwear to try to freeze your nuts off.

I get to run drills in this soon. Yay.

But first I get the pleasure of texting Tiffany to let her know I have the test. Maybe I should see if the dentist can fit me in for a root canal next. It'd fit with all the rest of today's shit.

I hurry to my car, turning it on as soon as I close the door, grateful that it's still fairly warm from my drive to the store. Its ability to block the wind is enough to make it feel at least ten degrees warmer anyway.

Now it's time for my evisceration at the hands of my ... son's mother.

Part of me still balks at thinking of him as my son. How could I even have a son? A three-year-old son at that?

But it's true. He's mine. It's as clear as day. The test is

merely a formality in case anyone tries to question it.

Like my parents, for example. I'm not sure how they'll react. But I sure as hell know they'll want more proof than similar baby pictures.

Me: I have the paternity test kit. When can I get it to you?

I sit in the parking lot and stare at my phone, wondering if I'll get a response at all. But at least the message shows as delivered, so it looks like she unblocked my number. That's something I guess.

After five minutes with no answer, I back out of the parking lot and head to campus for my two o'clock. Maybe she's in class right now and she'll respond when she's done. I don't know her schedule aside from the theatre class she has with Jackson.

Which means I can always find her tomorrow if she doesn't answer me today.

CHAPTER TWELVE

Tiffany

I stare at my phone, reading and rereading the message from Grayson.

Grayson: I have the paternity test kit. When can I get it to you?

Hmm, never? Never's good for me. Crawl back into the football stadium and leave me alone, please.

Though only part of me actually wants that. The part of me that fears change and doesn't know what he intends to do once he sees the positive results of that test.

But a tiny part of me wonders if it might be okay. If he's telling the truth and he really didn't know back then and he really did just find out, it might even be a good thing. Ben's too young to really start asking questions yet, but it's only a matter of time. One of these days he'll want to know about his dad, and wouldn't it be nice if he got the answer before the questions even came up? Wouldn't that be better than learning your dad is a deadbeat? Or me making up lies to cover up that fact?

Either way, it looks like the deadbeat is around, at least for now. It's the *for now* part that gives me pause, though. Because it would be better for him to just stay away if he has no intention of following through. A deadbeat who abandoned you before you were even born is bad enough, but it seems like having someone drift in and out of your life, never keeping promises, never making you a priority would be even worse.

Sucking in a deep breath, my stomach swirling with nausea, I text Grayson back.

Me: I'm available now

He responds immediately. He sent the text almost an hour ago. Is he just sitting around waiting for me to text him back? Does that make me feel good or terrible?

Grayson: I'm in class right now. Can we meet after?
Me: No. I have to pick up Ben.
Grayson: I could come with you
Me: I don't think that's a good idea
Grayson: It was fine yesterday
Me: And you said it would be just one time

He doesn't respond for several minutes, and I'm

about to put my phone away and ignore it, because he's the one who wants to meet. It's not my job to be accommodating.

Grayson: I could drop it off at your house later tonight

Absolutely not. No fucking way. I haven't even told my parents about Grayson showing up. God, I don't even know *how* to tell them. Or how to tell Ben. My stomach clenches and swirls at the thought, nausea swamping me, cold sweat breaking out under my sweater.

Everything's been fine. Life was fine. Why does he have to show up and ruin everything?

Tiffany: Fine. Meet me at the bench in front of the Early Education Center after your class

I can just imagine those sinful lips curling into a smug grin at his victory. And I can also imagine how much I want to slap that grin off his face.

* * *

Grayson strolls up looking warm in his puffy coat and track pants, the smile I imagined earlier tugging at his lips.

I narrow my eyes. I don't need him being all cute and pretty right now.

When he's standing in front of me, he pulls his backpack around, unzips it, and pulls out a plastic grocery sack.

I take it from his outstretched hand, peeking inside to find a receipt nestled next to a box featuring a picture of a man holding up a child. The paternity test, it seems. They make it look so cheerful and happy, and not terrifying and life altering. Marketing lies.

Lifting my eyes to Grayson's, I give him a closed-mouth smile. "Thanks. Gotta go." I swivel on my heel and march for the door, hoping against hope that he'll take the hint and leave.

No such luck. "Hold up," he calls, jogging a few steps to catch up to me, his breath visible in front of him.

I don't bother holding back my eye roll. "Really? I thought you just wanted to give me the test."

Shaking his head, he chuckles. He actually fucking chuckles like the idea that he'd leave me alone is adorable and amusing. "Was yesterday really so terrible?"

It wasn't, but I'm not going to admit anything of the sort. Besides, he was with us for like five minutes.

Fortunately, getting into the building and to Ben's classroom before the pickup cut off time saves me from answering or acknowledging his question.

Once again, Grayson waits in the hall, watching through the open half of the Dutch door while I collect Ben and check in with his teacher. Ben turns in my arms, patting my shoulder with excitement. "Look, Mommy! Look! It's your friend from yesterday! Will he swing me again? Please please please please please?"

Miss Kate gives me an amused, knowing look. "Your *friend* seems to have made a good impression on Ben."

I hope my grimace passes as a smile. "Mmm. Yeah. It seems so." I am absolutely not getting into this with Ben's teacher right now, though she will have to be told eventually. The upheaval in Ben's life is reason enough to tell her, but—another cold swirl of nausea roils in my belly—if Grayson pursues some kind of custody arrangement, he'll need to be added to the list of emergency contacts and approved pickup people.

God, so much could change just from one chance encounter.

Ha. If that isn't the story of my life right there.

Wrapping an arm around Ben, I squeeze him tight, and he squirms. "Mooom," he protests. "Put me down. I wanna say hi to your friend."

"Alright, Benny. Sorry." My voice is hoarse, and I clear my throat, grateful that Miss Kate has already moved on to another parent so I don't have to worry about her curiosity over my reaction.

Bending, I set Ben on his feet, and he immediately takes off to talk to Grayson, jumping up and down with his excitement. Grayson's face lights up, and he reaches over the door to give Ben a high five.

I drag myself to the cubbies to collect Ben's coat and backpack, then head for the door. Forcing my voice to be cheerful and pretending to be unconcerned with the near stranger trying to stake a claim on my son, I smile and hold out Ben's coat. "It's chilly. Let's put your coat on before we go out, okay?"

Distractedly, because he's still chattering away to Grayson, telling him all about the playground equipment and how many times he went down the slide today and what he had for snack after, Ben shoves his arms in his sleeves. I squat down and zip it for him, pulling his mittens out of his backpack and holding them out for him to shove his hands into, which he does with barely a glance in my direction, bouncing all the while and making the task ten times harder than normal.

"Benny." No response. I pat his arm and turn him to face me. "Ben. I need you to talk to me for a sec, okay?"

His face screws up, his mouth turned down. "What?"

I raise an eyebrow. "Is that how we talk to each other?"

He sighs heavily. "Sorry, Mom."

"Do you want your hat or your hood?"

"Hat!" he yells, bouncing back toward Grayson.

Pulling out his hat, I stand and stuff it on his head from behind.

Irritated, he glares back at me, swiping his hair out of his face.

Biting back my laugh, I help tuck his hair out of the way. "Don't turn away when you know I need to put your hat on."

Grayson meets my eyes and gives me a blinding smile. But when my answering smile is stiff, his falters, turning strained, hitching back up as he faces Ben again.

When I put my hand on the doorknob, Grayson steps out of the way, and Ben runs right for him, grabbing at his hand. My heart clenches. Is it really so easy to lose my son to this random guy?

"Swing me! Swing me! Swing me!" Ben demands,

jumping up and down while holding onto Grayson's hand.

Grayson chuckles and glances at me.

I give him another tight smile and pull the door closed behind me, making sure it's latched. "Let's get outside first."

"Yay!" cheers Ben as he takes off running for the door.

"Walk, please!" I remind him, but it makes no difference, because he's already holding onto the door and jumping up and down in anticipation of swinging all the way to the car again.

I should probably be grateful that Grayson wants a good relationship with his son. But more than anything, I'm mad that he couldn't just leave us alone. That Jackson couldn't keep his suspicions to himself. That Grayson couldn't just be the deadbeat asshole he's been for the last four years. That he has to give me hope and a glimpse of how life might've been if he'd gotten my messages.

Because I don't know how I'm going to handle having this hot guy who I've hated for years in my life all the time, making my son giddy with excitement at the sight of him. And if Gray starts showing up for pickup daily, people are going to think things. Ask questions.

I know Ben's going to mention "Mommy's friend" to his grandparents soon—because what three-year-old knows how to keep a secret?—and I'll be fielding more questions than I'm ready for far too soon.

I think I'm going to puke.

CHAPTER THIRTEEN

Gray

My breath catches when I check my phone and see the email that the results of the paternity tests are available.

"Everything alright?" Mom asks, setting the dish of mixed veggies on the table next to me so I can serve myself some.

I jerk my head in her direction. "Yeah. Fine. Great." *Because that was super convincing.* After scooping a serving of vegetables onto my plate, I pass the bowl to Piper, who's also staring at me with her brows furrowed. Clearly I'm doing a shit job of covering my distraction and anxiety about the test results.

It's silly. I know they're going to come back that I'm the father. I mean, I'm 99.99% sure. But still. This is confirmation.

"We don't usually have phones out at dinner," she grumbles.

Because I'm still on my sister's shit list, she takes any and every opportunity to make me feel like an ass. Which, I sorta did the same thing to her not that long ago—or at least that's how she sees it—so it's to be expected.

Right now I'm really fucking tired of it, but I'm not going to get into it with her at Thursday dinner with our parents. Especially not with Cal McAdam sitting next to her and glaring at me. I've put up with his presence at these things and in my sister's life because he really does seem to care about her even if he still hates my guts. I think our animosity is reflexive more than anything at this point. But that's another thing I'm not bringing up at Thursday dinner.

Pulling my napkin out of my lap, I set it on the table next to my plate. "Sorry." I scoot my chair back and stand. "I'll be right back."

Without waiting for a response, I leave the dining room and head for the stairs, taking them two at a time and heading for my old bedroom. I need to see the test results *now*. I'm not waiting until after dinner. And unless I want to spill the beans right now, I need to look at them in private. Because Piper would bitch at me for having my phone out at the table again, and the only way to shut her up would be to tell the truth, and I'm not ready for that. Not right now. Not when I don't know for sure. And not at Thursday dinner.

Opening the email app, I tap on the link, put in my login information, and stare at the screen while the little circle goes around and around.

It's a match.

I blink at the screen and read it again a few more times to make sure I'm not missing something or misunderstanding something.

But I'm not. I read it right the first time.

It's a match. I'm a match.

Ben's my son.

Holy shit.

My phone slips from numb fingers.

It's one thing to think it's possible, likely even. It's another to have it written out in black and white in front of my face.

Covering my mouth with my hand, I suck in a deep breath, not sure if I'm holding back laughter, shouting, or tears.

I have a son. A three-year-old son. Who I've seen twice in his entire life.

Holy fucking shit.

I have a son.

And his mother hates my guts.

* * *

I manage to make it through dinner with minimal awkwardness, brushing off the concerned looks by saying a friend had a health scare, but the tests all came back fine and they wanted me to know.

Of course that piqued Cal's interest, and I had to lie my ass off and say it was someone from Ohio. Since I was lying my ass off anyway, who cares, right?

But I'm vibrating with suppressed emotion as I walk into my apartment, pulling my phone out of my coat pocket and staring at it. Should I call Tiffany? Text her? What's the protocol for informing your son's mother that you're the father? Does this happen often enough for there to be a protocol?

My thumb hovers over her name for a long time, but in the end I sigh and decide to text her. Probably most people would recommend a phone call, or better yet, an in-person meeting. But I know that she won't want either of those options, and trying to push it will just piss her off more.

She already resents having me around at all, though she's going to have to get herself on over that since I'm not going anywhere. I think part of her still believes that I knowingly abandoned her before. I can't really blame her. It pisses me off, though, because I'd never do that. And with incontrovertible proof in my hands? No way in hell would I abandon them now.

Me: I got the test results today

I take off my coat and unbutton my shirt, stripping off the nicer clothes I wear for dinner at my parents' house and changing into a pair of sweats to relax in now that I'm home.

Tiffany: And?

I can't help snorting with amusement at that response. She was certain I was the father when she found out she was pregnant. I can only assume it's because either there weren't other possibilities or she'd already ruled them out. There's no way she doesn't already know the answer. But I text it to her anyway.

Me: It's a match. I'm Ben's father

I stare at my phone, watching the three dots appear and disappear and reappear again.

Tiffany: What now?

What now indeed? I'm not sure how to answer that question, except …

Me: I want to get to know him. I want him to know I'm his dad. I want to be part of his life.

I also want to take care of her, help her however I can, but I don't know how well she'd respond to that at this point. Given her not-so-thinly veiled animosity toward me the handful of times we've spoken, I doubt she'd take it well. So that conversation can wait.

When she doesn't respond for over ten minutes, I sigh. I don't get why she'd be hesitant. Isn't this what she wanted from the beginning? Me to be involved? Otherwise, why even bother attempting to tell me? It's not my fault that her attempts failed. I didn't choose to be absent. I didn't decide to abandon her and my unborn child. And now that I know, I want to do the right thing.

Why is that so terrible?

Clenching my jaw, I type out and send another message.

Me: We need to get together and plan how we're going to handle this. Pick a location. I'm available tomorrow after five.

Tiffany: Fine

CHAPTER FOURTEEN

Tiffany

"Mommy, what's wrong with your face?"

I tear my gaze from my phone and look down at my son snuggled against me on his bed. He reaches up and squishes my cheeks. "You look funny. What's wrong?"

Turning my head, I pretend to snarf his fingers, making him giggle and bringing me out of my funk enough to smile. I tuck my phone under my leg again. I'll deal with Grayson later. The familiar nausea at the thought of dealing with the reality bearing down on me fills my belly again.

"Everything's fine," I manage to say in a normal voice. "Pick one more story, and then it's bedtime, okay?"

He holds up two fingers, grinning. "Two stories."

Grabbing his fingers, I bring them to my mouth for a

kiss. "One story and a song after lights out."

He sighs and says, "Fine," in a pouty voice, climbing out of bed and going to his bookshelf, where he picks out *Dragons Love Tacos*.

I read the story twice—it's short and when he asks for it again so sweetly, I can't bring myself to say no. He snuggles under his covers, pulling his favorite dinosaur stuffy close while I turn off the overhead light, the multicolored stars shining from his nightlight filling the ceiling. Then I sit down on the edge of his bed and stroke his back while singing the song I made up for him when he was a baby. He's always been fussy about falling asleep, and I started rocking and singing random things to him when he was only a few weeks old, and some of those random things coalesced into what's now his favorite bedtime song.

We've been working on him falling asleep on his own lately, even though he still gets up in the middle of the night and wanders into my room most nights. But tonight, I stay until he falls asleep, softly singing his song and rubbing his back with long, slow strokes. Even after his eyes are closed and his breathing evens out, I stay and stare at his round cheeks and the way his hair curls behind his ears, tears filling my eyes at the thought of sharing custody of my precious baby with anyone else, even if that person is his father.

What's he going to want?

Pushing that thought aside, I leave Ben's room, quietly closing his door behind me. I'll find out what

Grayson wants tomorrow. And I'll just have to figure out how to deal with it then.

Mom looks up when I come into the living room and gives me a soft smile. "Took a while to get him down tonight?"

I shrug, gathering up a few of Ben's toys that didn't get picked up before bed and putting them in the basket next to the entertainment center. "Not really. I just like watching him sleep sometimes."

Her smile grows wider. "They're so sweet when they're sleeping. Makes you wonder how something so full of energy all day long ends up like that at the end of the day, doesn't it?"

Laughing softly, I nod. "Yeah." Of course that's not the real reason I want nothing more than to hold my son close as often as possible right now. But I haven't told Mom about Grayson yet, and I'm not going to until I know what's happening.

Part of me wants to, though. She's been amazingly supportive all along, never pushing me to do anything I wasn't comfortable with, except for those few times where it was needed. Like when I was dragging my feet about picking out a car seat and other baby gear in my third trimester. She ordered me into the car despite my heavy sighs and eye rolling and general annoying teenage behavior, drove me to a department store, and made me look at all of the options there, looking up the reviews online of the ones I found most appealing and forcing me to decide on a car seat, a crib, and a changing table that afternoon.

But I don't want her to decide that this issue is one where she needs to take charge as my mother and force me to confront the thing I don't want to deal with.

In this case, I'm the mother. I'm the one who has to confront this situation. I don't need anyone else adding to the pressure.

"You alright?" Mom asks, obviously noticing my quiet pensiveness.

I give her a bright smile. "Yeah, fine. Just tired."

She nods. "Do you still have homework for tonight? Or can you go to bed?"

Sighing, I stand. "Not too much. Just some reading. I'm going to grab a snack and get to it, because bed sounds good." I give her a kiss on the cheek and head to the kitchen. Dad's already in bed since he has zero hour weight training with his football team in the morning. Doesn't matter that the season's over until next fall. They're in the weight room at seven in the morning all year.

While I do have some reading to do, I mostly just want to retreat to my room to sit with the reality that soon I'll have to tell my parents about Grayson. And tell Ben about Grayson.

Suddenly food doesn't sound appealing at all.

* * *

I'm a wreck. I've been checking my phone almost nonstop since I got home from class earlier, trying to focus on spending time with Ben, but all I'm doing is dreading my meeting with Grayson.

At four thirty, I give Ben a quick hug and stand from the couch, forcing myself not to hold him any tighter or longer than usual. He wouldn't like it, and my parents are under the impression that I'm meeting a friend for dinner—actually, I'm pretty sure they believe I'm going on a date—and would think I'm acting weird.

In my room, I stare at my reflection for a moment, trying to decide if I should add to my makeup. For classes, I don't usually bother with much, maybe concealer if I'm having a breakout, a quick swipe of mascara so my blonde eyelashes are visible and maybe a neutral lip color to make me look more awake and adult than I usually feel.

But I feel the need for … more. Not because I'm trying to impress Grayson, because I very firmly am not. Why would I even want to impress the very attractive star quarterback of Marycliff University, right? He's my son's absentee father who's suddenly determined to be involved. Yes, yes, I know he says he didn't know, but it's difficult to let go of my anger and hatred toward him just like that. It's not a light switch that can be turned off with a few magic words.

I need assurances that he won't abandon us again. And words aren't enough.

Getting ready for this meeting feels like preparing for

battle. I need something to boost my confidence, and I've always felt most confident when I look great.

Despite the fact that this will just confirm to my parents I'm going on a date with someone, I flip through my closet and pull out my blue V-neck knit dress that brings out my eyes. Quickly stripping out of my top, I pull on the dress, happy with how it layers over my charcoal gray leggings. Paired with boots and a scarf it's perfect no matter where we end up. Hopefully we won't be spending too much time outside, but it's best to be prepared.

Turning back to my mirror, I take the time to put on eyeliner, a little bit of eye shadow to really highlight my eyes, and a couple more coats of mascara followed by my favorite lip stain.

Checking the time again, I have enough time to let my hair out of its usual bun and twist the sides into two braids that meet in the back, the rest of my curls hanging down my back, making me look effortlessly put together.

With a nod at my reflection I feel slightly better. Just a little, but I'll take whatever boost I can get right now.

Grabbing my black knee high boots from my closet, I sit on the edge of my bed and put them on, toss the important things in a small clutch instead of the giant tote I usually carry, and with a deep breath, I exit my room.

Mom pokes her head out of the kitchen when I get back to the living room, and Dad looks up from the book he's reading in his favorite chair while Ben watches *Dinosaur Train*.

"You look beautiful," Mom says, crossing to me and giving me a hug and a kiss on the cheek.

"Thanks, Mom." I give her a wan smile, because I know she means well and wants me to be happy. And I hate that I'm essentially lying to my parents by not telling them what's really going on. But I can't. Not yet. Soon, though. Probably tonight. Tomorrow at the latest. Because this conversation with Grayson is going to change everything.

CHAPTER FIFTEEN

Gray

Despite telling Tiffany that she could pick our meeting location, she never did, so I finally asked her to meet me outside the athletics center, since that's where I've been all afternoon.

I'm starving after running drills and working out. I'm hoping I can convince her to get dinner somewhere, either out or, if she's okay with it, back at my place.

At my place we'd have privacy for our discussion, plus I'd have my pre-prepped post-workout meal, but she might feel more comfortable being in public with me since we're virtually strangers.

I pull out my phone to check the time, wondering what the chances are of her standing me up since it's already 5:07.

But when I lift my head, there she is, looking like some

combination of catalog model and fallen angel, her blonde curls blowing around her head from the cold wind whipping through the corridor created by the trees and buildings that lead to the athletic center. Kick ass boots encase her long, lean legs, and the hem of her dress peeks out from beneath her wool coat, flaring as she walks.

She looks like she's ready to go out somewhere, and I can't help glancing down at my very casual post-workout attire of joggers, sweatshirt, and unzipped puffy coat in varying shades of gray and black with the bold exception of the red lettering on my Marycliff football sweatshirt.

Maybe I should just plan on eating the protein bar I carry in my bag for emergencies, because what are the odds she'll want to be seen in public with me dressed like that?

When she's right in front of me, her face a neutral mask, I gulp and straighten my shoulders, offering a tentative smile. "Hey."

"Hey," she returns, her voice flat, deflating any hope I had of this being a positive encounter. Some part of me still hoped she might be into me again like that night we first met. Despite her hostility now, I know she's charming and sweet when she wants to be. I had that directed at me once upon a time, and I thought maybe I could convince her to again. Guess not.

She glances around and pulls her hair to one side, holding it so the wind doesn't whip it into her face, then refocuses on me. "Where are we doing this?"

So direct and to the point. Blunt. No fiery fury like last week and definitely not the smiling girl who danced with me at that party. But a lot has happened since then. She's not licking her wounds from a bad breakup and looking for something to distract her. She's a woman, a mother, and she sees me as a threat. Something to be dealt with.

My teeth grind together at that realization. I don't want things to be shitty between us. I was serious that night years ago when I told her I wanted her number before she left, and I'd been disappointed that she didn't follow through. But I figured maybe she didn't want to get involved with anyone else, fresh off her breakup. Or maybe she got back together with her ex. Or maybe she'd just moved on. Regardless, the night we met was a fond memory, even after it was relegated to the annals of high school shenanigans.

I never expected to see her again, much less find out that she's the mother of my kid.

She clearly never expected to hear from me either, especially after how my high school coach treated her. I have to force myself not to grind my teeth or flex my fists at the fresh wave of rage that washes over me from the way he inserted himself and decided making me a deadbeat was in my best interests.

Tilting her head, she raises her brows, and I can't help but get lost in her icy blue eyes.

"What do you tell people?" I ask.

My question clearly catches her off guard, because her eyebrows twitch together in confusion. "What are you talking about?"

I clear my throat. "About me. I mean, about Ben's father." Lifting a hand, I gesture vaguely at her. "He looks nothing like you. Do people say things? Ask about me?"

Ducking her head, she looks away and crosses her arms, her neutral mask faltering for a moment before sliding back into place. "I tell them the truth, that his father's not in the picture. Most people just tell me how cute he is, ask if he's mine, and say he must take after his father." She looks at me again. "I just say thanks and smile, because random strangers aren't entitled to details about my life."

I grunt in response. It's a version of the truth, and far more charitable toward me than I have a right to expect given the way she was fobbed off. Her family must hate me too, since I'm sure they all believe the same story.

God, that kills me.

I've always been the responsible one. The guy other people count on to do the right thing. It grated enough that my second string quarterback had it in for me all season, but I could ignore that for the most part, because it was clear that was all about him and nothing to do with me personally.

But this? They believe I'm a terrible person because they were told I wanted nothing to do with Tiffany and Ben. That I abandoned them, choosing to be a selfish little shit and take the easy way out while leaving her to deal with a lifetime of consequences.

I'm not that guy. And I hate that anyone would think I am. I just don't know how to change her mind.

Tiffany stares at me a moment longer, then sighs. "Is this going to be a short conversation? Because I'm cold, and I'd prefer if we moved inside somewhere if it's going to take longer than a few minutes."

Grunting again, I gesture toward the parking lot behind the athletics complex and slowly start heading that way. After a moment, she falls in step beside me. "Are you hungry? I'm hungry."

Even though I asked a question, I plow ahead without giving her time to answer, hoping if I just keep talking, I'll be able to convince her to have dinner with me. To give her a chance to get to know me, to see me for the guy I really am, not the shitty fuckface she's believed me to be all this time. "I had a long workout today, and I need food. We could go somewhere and have dinner, or if you'd prefer to have our conversation in private, we could go to my apartment. I can make something quick for dinner."

Her lips are parted in surprise when I look back at her, and a flash of memory hits me like a punch in the solar plexus, the feel of those lips under mine, the way she sucked on my tongue and fed hers back to me when we kissed. Damn, she was a good kisser in high school. How much better would she be now?

But kissing's not on the menu, and I need to make sure I remember that.

For one thing, she hates me. Has hated me for years now. And for another, this is about Ben.

She clears her throat, and when I glance back, I realize she's stopped. Her eyes jump to mine, and I can't help wondering what she was looking at. Was she ogling my ass?

I bite back a smile, forcing myself to remain neutral as

well, even if I get a surge of pride and excitement at the thought of her checking me out. At least the attraction between us is still mutual, even if I know we won't act on it.

"Where were you thinking of going for dinner?"

I was right. She does prefer to be somewhere public.

Shrugging, I hitch my backpack higher on my shoulder. "I'll eat pretty much anything, though my meal plan wants me to eat mostly lean meats and veggies with some carbs to balance it out. I'm due a cheat day, though, so I can splurge on something at a restaurant. Anywhere you're partial to? Or I can just pick and drive us."

She tilts her chin up, her eyes narrowing. "I wasn't planning on riding with you."

"Okay." I shrug like it's no big deal, even though I would actually like her to ride with me. We could start hashing out details in the car. And if things get too heated to continue in a public restaurant, we can move to the car so we don't have to worry about people listening in on our business.

Plus, I want the opportunity to break through that neutral wall she's erected to keep me at bay. To show her that I'm a good guy who'd make a good father if given half a chance. But I can't do that if she won't give me the time of day.

I suppose I should be grateful she agreed to this meeting at all and is even willing to eat dinner with me, though. Maybe eventually she'll come around.

Glancing in the direction she came from, which is the opposite direction of my car, I tilt my head toward the parking lot behind me again. "Let me give you a ride to your car at least, and we can decide where to go on the way there."

Her sigh of defeat shouldn't make me feel as happy as it does, but I can't help it. Every little victory buoys me and makes me feel like, as shitty as things are right now, there might be hope for something better eventually. Maybe not soon, but eventually.

I did some googling about co-parenting, and everything says it works best if the parents can have a cordial relationship. I'll settle for cordial if that's all I can get. But I'd prefer friendly. Or … I dunno … the part of me that's always found Tiffany attractive, the part of me who felt the draw to her when I walked into that party and saw her standing with her friend, the part of me who couldn't believe his luck when she not only danced with me but let me lead her to a bedroom …

That part of me wants to see what might've happened between us if she'd given me her number that night.

A pang of longing hits me. Because if she had given me her number, I would've called her. And she would've been able to tell me she was pregnant. And I could've been there for her all along.

Pulling my keys out of my pocket, I stuff down those feelings. When we reach my car, I unlock it and hold the passenger door open for her.

With her arms still crossed and eyes still narrowed in that glare, she stops in front of the door and stares at me. "You don't have to do this, you know."

I raise my eyebrows, returning her impassive mask

with one of my own. "Do what exactly?"

She waves a hand at me. "The whole gentleman act. Offering to take me to dinner. Opening my door. This isn't a date, and I'm not going to fall all over myself in gratitude for a meal and door holding and hand my son over to you like that."

"That's not—" I start to protest, but she shakes her head and cuts me off.

"Just don't, okay? You don't need to woo me. This isn't about us. It's about Ben. Don't treat me like a potential conquest. Just be normal. It'll be easier on all of us that way."

My brows pull together as she climbs into the car, leaving me to puzzle over that barb. A potential conquest? Is that what she thinks this is? I thought I was just being gentlemanly.

Rounding the car, I climb into the driver's seat and start the ignition before facing her, my hands gripping the steering wheel. "I'd hoped that we could have a polite conversation. I'm being nice. I'm not trying to manipulate you into anything." I pause, waiting for a response, and when all she does is snort, I grind my teeth.

"It's not like I need to be extra nice or manipulative anyway," I mutter, irritation and frustration rising up inside me. Getting the better of me. Even as the words leave my mouth, I know this isn't the best way to win her over, but I can't seem to stop them. "We both know that I'm Ben's father. I have parental rights. The DNA test proves it. And even if it's not admissible in court, I'm sure it's enough evidence for a judge to order an admissible test. And then, what? We let some random stranger decide what's best for Ben? Is that really what you want?"

With her arms crossed over her chest, her eyes fall closed. She expels a breath like I hit her in the gut, and guilt twists in mine. "No," she says at length on a hoarse whisper. "No, I don't want that."

We sit for another moment, me staring at her, her keeping her eyes closed, her shoulders hunched as though to ward off an attack while I try to figure out how to get us back on the more positive footing I thought we were achieving before I made the horrific mistake of—*gasp*—opening her door for her. A literal minute ago I felt hopeful, and just like that, we're back in the shit.

She has all the cards here. I want us to get along. Threatening to take her to court seems like a bad way to go about that.

She blinks her eyes open and sniffs—oh god, is she going to cry?

Studiously avoiding my gaze, she buckles her seatbelt. "I'm parked by the administration building. Pick where you want to have dinner, and I'll follow you."

I keep looking at her, hoping she'll look at me so I can offer a real apology, but she won't. Finally, with a sigh, I buckle my own seatbelt and pull out of the parking spot. "I'm sorry," I offer quietly as I slowly make my way through the parking lot.

She doesn't respond, sitting with her arms crossed and her face turned to her window.

"I'd really like for us to get along," I try again. "Is there any way I can convince you to ride with me to the restaurant?

"No." It's flat and definitive and doesn't make me feel great about our upcoming negotiations, but at least it's marginally better than silence. Marginally.

CHAPTER SIXTEEN

Tiffany

The drive to a quick service burrito place close to campus gives me a brief reprieve from Grayson's overwhelming presence.

He's determined and uncowed by my glares and rudeness. Dammit. I was half hoping that if I were unpleasant enough, maybe he'd just give up and leave us alone.

But it's clear he won't do that, and if he's threatening to take me to court to sue for parental rights … I'm going to have to suck it up and play ball.

That thought still makes me sick, and even though the smell of spiced meats would normally make my mouth water, right now it reminds me of when I had morning sickness with Ben and any strong smells made me want to puke. My dad likes to snack on chips and salsa, and just being in the same room with him eating that would make me want to hurl. For a few months, he was only allowed to eat his favorite salsa when I wasn't around and he had to immediately wash the dish after.

Would Grayson have done that for me if he'd been around?

I swat the thought away as I look around for him. He should've had the opportunity—would've if I'd gotten my way. I'm still not sure I believe his excuse that he never found out.

And even if it's true, the fact that he wants to see his son now doesn't necessarily mean anything. It could just be some kind of ego boost for him. Possessiveness, wanting what's his, and not anything to do with what's best for Ben.

Drawing my determination to protect my son at all costs around me like a cloak, I head for the corner booth where Grayson has parked, a plastic number tent sitting on the edge of the table.

He stands when I get close and gestures to the front counter. "I didn't know what you'd want, but I can get it for you if you want to order something."

Shaking my head, I slide onto the bench opposite him, setting my clutch next to me and folding my hands in my lap. "I'm not hungry."

"Are you sure?" He sinks onto his bench, but doesn't scoot all the way in, his brows drawn together.

With a huffy sigh, I shake my head again. "I already told you, this is unnecessary. If I want food, I'm perfectly capable of getting it myself. I'm not hungry. Can we please just get this over with?"

His lips firm, his brows drawing down as he slides all the way into his seat, a muscle in his jaw bulging.

He's irritated? Too damn bad. I've been irritated since I saw him a few weeks ago, and my irritation's only gotten worse.

Undeterred by his subtle display of displeasure, I put my arms on the table and lean close to him, pitching my voice so we won't easily be overheard by the few people in the mostly empty restaurant.

"Look. I understand that you want to get to know Ben. He's an awesome kid, so I can't really blame you. But you have to understand that I've made the decision not to introduce Ben to people who don't have an interest in being in his life long term. Which means, when I date, I have to be certain about the relationship before bringing Ben into it. If you're not going to stick around, I'm not interested in letting him get attached to you, only for you to buzz off in a few months and break his little heart."

He sucks in a breath, straightening in his seat, his dark eyes narrowed and fiery as he processes what I've said.

"I have no intention of disappearing," he says at length.

It's my turn to narrow my eyes. "You say that, and yet I'm quite certain that you're planning on entering the NFL draft soon. Or did I mishear all the rumors flying around about you?"

Even if I'd wanted to avoid hearing about Grayson, since my dad's a high school football coach, he follows Marycliff's seasons very closely. Many of his players have stayed close to home and played for Marycliff over the years. And every time Grayson's name is mentioned, my normally placid father starts pacing the living room, clenching his fists and grinding his molars like he'd enjoy nothing more than to tear Grayson to pieces and punch anyone who mentions him in the mouth.

A slow smile spreads across his face, and I firmly ignore the warmth it ignites in my belly, though the fact that it replaces my nausea is welcome.

"You've been paying attention to rumors about me?"

Scoffing, I sit back and cross my arms. "It's hard not to when everyone talks about it."

He leans forward, propping himself on his crossed forearms, following my retreat, making that warmth in my belly rise to a simmer. "You've been paying attention, though." He examines me slowly, his eyes skating over my face, lingering on my lips before returning to my eyes. "If I didn't know better, I'd think you might like me."

Pursing my lips, I shake my head. Any chance of me actually liking him ended when I was eighteen and pregnant, learning that the father of my child denied even knowing me. "May I remind you that we're not on a date. And we're here to discuss something that directly impacts the life of an innocent child. We're not here for you to flirt with me."

He seems to deflate, hanging his head and staring at the table. "You're right," he mutters a moment later. "I'm sorry."

There's a pause as a young woman with long brown hair in a high ponytail brings out Grayson's food.

He gives her a charming smile and a warm, "Thank you."

I look away, not wanting to watch him flirt with the pretty waitress.

"Are you sure you don't want anything?" Grayson asks as he gathers up the burrito in his hands, looking at me with raised eyebrows, waiting for my answer before devouring his food.

His stomach rumbles loudly, making me chuckle as I wave him off. "I told you I'm fine. Eat your dinner. You're clearly starving."

He gives me the same charming smile he flashed at the waitress before taking a big bite. "My mom tells me I'm still a growing boy," he says between bites.

I can't help smiling back at him, caught up in the lightness of the moment despite our history and the seriousness of what we're here to discuss. His smile and boyish charm make it easy to forget all the bad lying between us.

This time it's Grayson who brings us back on topic. "Look, I know you have a whole routine, and I'm not ..." He looks around, searching for words. "I'm not trying to take him from you. I just want to get to know him. I want ... access. And I want to figure out how much I owe you for the last few years you've been on your own with him."

Instinctively, I shake my head. "I don't think—"

But he cuts me off. "I'm going to play professional football," he says matter-of-factly, like it's already decided.

At my spluttering scoff, he just nods as he takes a sip of water then meets my eyes. "It's just a matter of for who and what my contract will look like. They've been scouting me for the last couple of years, and leading Marycliff all the way to a bowl game this year has demonstrated that I have what it takes to lead a"—he pauses, once again searching for words—"an inexperienced team to a solid season. The team with the worst record gets first pick, and they want to pick solid players that can bring up their standings the next season."

Nodding, I swallow, wishing I had a drink too. "Yeah." My voice cracks. I clear my throat and try again. "Yeah. I know. My dad's a football coach. I know the basics of how it all works."

He nods too, finishing another bite. "So. I'm not saying I'll be the first pick or anything, but the review committee told Coach Reese they expect me to go in the first or second round."

Normally hearing a guy detail his pro football prospects would sound braggy, but he's not giving off that vibe at all. It's all very nonchalant and normal sounding, like everyone discusses the likelihood of being a first or second round NFL draft pick.

All I can do is blink at him.

"My point," he says around a mouthful of food, then swallows, chasing it with another sip of water. "My point is that I'll have plenty of money to help support Ben, and by extension, you. I'm his father. He's my responsibility too."

"Alright," I croak. I mean, if he wants to send me

monthly child support checks, that'll just make it easier to get my own place once I've graduated and found a job, right? And at least that'll be one less thing for my dad to get up in arms about. I'm sure he'd insist that Grayson start paying child support immediately if he knew I were in contact with him, especially since he's demanding access to Ben.

I rub my hands up and down my thighs, not sure what happens now. Grayson watches me in silence.

"Okay," I agree again, nodding. "If you want to help pay for things for Ben, I won't fight you on that."

He snorts, shaking his head, a crooked smile tipping up one corner of his mouth. "Meaning you will fight me on other things?"

Instead of answering, I ask a question of my own. "What is it you actually want?" I need to know, because I can't make any plans until I know the answer to that question. "What kind of custody and visitation plan do you have in mind?"

He gives me a look like a deer caught in headlights, and I can't decide whether I want to sigh or laugh more. Because clearly he hasn't really thought much beyond the caveman level of, "Child! Mine!" and therefore hasn't considered the full implications of what that means aside from financial support.

Taking a deep breath, I focus my gaze on my hands on the table. "You've said you want to see Ben. I'm pretty sure walking us from his classroom to my car isn't what you mean by that. And he'll need to be told that you're his father, I—" I suck in another deep breath, closing my eyes and forcing out the words. "I intend to do that. But you're basically a stranger, so that's going to be a big deal for him."

Warm fingers wrapping around mine make me open my eyes, and I look down to see Grayson's thumb rubbing the back of my hand. He gives me one last squeeze and withdraws, making my fingers feel even colder than they did before.

How does he do that? I should be furious with him. Cold and unfeeling. And with a few smiles, a couple of cute comments, and a simple comforting gesture, he's already starting to break down the walls I erected years ago.

His voice breaks into my thoughts. "Why don't we plan some activity for the three of us together? We can break the news to him there and then have a regular schedule like that for a while to let him get to know me. We'll move to one-on-one time when he's comfortable with me. Does that sound okay?"

I meet his eyes, hardly believing how reasonable he sounds after threatening to take me to court like half an hour ago. Licking my lips, I nod—and I don't miss the way his gaze zeroes in on my mouth before he drags his eyes back to mine.

"Okay," I agree. "I think that sounds like a good plan."

Grayson releases a breath and gives me a small smile. "Good. Okay. Now that's settled, will you please let me buy you something to eat?"

CHAPTER SEVENTEEN

Gray

Tiffany and I part ways in the parking lot after she finally let me buy her a small burrito. I'm not entirely sure why it matters so much to me that she let me feed her, but it does. And even though I know this isn't a date—she reminded me of that fact enough times, after all—for some reason, walking her to her car and watching her drive away feels all wrong.

She let me comfort her when she was upset. It wasn't much, really. A small gesture, covering her hand with mine and stroking her soft skin. But she didn't flinch away or act like she wanted to slap me. On the contrary, she seemed almost grateful.

After we reached our agreement to start with a first meeting, she relaxed quite a bit, giving me a glimpse of how she must be with everyone else. When I'd first walked up on her and Jackson that one day, she'd been laughing at something he'd said before she noticed me. Until today, I haven't seen her smile since.

When we walked up to the counter together so she could decide what to eat—a chorizo con huevos burrito—I had to restrain myself from escorting her through the line with my hand on her back. It's ridiculous, given everything, but having her with me somehow just feels … right. I can't explain it even to myself.

So when she finished her food, I only managed to get her to hang out with me for a few more minutes before she said she had to go.

As she drives away, I can admit to myself that I'm not ready for our time together to be over. And it definitely shouldn't end with her driving away without a backwards glance.

Letting out a sigh, I climb into my car. Her main question runs through my brain, and I sit in the parking lot telling myself I'm letting the car warm up when in reality I'm just loathe to go home to my sad little apartment with its secondhand furniture and bare walls. It's not a home. It's a place to crash.

What is it you actually want?

That's what she asked, and somehow the directness of the question caught me off guard. All I'd thought about was just wanting to see Ben. Get to know him. Let him get to know me. I hadn't really thought about the specifics and logistics of how that would work and what that would mean.

The word *custody* never even entered my head. Much

less *visitation schedule*. It all sounds so formal. So adult.

And suddenly I feel like a big dumb kid.

I don't like it. I don't like it at all.

I'm used to being in control. In my life, on the football field, in school. I know what's expected, I know where I need to be and when I need to be there, I know what needs to be done. I have playbooks and rule books and people to keep me in check. I know how to prioritize what needs to happen and when, I know how to evaluate a situation and call an audible to get my team the best outcome, I know how to change things up as needed so I can do the right thing. And if I make a bad call, I know there are people around me to help get me back on track.

But custody? Visitation? Parenting?

I don't have any playbooks or coaches for that. I don't know where the right track is, much less how to stay on it, or how to know if I've gotten off of it.

I've met the kid twice and swung him through the parking lot. And while being responsible for that level of sheer delight is intoxicating in the best way, *custody* and *visitation schedules* are things that parents deal with.

Obviously that's the clear goal of meeting with Tiffany and trying to start hashing things out, but it didn't really hit me until now.

What is it you actually want?

That's the million dollar question.

Slowly, I buckle my seatbelt and pull out of the driveway. But instead of heading for my apartment, I go in the opposite direction, toward my parents' house.

If I could have anything I wanted, it would be for

Tiffany to have given me a chance back in high school. But that's clearly impossible. And despite our moment of … friendliness, she obviously wants nothing to do with me now either.

Beyond that, I want the opportunity to get to know my son. That seems entirely abstract right now, though. And I don't know if I can come up with a better answer until after that piece is in place.

The other thing I want is support from people who care about me. And as much as I'm not looking forward to telling my parents, I don't think I can put it off any longer.

* * *

"Hello?" I call as I open my parents' door and let myself in. I grew up here, so it still feels like home, but I also feel strange just barging in since I don't actually live here anymore.

Mom pokes her head out of the kitchen, then emerges fully, smiling as she wipes her hands on a towel. "Gray. This is a surprise." She gives me a quick hug. "Are you here for dinner? We're just finishing up, but there's plenty if you want to sit down. I can make you a plate."

"No, I ate already." I clear my throat, which makes Mom stop on her way back into the kitchen, turning to examine me closely.

"Is everything alright?"

Ducking my head in a quick nod, I run my hand through my hair, unable to control the nerves and adrenaline racing through my system. I'm no stranger to a racing heartbeat and pounding blood, but I usually have some outlet for it. Somewhere to direct all this energy. But now? It's just … stuck. In my body.

With my hand in my pocket, I jiggle my keys, which only makes my mom stare at me longer.

"Is Dad home?" I ask, forcing the words through my tight throat.

She steps back and nods. "Yes. He's in the kitchen."

God, how are they going to react?

I've never really been on the receiving end of their anger or disappointment before.

Sure, I got reprimanded occasionally as a kid, but it was just normal kid stuff like *be nice to your sister* and *clean your room*. I did get a bit of secondhand censure whenever Piper got herself into trouble, because it was my job to look out for her when Mom and Dad weren't around, but they also know that Piper's as stubborn as they come and no one can really control her, them included.

But this? Telling them I just found out I have a kid? This is something else altogether.

And whatever else Piper's done, she doesn't have a secret baby, so this is all new territory for all of us, and I have no idea what to expect.

It's the not knowing that's killing me, to be honest.

Mom leads the way into the kitchen, where Dad sits at the table looking at something on his tablet.

He lifts his head when I enter the room, glancing between Mom and me, his gaze sharpening as he takes us in.

"Gray? Everything alright?"

"I asked him that," Mom answers for me, "but all he did was ask if you were here. So here we are." She sits in her usual seat, and I take the one opposite, reaching out and rolling up the corner of the brocade placemat at my seat.

Mom and Dad wait patiently while I roll and unroll the corner of the placemat a few times, but after a moment, Dad clears his throat. "Did something happen?"

I tilt my head to the side, because while yes, something did happen, the thing that happened was four years ago, so …

Blowing out a breath, I sit back in my chair, my hands scrubbing my thighs. "Um, I got some news."

Mom reaches for Dad's hand, and he wraps his fingers around hers, both of them bracing themselves. "What kind of news?" Mom asks, her voice more subdued than normal.

"Um, so, uh …" Unable to sit still, I stand and start pacing behind my chair, running both hands through my hair.

"Gray? Are you … are you … sick?" Mom asks, almost choking on the words.

I shake my head. "No. No, it's not that."

"Is it football?" Dad asks, both of them seeming less tense since I've successfully reassured them I'm not dying. God, I'm fucking this up. I can't even talk to my parents. How am I going to talk to a kid and say the right things? What if I fuck him up too?

But I shake my head again. "No, it's not football. It's …

shit," I mutter, not even caring that I'm cursing in front of my parents. I stop pacing, closing my eyes as I turn to face them, but open them to deliver the news. "Um, well, I, uh, I have a kid."

I've been wracking my brain for some way to lead up to it, but ultimately I can't come up with anything, so there it is, stammering, but summed up in just four tiny words. All single syllables too.

Holy shit. Holy shit holy shit holy shit.

I sit down heavily as my parents sag in their seats, their faces blank masks of shock.

Yeah, that's about how I feel about the whole thing too.

"I'm sorry, can you repeat that?" Mom says. "I think I must've misheard you."

"There's a girl. Tiffany. We met in high school. Well, I mean, *met* might be too strong of a word. We … were at a party together. Things … progressed." God, I'm talking to my parents about a high school hookup. Can life get any worse? I mean, maybe? But I can't think how right at the moment.

I clear my throat. "Anyway. I never saw her again until recently. She, um, she has a kid. He's three. And he's my son."

My parents just stare at me, Mom blinking owlishly, a range of indecipherable thoughts crossing Dad's face.

After a long moment, he clears his throat. "You're sure? Because with you poised to do well in the draft—"

I cut him off with a slash of my hand and a jerk of my head before he can finish that thought. While Tiffany wanted me to be involved originally, it's clear that she accepted my supposed lack of interest and has been competently handling things herself. I can't imagine that fierce and fiery woman trying to shake me down for money.

"I'm sure. We did a test."

"What kind of test did you do?" Dad asks.

I flip a hand. "One I picked up at the pharmacy. I got the results last Thursday."

"Thursday," Mom breathes, looking around, her gaze abstract. "Why didn't you say something?" She refocuses on me. "Why didn't you tell us then?"

Lifting one shoulder, I turn my hand palm up on the table. "I didn't want to announce it in front of everyone and ruin Thursday dinner. And I wasn't sure exactly what would happen."

"Does that mean you're sure now?" Dad asks.

I flip my hand back over and tap my fingers on the table. "Not exactly. I mean, not all the logistics and details, but I met with Tiffany tonight, and we're going to start slowly with me getting to know him and him getting to know me and then plan next steps from there with custody and visitation." There are those words again. God, I feel like when my dad would put one of his ties on me, and I'd stomp around the house in his dress shoes pretending to be an architect and trying to boss around Piper. Of course, she'd just stick out her tongue at me and do whatever she wanted. Except this time I'm pretending to be a dad.

Hopefully Ben reacts better to me than Piper did.

"That's ... good, I guess," says Mom.

I nod mutely to acknowledge the statement, and we all sit in silence, no one knowing what to say or how to deal with this.

"We should contact an attorney," Dad says. "I'll ask Mike if he knows any good family law attorneys." Mike is the contract attorney at Dad's firm. Leave it to Dad to go into problem solving mode.

I suck in a breath, ready to protest, but Dad holds up his hand. "I know you said you're figuring things out, but these things can be messy, and it's in everyone's best interests, including the child's, to have all the details in writing." And before I can utter another word, Dad picks up his phone and taps out a message, obviously following through immediately on texting Mike.

He meets my eyes as he places his phone back on the table. "I'll get in touch with Mike's recommendations tomorrow, and we'll make a plan of action for the best way to deal with this."

Is this how Piper felt when Mom and Dad came in and withdrew her from school down in California last year? This sense of paralysis and loss of control? Like all your choices are being taken away?

Though if the worst I'm dealing with is my dad insisting on getting family attorney recommendations, I'm getting off pretty easy. My parents look upset, but no one's screaming or crying or ... doing anything. They're remarkably calm.

What would they do if it were Piper announcing she's pregnant?

God, I can't even imagine how badly they'd lose their minds.

No wonder Piper was so pissed at everyone last semester. And then I betrayed her more …

I really need to apologize to her again. Another thing to add to the to-do list.

"What's his name?" Mom asks, leaning on the table, her hands twisted together. "Your … son. What's his name?"

"Ben. Benjamin. His mom sometimes calls him Benny."

"Ben," Mom repeats softly, looking at dad. "We have a grandson."

Yeah. Yeah, they do.

I swallow hard, watching the unspoken communication between them before Mom meets my eyes again. "We'd like to meet him too." She lifts her chin, as though expecting me to push back.

But I nod. Because of course they want to meet their grandson. How could they not?

CHAPTER EIGHTEEN

Tiffany

I can't quite decide what I'm feeling as I drive home.
Some weird combination of relief and anxiety. Relief
that Grayson doesn't expect overnight visits right away,
and despite his threat of involving the courts, he seems to
view that as a last resort. And having my ability to
participate in the decision making process taken away
from me ... well, that's my worst nightmare. As much as
I hate it, it's better to cooperate, especially since Grayson
appears to be stubborn and insistent that he be allowed
access to Ben.

Stupid ... man. Couldn't he just have stayed away?
We were doing fine without him. Yeah, sure, I've hated
him for years because of his abandonment, but that
doesn't mean I wanted him to grow a conscience and
decide to be involved. And I *especially* don't need his flirty

smiles, his insistence on buying me food, and the warmth of his touch that seems branded on my skin. It's like he wants to take care of me, and I'm not in the market to be taken care of anyway, and if I were, he wouldn't be on the list of applicants.

Why'd he come to Marycliff anyway?

That's actually a really good question. Why *did* he leave what had to be a good thing going for him in Ohio and come back here?

But that's a question for another time, because I'm home, and I'm going to have to tell my parents that Grayson wants to be involved with Ben now. They're going to be so pissed. And to make it worse, I need to talk to them without Ben, so I'll have to wait until after he's asleep to break the news. Which means I have to stew in my feelings for the next few hours, and they won't be able to vent their rage out loud when I do tell them.

Actually, maybe it's better this way.

Climbing out of my car, I make an action plan on my way to the front door. Even though I'm still not one hundred percent convinced, I'm going to go with the story that his coach never told him, he didn't know, and he just found out and wants to do the right thing.

I have no idea why I feel the need to defend him or put him in the best light. I shouldn't. I don't actually *like* him or anything. Although he was really sweet at dinner with insisting on paying and chatting with me like we're old friends and standing in the parking lot, watching me drive away, naked longing on his face like he was afraid he might never see me again.

That's the look you give your girlfriend as she drives off to college in a different state. Or your boyfriend who just enlisted in the military and is leaving for boot camp. Not the kind of look you give the estranged mother of the child you just discovered …

"How was your date?" Mom asks from her spot on the floor where she's doing a peg puzzle with Ben when I get inside.

Ben looks up, a wide grin on his face. "Mommy!"

I scoop him off the floor for a big hug. "Not a date, Mom," I remind her over his shoulder. "I just met up with a friend." The slight hesitation before the last word doesn't help my case at all, though.

Mom picks up on it, giving me a doubtful look. "Friend. Right." She passes Ben another puzzle piece when I put him back on the floor. "Is this a *friend* I've met?"

Rolling my eyes at her emphasis, I perch on the edge of Dad's chair and watch Ben try a few angles to line up the monkey with its slot before getting it right. "No. Where's Dad?"

"Bathroom." Mom passes Ben an elephant next.

"El-phant!" Ben crows. Mom makes an elephant sound, he doubles over in a fit of giggles, and I join in the laughter. It's a welcome release of the tension from anticipating the unpleasant conversation that I know will be coming when I tell my parents who my "friend" really is.

And then … I have to figure out how to tell Ben.

Does Grayson want to be there for that conversation?

We didn't talk about that.

Pulling out my phone, I fire off a quick text to ask him, ignoring my mother's knowing smile. "I'm gonna go change," I announce, and head for my bedroom to get back into my usual loungewear.

The evening seems to somehow both rush by at warp speed and drag on forever with Ben protesting the usual bedtime routine like it's something brand new and not what we've been doing every night for literal years. But I finally get him settled into bed after three stories, a song, and endless back rubs. I don't have it in me to try to get him to go to sleep without me tonight. Not with the reality of him spending nights somewhere else looming over us. Not with the upcoming conversation with my parents I don't want to have but can't conscionably put off any longer.

Plus the singing and rhythmic stroking of his back is as soothing for me as it is for him. And even though my stomach immediately ties itself in knots when I stand and quietly move to the bedroom door, the dread is a little more manageable. So that's something, at least.

The relief is short lived, though, when I find my parents bustling around the kitchen, Mom finishing up with the dishes, Dad gathering up today's newspaper to put in the recycle bin, ready for a fresh paper in the morning.

I stand in the doorway and watch them until Dad looks up and notices me. "Hey, sweet pea. Need something?"

Licking my lips, I force myself to nod. "Yeah." I clear

the frog from my throat. "Yeah. I … can I talk to you both? I, um, have some news."

I don't miss the concerned look my parents exchange as Mom puts the last glass in the dishwasher, closes it, and dries her hands on the towel hanging below the sink.

Sinking into my usual spot at the kitchen table, I take in the familiar sights of our kitchen and the nods to farmhouse decor with the milk and eggs signs hanging on the wall and the rooster napkin holder in the center of the oval table surrounded by matching oak Windsor back chairs. The seat at the end of the table is now Ben's, his little blue booster seat a permanent fixture there.

I stare at his spot for a moment, imagining dinners at this table without him, and the thought makes my heart clench. How soon will that start? Grayson said he wants to let Ben get comfortable with him before doing one-on-one visits, which is good, obviously. But how long will it take Grayson to decide that Ben's comfortable enough? And will my opinion matter? What if he decides one play date is enough and wants Ben to spend weekends with him like next week? Does he even have a place for Ben to stay? Where does he live? A week isn't enough time to get a bed and toys and toddler proof a place, is it? Not with classes and his training schedule and homework. Right? He said he doesn't have a roommate, so I don't have to worry about that at least, I guess.

"Tiffany?" Mom's soft voice interrupts my spiraling thoughts, and she reaches across the table to place her hand on top of mine. "What's going on?"

Sucking in a deep breath, I look at each of my parents

in turn. "Grayson Kilpatrick wants to be involved in Ben's life."

Mom just blinks at me, my words not making sense.

Dad stares blankly, equally in shock. Then he jerks his head, his chair scraping on the floor as he pushes it back to stand. He moves behind it, puts both hands on the back and squeezes until his knuckles turn white, his head down.

Folding my hands in front of me, I open my mouth, wanting to say something, but my planned defense flies out of my head, and I can't find the words.

"Why now?" Mom whispers hoarsely at last. "He left. He pretended he didn't even know you. Why does he care now?"

Dad throws a hand in Mom's direction in wordless agreement with her question, his arm shaking with tension.

Clearing my throat, I shake my head. "He says he never knew. Before. His coach didn't actually talk to him. He had no idea until recently, and now that he knows, he wants to do the right thing."

Dad snarls. "I should've known." He bangs the heel of his palm on the back of his chair. "That rat-faced, backstabbing bastard. I should've known better than to trust him. I should've insisted on talking to that damn kid myself."

Even though his comments are obviously directed more at himself than anyone else, I guess if Dad blames Coach Lawson or himself more than Grayson, at least he won't try to cut Grayson's balls off if and when they ever come face to face.

Mom reaches out a hand, and Dad grabs it and gives it a squeeze before letting go to resume pacing. She turns her attention to me, her eyes narrowing as she connects more dots. "Your date tonight. Is that who you were meeting?"

I nod again. "Yes. It wasn't a date. It was us figuring out how to include him in our life."

"So he wants to be involved." Dad sounds resigned.

For some reason that irritates the hell out of me. Shouldn't they want Grayson to be involved? Isn't it good? Good for Ben, at the very least, and potentially good for everyone? If he's around and actually stepping into his role as a parent, that means my parents won't have to pick up the slack for me nearly as much. They're starting to talk about retiring. Wouldn't they enjoy being able to just relax and have the house to themselves rather than helping raise another kid?

Pushing aside my irrational irritation, I keep my voice level, lifting my chin to address my father. "Yes. He does. We already did a paternity test to confirm that he's the father, so it's all official and everything."

"What did you decide?" That's Mom again, the pragmatic one. I know she's already contemplating what this means for the childcare schedule.

I fill them in on the gist of our conversation tonight, and Mom pulls out her phone while I'm still talking. "Uh ... something important going on, Mom?"

She gives me a pursed lip glare. "I'm looking up family attorneys."

My stomach clenches and my heart rate picks back up. "Why?" The question comes out sharper than I intend.

"Because," she says like the answer should be obvious, "whatever you work out needs to be formalized. We need to at least consult an attorney about the legalities and implications before you agree to anything more."

I open my mouth, because that sounds terrifying, but I close it without speaking.

"She has a good point," Dad says, sinking back into his chair, now being the quiet, soothing one. "I'm glad that Ben's dad wants to be involved. While what happened with you certainly lowered my opinion of him, prior to that I thought he seemed like a good kid. Responsible, reliable, steady on the field. But he's also young and poised to start a career as a professional athlete. It would be in everyone's best interests for you to have everything in writing, and an attorney can help us decide what type of language and provisions we need to include." His voice taking on that dark, angry edge again, he continues. "Besides, this way we'll ensure that he can't just pretend he doesn't know you if it's convenient again."

Looking down at my hands, I pick at one of my cuticles, blinking away the tears that rise to my eyes unbidden. All of this—confronting Grayson, telling my parents, discussing custody and visitation—is stirring up a lot of emotions, both old and new. The sick, sinking feeling when I was told he pretended not to know me. The fear, the worry, the facing down the unknown. All of that is back in full force. What if he decides to abandon us again? Or, I guess maybe for the first time?

Dad has a point about him leaving soon. He'll be an absentee father in some capacity no matter what. At least if there's a formal, legally binding agreement, I know that Ben will get taken care of.

Nodding again, I blow out a slow breath. "That's a good point."

We spend a few more minutes looking at potential attorneys and Mom says she's going to do more research on common custody arrangements. I feel like I should be the one doing that, but for right now I'm feeling overwhelmed enough that I'm happy to let her take the lead. At least if she's informed, I'll be able to bounce ideas off her as things evolve.

When we part ways to go to bed, the sick feeling in my gut has mostly subsided, and it's a relief to know that my parents have my back yet again. Not that I really doubted they would, but sharing big potentially negative news is always nerve racking.

Now the biggest unknown is how much Grayson's presence will change everything …

CHAPTER NINETEEN

Gray

Anticipation sings through my blood as I get out of my car in the mall parking lot, sending a quick text to Tiffany to let her know I'm on site and heading to the designated meeting place.

I'm not super thrilled that we're doing this at a mall playground, but she assured me that he would have lots of fun here. She said that after he burns off some energy we can get a snack in the food court, and since it's too cold to meet at a park, this is the next best option.

I suppose doing this in a neutral place is reasonable. Meeting at my apartment would be quieter, but I don't have anything to entertain a little kid, so it's probably not the best option. And really, it's not like I'm going to have deep philosophical conversations with a three-year-old. Right?

But any disappointment at her choice of meeting place is far outweighed by the nervousness and excitement that wells up inside me, setting my heart racing and my palms sweating. I get to see Tiffany again, which by itself fills me with nervous excitement. My attraction to her, inconvenient as it may be, has only gotten stronger since our dinner that wasn't a date. Our easy conversation only makes me want to chip away at that wall she has between us. I don't expect her to ever want to date me, but I'd like it if we could at least be friends.

Or at least that's what I keep telling myself.

My stomach roils nervously as I consider the other purpose of today's visit. We're going to tell Ben that I'm his father.

I have no idea what to expect or how he might react. Will he accept me right away? Will he ignore me? He was pretty excited to see me last time, but I'm smart enough to know that it's because he liked me swinging him really high with his mom. If Jackson, or hell, even Cal McAdam did that, he'd be just as thrilled to see them.

My phone chimes with an alert as I go in the mall's main entrance.

Tiffany: We're already at the playground. See you soon.

That means I'll have time to sit with Tiffany before we have the, "Ben, I am your father," conversation, though I'll be sure not to use the heavy-breathing Darth Vader impression when we say it. Will I be telling him? Or will she?

We never discussed the particulars.

Maybe I can ask her how she thinks we should deliver the news while we're watching Ben play. It'll give us something to talk about, though part of me wants to pick a lighter subject, something that will relax her and get her to open up to me again. I want more time with that Tiffany.

After consulting the map to find the play area, I go up the escalator and make my way to the end of the mall where there's an area sectioned off by purple half walls surrounding a big shiny foam looking tree. Kids climb up one side, go through a hole in the trunk, and slide down the other. Laughter rings out as I get closer, indistinct shouts from a half dozen little kids running and shrieking and playing.

A bench runs along the inside of the wall for parents to wait, and when I open the gate, Tiffany immediately looks up from her phone and gives me a cautious smile. "Hey. You made it."

Nodding, I take my coat off and sit in the free space next to her. She has a pile of coats on her other side and her big tote bag set on top of it, gaping open to reveal a package of baby wipes and a gallon Ziploc of various snacks.

I don't know that I would've even thought to bring snacks, much less baby wipes. Wait—is he still in diapers? What age do kids stop wearing diapers usually?

"Are you alright?" Tiffany asks, pulling me out of my staring and blinking.

"Yeah. Sorry. I, uh ..."

She offers me a sympathetic smile. "It can be kinda overwhelming, I know." She looks around the space at the other parents and kids. "It's not too crowded today, which is nice."

Ben comes running over, jumping up and down in front of us. "Mommy! Your friend is here!" He places his hands on her knees and continues bouncing up and down.

I can't help smiling at his antics. "Hey, buddy. Your mom invited me along to hang out with you today. Is that okay with you?"

He turns to me with wide brown eyes that mirror my own, nodding. "Mommy said you were gonna have a snack with us after." His little hands land on my knees now, and he jumps close to my face and shouts, "I love snacks!"

"Me too," I say with a laugh.

He pauses his jumping, holding his arms up above his head. "You gonna swing me while we walk?"

Stealing a glance at Tiffany, who's watching this exchange with an inscrutable expression on her face, I nod. "If your mom's okay with it."

He clasps his hands together and turns to his mom. "Please please please, Mommy, please please please."

Leaning forward, she pulls him in close for a hug. "How can I say no when you ask so nicely?"

"Yay!" The bouncing resumes, then he runs back into the fray, climbing into a boat and moving all around like he's being tossed at sea.

I may not know the first thing about diapers and packing the right amount of snacks and clean up supplies for a trip to a mall playground, but I already know I'd do just about anything to keep a smile on that kid's face.

"He's really cute," I say after watching him go down the slide a couple more times.

"He is," Tiffany agrees easily.

We watch him in relative silence for a while, and while it's not uncomfortable, the question of how we're going to tell Ben who I really am to him needles me like a thorn stuck under my clothes. If we can get that out of the way, maybe we can move from stilted silence to actual conversation.

"So what's your plan?" I ask at last.

She turns to me, her eyes as wide as Ben's were a few minutes ago, and suddenly I see echoes of her in his face as well. "My plan?"

I gesture around, encompassing us, Ben, and the play area. "We're telling him today, right? That was the impression I was under, at least. But this doesn't seem like the most conducive spot to have a conversation."

She ducks her head like she's trying to hide behind her hair, but it's piled on top of her head in a messy bun, so the move doesn't really work. "Yeah." She clears her throat. "There's not—" Looking up, she shakes her head and sighs. "I don't know what I'm doing here."

"That makes two of us," I mutter.

She shoots me a look, her lips quirked in a rueful smile, and for a brief shining moment, it feels like we're in this together. Not adversaries or whatever we've been, but like we're on the same side. "There's not exactly a handbook on this, you know? I actually poked around on the internet last night to see if there were any tips."

"And?" I tried that too, but didn't even know how to frame the question so Google would give me any answers that might help.

She shrugs. "And it's all very subjective. Go slow—which we've already agreed on—and validate your kid's feelings kind of stuff." Pressing her lips together, her eyes on Ben, she shakes her head. "I don't know that there's a right way, really. All we can do is our best." She looks at me again. "If you don't want to tell him here or in the food court, that's fine, I just …" She shrugs again. "I don't really know where would be better? Most things said familiar surroundings are best for young kids. But I still live with my parents, and I didn't think having them around would be helpful today. The park by their house is familiar, but it's too cold to be outside for long. So that left here."

Nodding, I slump down on the industrial carpet covered slab of wood masquerading as a bench to try to get comfortable, enjoying this fleeting feeling of camaraderie for as long as it'll last. "Makes sense," I say gamely. While I might not've been thrilled about a mall play area and food court as a first choice of venue, there really aren't a lot of options for neutral territory that's also familiar to Ben. Hearing her admit to winging it makes me feel better about the fact that I feel like I'm at sea in a life raft without even an oar, much less a motor to navigate the choppy waves.

She glances at me before looking at Ben again. "We can schedule something else. Tell him another time. If you want."

"No."

She looks at me, eyes wide at my barked negative. And just like that, I've fucked up whatever connection we shared. Dammit.

Forcing a deep breath, I try again. "Sorry. That came out harsher than I intended." I sit up straighter. "I don't want to wait. And I don't have any better suggestions of places to meet. I mean, there's my apartment, but that doesn't meet the familiar surroundings requirement, and I don't have any toys or anything there." Shit. Should I have gotten him a toy for today? I didn't even think about that until just now.

"Oh, that reminds me," Tiffany says, turning and digging through the bag next to her. She pulls something orange out and slides it toward me along the back of the bench. "Hurry, stick it in your pocket or under your coat before he sees it. He's got a sixth sense for anything you don't want him to see. Packing that in there and keeping him from noticing was a whole thing."

My fingers brush hers as I take the hard plastic toy from her hand, a zing of electricity passing between us.

Her lips part, and I'm ultra aware of how close we're sitting, how she's leaning toward me, how I could press my thigh to hers if I closed the few inches between us …

She jerks her hand away, turning toward her bag again, making a production of arranging everything just right.

I look down at what she handed me and find an orange and red triceratops in my hand.

"Hide it. Quick!" she hisses, and I obediently stuff it under the coat in my lap. She relaxes back against the wall, giving me some serious side eye. "You'll have to up your subterfuge if you're gonna be a dad."

"What?" Something about her referring to me as a dad is messing with my head, and none of her words make sense.

She chuckles, adjusting her position on the uncomfortable bench, and that rare glimpse of laughter from her dazzles me as much as her earlier words addled me. "I'm not saying you need to be a pathological liar or anything, but you gotta be able to hide toys and stuff. Otherwise he'll figure out you're Santa and the Easter Bunny before he turns four."

An answering grin pulls at my lips. "Thanks for the tip." An image comes to my mind of pulling out hidden presents for Christmas and setting them around a tree for Ben to find when he wakes up in the morning. I shake it off quickly, though, because in that vision Tiffany's with me, tiptoeing around, giggling and trying to stay quiet as we set everything out together. Which is definitely impossible.

I mean, would I want that anyway? I'm supposed to be focusing on my football career. I've purposely kept myself free of entanglements and relationships. Now ... I guess I'm firmly entangled whether I wanted to be or not.

And maybe I didn't want to before. But now that I know about Ben ... you couldn't pay me enough money to stay away.

My eyes are drawn to her profile, and I study her as she watches Ben, tracing the lines of her face with my eyes, remembering the feel of her plump lips under mine. Sure, it's been years, and maybe I'm embellishing the memory, but I remember thinking she was hot as fuck that night and how much fun it was to get to screw with my rival by dancing with his girlfriend. I caught him watching us, but when I kissed her it became far more about her than about screwing with him. And when she agreed to head to a bedroom ...

Ben comes running up, out of breath and sweaty, pulling me out of the memory of our night together. "Mommy! Mommy! I'm thirsty!"

"I bet you are." She pulls a blue water bottle out of her magic bag and hands it to him.

Drinking deeply, he turns his guileless face to me, studying me for a moment before pausing to say, "Hi."

"Hi." I'm sure my grin is big and dumb, but I don't even care. This kid is adorable and hilarious.

"You gonna have snacks with us?"

I nod, even though we've already covered this. "I

am."

He bounces up and down. "Yay!" After one more drink, he hands the water back to Tiffany.

"You ready for snacks now?" she asks.

He shakes his head and takes off running, shouting, "No!" over his shoulder on his way back to the slide.

Tiffany checks her phone. "Next time he comes over, I'll give him a ten minute warning, then we can go to the food court and get something to eat. We'll tell him then."

My heart rate picks up, and I take a deep breath, letting it out slowly. "What if he starts, I dunno, like screaming and crying or something?"

Tiffany looks at me and lets out a soft chuckle. "You think he'll be that upset at the prospect of finding out you're his dad?"

I give her an answering chuckle, looking down at my coat and fingering the plastic dinosaur hidden inside it. "Maybe? I don't know. I mean, won't it be a shock?"

Risking a glance at her, I see her pulling her mouth from side to side while she watches Ben and thinks about that. "Yes," she says slowly. "It probably will. But how we act about it will help him figure out how he should act too. If we act like it's normal and no big deal, he shouldn't freak out. He'll mostly want to know what that means for him." Her blue eyes meet mine. "Which, I suppose, we should figure out a little bit more first. Do we want to do a weekly time together like this? And"—she swallows hard, her eyes darting to the side as she considers her next statement—"I mean, you've already come with me to preschool pick up a couple of times. We could start making that a regular thing too. And depending on your schedule, add in a visit one afternoon during the week."

I have to clear my throat, stunned and happy and a little choked up at her willingness to offer … anything, really. It's way more generous than I would've expected from the rocky start to this phase of our relationship. Nodding, I clear my throat again. "That sounds … good. Yeah. Let's plan on that. We can adjust as everyone gets more comfortable and Ben gets to know me better."

She shoves my shoulder, a grin on her face that looks too forced to be genuine. "Aww, don't get all soft on me. You'll ruin your reputation if people here see the star quarterback with the NFL expectations crying at the mall's indoor playground."

Shaking my head, half my mouth lifting at her words, I reach out and pat her leg without thinking. "Don't worry. I won't do that." I stare down at my hand just resting on her leg like it belongs there. When I glance at her, she's just staring at it too. Jerking my hand away, I stuff it back under my coat. "Sorry," I mutter. Being with her feels so comfortable, touching her like that seems natural, but I need to remember that we don't have that kind of relationship. She made it clear the other night that she's not interested in me. Even if I'm attracted to her, that's one sided, and I need to deal with my own feelings and not push them at her.

She dismisses my apology with a wave of her hand. "You're fine. No apologies necessary. We're all still figuring out where we stand with each other."

Before I can respond, she stands and waves at Ben. "Ten minutes, bud," she calls, giving him a thumbs up. He holds his little thumb up in response, and Tiffany settles back into her spot on the bench.

Ten more minutes, then we'll find a table and tell Ben I'm his dad over soft pretzels and Orange Julius. No big deal, right?

Ha.

CHAPTER TWENTY

Tiffany

The imprint of Grayson's hand seems branded into my skin. It took a second for my brain to catch up to the sensation of his hand on my leg—the warm comfort of his touch—and the stupid horny part of me is sad that he removed his hand so quickly.

Which is ridiculous. I mean, really ridiculous. Sure, he's wanting to be a father to Ben, and that's good, as long as he follows through. Good for Ben more than for me.

But the memory of our night together has been playing in my head on repeat ever since Grayson showed up again. And the warmth of his hand on my leg brought all those initial feelings of attraction and boldness flooding back.

What would it be like now? He was good back then, and I can only imagine that he's had a lot more experience since then, what with all the attention I'm sure being a star athlete generates. Whereas I've been ... not getting much action. That must be why my vagina is trying to take over and do the thinking right now.

Because let's be honest, getting together with Grayson for any reason would be a terrible idea. He's supposed to be building a relationship with Ben, not with me. And would he even want a relationship with me anyway? He's off to the NFL in a matter of months. If things went sour between us, that would make it even more difficult to co-parent effectively.

And it's not like things are off to a great start as it is ...

No. It's good that he jerked away. Because us together is too risky. And our focus needs to be on Ben, and *only* Ben.

We don't speak while we wait for the clock to tick down for Ben to finish playing. I keep my eyes trained on Ben, watching him play with the other kids, running around, and generally wearing himself out in the best way, studiously ignoring the hot football player sitting next to me and the tension running between us. Though it's probably only me who feels it. I'm sure he was just being friendly with his leg pat, and I gave him horny eyes, and he jerked away to make it clear that's not what he's here for. And who can blame him? I already told him that I was absolutely not interested in him at all.

Checking my phone for the 384748th time in the last eight minutes, I decide it's close enough to ten and stand. I move to the base of the slide and wait for him to come down, offering my hand for a high five when he pops to his feet.

"Mommy! Mommy! Watch me do it again!"

"Alright. Last time, though, okay? Then snacks."

He runs to the stairs without answering, waiting for the two kids in front of him to go and move out of the way before taking his turn. Preschool has helped a lot with that. In the fall, he would've just barreled down on top of them unless I stood right next to him and made him wait.

Checking to make sure I'm watching, he lies down and slides down head first, arms out Superman style. When he gets to the bottom, he drags himself the rest of the way off and stands up, beaming. "Didja see? Didja see?"

"I did!" I can't help grinning at his enthusiasm. "Good job. Just don't do that on the big slide at school. You'll end up with a facefull of bark. Let's go get Grayson and then pick out what snacks we want."

"Can I get a corndog? I want a corndog!"

"Sure, sweetie. You can have a corndog."

"Yay!" He sprints for Grayson, bouncing up and down with his hands on Grayson's legs, yelling, "I get a corndog!"

The soft affection and indulgent smile on Grayson's face as he interacts with Ben fills me with warmth, intensifying my inconvenient attraction. I've never introduced a man to my son before. And while Grayson and I aren't anything to each other, this is the way I'd want someone I was serious about to react to my son. Happy to see him. Wanting to spend time with him.

Looking at him like he's the greatest thing in the world.

The memory of the warmth of Grayson's hand on my leg, the way he was with me that night years ago ... the part of me that grew up wishing Disney fairy tales could come true wonders if maybe something like that *could* happen for Grayson and me.

But I'm not that naive. Not anymore.

Maybe I was once. Back when I found out I was pregnant and thought maybe something could happen between us. He'd asked for my number, after all. I hadn't given it to him because I was fresh off my breakup with Carter and thought taking a break from guys was a smart move. Ha. How right I'd been. Too bad I didn't decide that until after I got knocked up. Not that I regret a moment of Ben's existence, but getting pregnant in your senior year of high school is certainly no picnic.

But that naive part of me died when Grayson denied ever meeting me. Or at least I thought it did ... I guess it's making a reappearance now. How inconvenient.

Clearing the clog out of my throat, I pull Ben's shoes out of my bag, squatting down to help him get them on. He's still distracted by Grayson, telling him all about how much fun he had playing and how excited he is for his corndog, so he repeatedly tries to put his right foot into his left shoe.

Grayson notices, and leans over to look at Ben's feet. "Wrong foot, buddy. Your mom needs your other foot."

I give him a quick smile of thanks, and our eyes catch and hold for a moment. It's probably my imagination combined with my recent thoughts, but I could swear that the same warmth and affection he directed at Ben is now channeled toward me as he returns my smile.

That shouldn't fill me with as much hope and happiness as it does. All the articles I read about co-parenting emphasized maintaining a businesslike relationship. Of course they were assuming divorced parents, but I figured given our animosity—or maybe just *my* animosity—that seemed like a good goal. But if he's going to touch me and smile at me and generally be a good guy, I'm not sure how long I'll be able to maintain my distance.

Once the first shoe is on, the second one goes faster, and I gather our coats and my bag, taking Ben by the hand to lead him out of the playground, Grayson trailing behind us.

Ben and I head to the place with the corndogs, while Grayson gestures he's going to get something from a different stand. With a corndog for Ben, a large container of fries, and a chocolate milk on a tray, I choose a table that's as out of the way as possible.

Tray in hand, Grayson looks around, his face lighting up when he spots us. My heart gives a funny thump in my chest. His smile warms me, but the reality of what we're about to do has my anxiety ratcheting up to an all time high, and suddenly French fries sound like a terrible choice. I'm not sure my stomach can handle much of anything right now.

Oblivious, Ben climbs onto the chair next to mine and sits on his knees, chanting, "Corndog, corndog, corndog," while I place it in front of him. He picks it up and takes a huge bite, grinning at Grayson around his mouthful as Grayson takes the seat across from Ben.

"Corndog. Nice," Grayson says approvingly while gathering up some kind of wrap in his hands.

He glances at me, eyebrows raised. "Not hungry?"

Shaking my head, I rub my hands on my thighs. "Nah. Not really."

The look he gives me is warm and full of understanding, and I don't like the way it feels like we're co-conspirators. With a firm internal voice, I remind myself that he's just here because of Ben. Not me. I'm the barrier between them, the thing blocking Grayson from having access, the gatekeeper he has to appease in order to see his son.

Ben chatters to Grayson, asking a million questions, because that's what he does, interrupting to tell stories about things he does at preschool—lately he's been all about Mount Saint Helens, because they made clay volcanoes in class last week and his teacher told them about the eruption and how there was ash everywhere. According to Ben, he was there when Mount Saint Helens erupted, though he says interrupted. Must've been in a past life.

Grayson's nodding and making sounds of awed wonder at appropriate intervals, hiding his smile at the talk of the "interruption." It's really sweet, but I'm dying inside, because I need to get this over with, but I also want Ben to finish eating first.

Grayson glances at me from time to time, and I do my best to give him reassuring smiles, but I think they probably come out looking more sick than anything. Once upon a time I could fake smile my way through almost anything. Since quitting cheerleading my senior year, I seem to have slowly lost that ability.

After he finishes his wrap, he lays his arm on the table, almost like he's reaching across for me, and I remember the way he did that when we had burritos the other night. The way he gently wrapped his fingers around my wrist and moved my hand away from my face when I was overcome.

Is this his way of offering support?

Even if it's not, I'll pretend it is. Because at this point, I'll take whatever I can get.

At long last, Ben nibbles the last of his cornbread covered hot dog off its stick and proceeds to tap the stick on every available surface. Grayson glances at me, apprehension clouding his gaze.

Sucking in a deep breath, I decide it's time to rip off the Band-Aid, so to speak. "Hey, Ben," I say lightly and wait for him to glance at me so I know he's listening. "How would you like it if you got to see Mommy's friend Grayson a lot more often."

Ben looks between Grayson and me. "Sure." Then to Grayson. "Will you swing me?"

Laughing, Grayson wipes his hands on a napkin, even though he already did that, crumples it up and drops it on his tray. "As often as you want." Despite his easy answer, I can see the lines of tension drawing his muscles up tight.

Ben sits up straighter, excitement lighting his face. "I

want it *every day!*"

That provokes more chuckles from Grayson, but again, all I can muster is a sickly smile.

"I don't know if we can do *every* day," I tell Ben. "Grayson has classes and football and other things he needs to do too."

"You play football?" Ben asks, perking up at that word. "My grampa plays football. Right, Mommy?"

I nod. "Yeah. He coaches more than he plays these days. But you and he like to play football together, don't you?" Ben nods eagerly, looking at Grayson to see his reaction.

"I could play football with you too," Grayson says, and Ben's eyes grow comically wide.

"Really?" This kid is in heaven.

"Really," Grayson confirms, his smile wide, and he glances at me like he wants me to share in his pleasure.

"Maybe you guys can do football next weekend," I suggest.

Ben wiggles in his seat, overflowing with excitement. "Can we, Mommy? Please?"

I gesture at Grayson. "If it's okay with Grayson."

At his nod, I suck in another breath. Because now it's time to drop the bomb.

Leaning down so I'm closer to Ben's level, I peer into his face. "Ben, there's something important I want to tell you."

I hear Grayson inhale sharply, then cough like he aspirated some crumbs. Straightening, I glance at him, eyebrows raised. "You alright?"

Nodding, Grayson waves me off. "Go on," he says, voice hoarse. "Keep going."

Right. Here goes nothin'.

"You know how Grampa is Mommy's Dad?" I ask Ben.

His eyebrows pinch together. "And Gramma is your Mommy, right?"

"Right. Well, did you know you have a daddy too?"

Ben's eyes grow huge again, and then he's back to confusion, shaking his head. "No, I don't. I have a mommy and a gramma and a grampa. That's my family."

"That's true," I hedge, risking a glance at Grayson, who sits impassively, waiting for me to spit it out. They did a whole thing about family relationships in preschool before winter break. That was really the first time the question of Ben's dad has come up. And I did my best to brush it aside and gloss over the lack, emphasizing that he's lucky since he gets to live with *three* grownups who love and care about him, and not just one or two.

And now that's kinda coming back to bite me in the ass.

"But everybody has a dad, because it takes a mommy and a daddy to make a baby. It's just …" I pause, mouth open, not quite sure what to say or how much to explain. "Your daddy had to be away for a while."

"How come?" Oh, my heart is dying from his sweet little innocent face wanting to understand things that he really can't.

He abandoned us. He didn't want us. But that's maybe not true, after all. And even if it were, I couldn't tell my son that, even if Grayson weren't sitting right here.

A glance at Grayson reveals that his mouth is also open like he's about to say something, but similarly can't figure out what exactly that should be.

So I go with something easy. "Sometimes grownups have to do things, and sometimes those things take them away from their kids. Anyway, the point is, your daddy is back, and he wants to spend time with you."

Brows pinched together again, Ben cocks his head. "Where is he?"

"Right here," says Grayson, his voice low and gruff like he's trying and not quite succeeding at holding back his emotions.

Ben cocks his head and studies Grayson. "You're my daddy?"

CHAPTER TWENTY-ONE

Gray

That word, that question, from that guileless face in that cute little kid voice … My heart thumps hard as my insides rearrange themselves to make room for this little guy who's burrowing his way in without even trying.

I nod and clear my throat. "Yeah. Yeah, bud. I'm your dad. Oh, and I, uh, got you something." I set the dinosaur on the table in front of him, hating the lie that I got it. His mom got it to help me look good.

Which is totally unexpected. Why would she be wanting to help me look good? Wouldn't it be easier on her if Ben *didn't* like me? So the fact that she even *thought* about helping me out and then went to the trouble of hiding a toy from him so I can pass it off as a gift from me has my feelings even more twisted up. I'm already falling for this kid. And my attraction to Tiffany is undeniable. But there's a difference between attraction and feelings. I've been attracted to plenty of women and not acted on it. If she's going to do things like this, help me out like this, there's a real possibility that feelings will enter the mix, and I don't know how to handle that.

Ben picks up the dinosaur and makes a roaring sound, then looks between me and his mom. "Can we get ice cream?"

Tiffany stills, staring at him for a second, and when she glances at me, her lips twitch in amusement. "Umm," her voice shakes a little, but then she comes to a decision. "Sure. Yeah. Yes, let's get ice cream."

Hopping out of his seat, Ben takes off for the ice cream place. Tiffany gives me a bewildered look before following after him.

I rise more slowly, uncertain if I should go with them or not. But then Ben runs back in my direction, past Tiffany standing with her hands on her hips, an indulgent smile on her face.

"Mommy's friend!" he yells. "Come on! Ice cream!"

Mommy's friend. I guess that explains his nonchalance in the face of life changing information. No screaming or crying. Only a few minutes of confusion followed by ice cream. Me as his dad doesn't make sense to him. Not yet, anyway.

Determination fills me. He'll learn what it means to have a dad eventually. I'll make sure of that, at least.

Giving him a smile, I hold out my hand for his. "Call me Gray," I tell him. That seems safest since he hasn't quite grasped the idea that I'm his dad.

"I've got the ice cream," I tell Tiffany as she falls in step beside us. She nods and picks up Ben, holding him up so he can point at the flavor he wants.

Tiffany gives me another glance, her brows raised in question, and when I nod, she orders a cone for herself. I hesitate, because this wasn't part of my meal plan today, but decide to splurge on a small cone as well.

Ben eats his ice cream cone with relish, while Tiffany and I are more subdued. I'm not sure how she's feeling, but I'd built this up in my head a lot, expecting to have to deal with a lot of questions or emotions, but Ben seems ... entirely unfazed. More concerned with corndogs and ice cream than the question of his paternity. Of course, he's three, so I guess it doesn't mean that much to him.

After we finish our ice cream, Tiffany cleans up Ben with the wipes from her bag and takes him to the bathroom, which I'm guessing means he uses the toilet and doesn't wear diapers still, but I should probably ask just to be sure. I also need to make a list of things that I'll need for him before he stays with me for any length of time. I mean, we're going to be doing visits all together for ... a while. We haven't settled on what that'll mean in practice. I guess we're being flexible and seeing how Ben handles everything.

As promised, Tiffany and I swing Ben from the exit to the car with him giggling all the way. I wait, watching her strap him into his car seat, then she stands and stares at me for a moment, arms crossed against the cold, the tip of her nose a little pink from the time we've been out here already.

I stuff my hands in my pockets so I don't reach for her. Because everything in me wants to wrap my arms around her and hold her close. Maybe it's not so much that feelings are possible. Feelings seem to have already entered the chat. "Thanks," I manage to get out gruffly. "For this."

She nods, avoiding my gaze and tucking a stray strand of hair behind her ear. "Yeah. Sure. Of course. Thanks for buying the ice cream."

"No problem."

"So, uh, next weekend, then?"

I nod, hating the stilted quality of our conversation. Hating that I don't have access to either of them whenever I want. "And preschool pickup. So I guess I'll see you on Monday."

Her eyes widen a fraction, then she's nodding again. "Right. Yeah, of course. See you Monday."

I step back, giving her room to get to her door, then move to stand near Ben's window so I can wave at him as they drive away.

He waves back, a big grin on his face, thrilled with the attention. I force myself to smile back until I can't see him anymore. But I don't feel like smiling. I feel somehow bereft after only two hours with the both of them.

I promised football with him next Saturday, so we won't be meeting at the mall playground again unless the weather's truly terrible. At least I have the promise of seeing him a few minutes a day to look forward to. And in that time, I can hash out with Tiffany where we should get together next weekend.

And hopefully rein in my entirely inappropriate and unwelcome feelings toward her.

* * *

The next two weeks pass in a blur. I meet Tiffany every day to pick up Ben from preschool, swinging him out to the car every day as promised. And every day they burrow their way into my heart a little more.

With Ben, that's not a problem. Yeah, we're taking things slow, but he's my kid. I'm supposed to think he's the greatest thing in the world, right?

But with Tiffany … spending time with her every afternoon, finding ways to make her laugh or smile, it makes it more difficult to keep my feelings—and my hands—to myself. And when her face starts lighting up at the sight of me, I feel a thrill of victory tempered by a profound sense of disappointment that it won't ever be anything more.

She keeps her distance, carefully out of touching range, and I keep my hands in my pockets to remind myself that I'm not supposed to touch her no matter how much I want to. Every day I have to restrain myself from pulling her close and wrapping an arm around her. And when we say goodbye, I stop myself from hugging her and placing a kiss on the tip of her nose, or her forehead … or her lips.

Seeing her and Ben has quickly become the highlight of my day, even if it's over almost as soon as it starts and full of unfulfilled longing.

The pressure of my own desires is compounded by my parents wanting to meet their grandson. They haven't been hounding me or anything, giving me time and space to get things settled, and I've been giving them updates and pictures. But I know they're anxious to meet Ben, and that knowledge weighs on me.

I worry that asking right now would upset the delicate friendship I've struck up with Tiffany. And I'm not willing to do anything that would send us back to the stilted awkwardness of those first few meetings. Not when she greets me with smiles and falls into easy conversation like we're old friends, texting me photos of Ben making silly faces or drawings he's made when we're apart.

Our day at the park playing football with Ben went goes a long way toward getting Tiffany on my team. She helps coach me on how her dad plays football with him after laughing at me standing and staring at Ben open mouthed when we got out in the grass, all bundled up in sweatshirts against the chill despite the unseasonable sunshine.

My regulation sized football is obviously way too big for him, and Tiffany came prepared with the Nerf ball he uses with her dad.

Saying goodbye at the end of our visit is the most painful part. I actually got to touch her under the guise of playing football, her thick layers making her cuter rather than less attractive, and it takes everything in me not to wrap my arms around her and bury my face in her hair.

But I manage to restrain myself. Barely.

For our next visit, the weather is bad—just enough above freezing for the drizzle to be rain instead of snow and cold enough to be nothing but miserable—so she's bringing Ben over to my apartment for the first time.

I've acquired a handful of toys—some blocks and Duplos I got from my mom that were mine and Piper's when we were kids plus a Little People plane and a few wooden peg puzzles that looked nice when I saw them at the store. Walking up and down the toy aisle was overwhelming, though. There are so many choices. And I don't know Ben well enough to know what he'll like.

The one thing I was confident about was getting him his own little foam football stamped with MU and a kids' Marycliff Football jersey from the campus store. The jersey might be big on him since they didn't have toddler sizes, but I want him to have it anyway. Maybe it's silly since my one and only football season here is over, but I feel just as much a part of this school as I did in Ohio. Maybe more so since I grew up going to Marycliff football games and taking part in the special camps they put on when I was in junior high and high school.

When Coach Reese said he was coming here and offered to bring me with him, making the decision was a no brainer once I heard Piper was coming back here. She'd dreamed of escaping all through high school, so I knew she hated getting dragged home. Helping out her and Coach Reese at the same time while taking advantage of an opportunity to show what kind of leader I can be on the field in a way that Ohio wouldn't provide seemed like a win all around.

And now that I know about Ben, I'm extra glad I decided to come home. If I hadn't, I could've easily gone my whole life without even knowing he exists.

A knock on the door pulls me out of my thoughts.

They're here.

With my heart racing with anticipation, I cross the room and pull the door open, captivated by Tiffany's smile. "Hey," she says.

All I have time to get out is, "Hey," before Ben barrels into me, wrapping his arms around my legs, his head just low enough that my junk is safe. Barely.

Because he's the real reason they're here, I let him claim my attention despite the fact that I want to greet Tiffany with the same amount of enthusiasm Ben has for me. Okay, maybe I don't want to headbutt her junk, but ... *Shutting down that train of thought right away.*

"Hey, little man!" I say to Ben. Reaching down, I grab him under the armpits and lift him up, tossing him in the air above my head and making him giggle.

"He hasn't had anyone do that for him in quite a while," Tiffany muses as she closes the door, a smile in her voice.

"Oh yeah?" Pretending to drop Ben and catching him, setting off another squeal followed by a round of giggles, I set him on the floor and point him in the direction of the living room. "Go check out what's over there." As he runs off, I straighten and return my attention to Tiffany.

She's wearing a green sweater with a low scoop neck that looks soft as a cloud and displays a tantalizing amount of cleavage paired with her black leggings with the subtle leopard print. I've seen her in them a few times now. They must be one of her favorites. With the way they show off her ass, they're one of my favorites too.

"He's gotten too heavy for me to toss in the air like that," she continues, claiming a kitchen chair to hold their coats and her magic bag of tricks. "My dad too." She looks up at me with a warm, happy smile. "He still asks sometimes, so it's nice that someone can do it."

Moving next to me, she looks into the living room where Ben's getting into the toys I've managed to acquire. "Wow." I don't miss the appreciation in her tone even though she tries to downplay it by saying, "You really didn't have to go to all that trouble."

"It's no trouble," I say with a shrug. "About half that stuff is toys my mom saved from when my sister and I were kids. I just got a few more things to fill in the gaps. I want him to be comfortable and have fun here."

When she looks up at me, appreciation and affection in her gaze, I force myself not to bend my head and claim her sweet pink lips.

If I remember right, in high school she tasted sweet, like she had on some kind of flavored lip gloss. Does she still wear flavored gloss? Or has she moved on from that?

"Mommy, look!" Ben squeals, and she jerks her head in his direction, interrupting whatever was passing between us.

I know what I'd want to pass between us. But despite the fact that she seems to have accepted that I didn't know about Ben before and her friendliness toward me, I don't think she's interested in having any kind of relationship with me beyond co-parents.

Sitting on the couch, I watch Ben show Tiffany all the toys I've gotten for him to play with here. After he's finished, I pull out the gift bag I put the football and jersey in. They're special, so I thought I'd dress them up. "I have one more thing for you."

Ben's eyes grow big and round, and Tiffany looks skeptical. "Grayson ..." she starts, her voice full of doubt, but before she can say more than my name, Ben yanks the tissue paper out of the bag and reaches inside, coming up with the football.

Immediately he turns to Tiffany, bouncing like he might be part Tigger. "Mommy! Mommy! Look! Look! A football! Wif letters on it!"

He shoves the little football in Tiffany's face, and she takes it gingerly from his fingers with a nervous chuckle. "That's pretty great. What do we say when someone gives us a present?"

Turning to me, still bouncing like crazy, he shouts, "Thank you! Thank you!" And then launches himself into my chest.

I catch him, laughing, falling back against the cushions mostly for show, though he did catch me off guard enough that I don't have to fake it. I just don't have to fight against the urge to fall back. "Oof. You pushed me over!"

He giggles and climbs off of me.

Hooking a finger in the gift bag, I tip it toward him. "Take a look. There's more."

Eyes round again, he peeks in the bag and pulls out the jersey. "Mom! Mama! A shirt!"

She laughs as he holds it up. "Well, you'll definitely be able to wear it for a long time."

And she's right. It looks more like a dress than a shirt at this point, and I can't help smiling. "Check out the back."

Ben holds it up and looks at it. "More ABC's, Mama!"

Tiffany chuckles. "Turn it around and let me see."

He does as she asks, and I swallow hard as she takes it in. "That's my name on the jersey," I tell him. "That way when you wear it, you can be like me."

The look Tiffany gives me is unreadable, but she clears her throat and looks at Ben. "That's pretty cool, isn't it Benny Boo?"

"Supa cool!" he shouts, taking the jersey to his mom. "I wanna wear it!"

The jersey does look more like a dress, but seeing him with my name and number emblazoned on his back does something to me, and I know it's affecting Tiffany too. I'm just not sure if that's good or bad.

After a few minutes, she murmurs that she needs water and heads for the kitchen. Happily playing with Duplos, Ben doesn't even notice.

Needing to make sure that she's not upset, I follow her and find her standing with her hands braced on the counter, her head down.

"Hey." I pitch my voice low, hoping I don't startle her.

But she was apparently lost in thought or emotion and didn't hear my footsteps, because she about jumps out of her skin and spins around, her hand to her chest. "Grayson! Holy crap! You scared me."

I offer a crooked smile. "Sorry. Just wanted to make sure you found the glasses alright."

She looks around at the cabinets, clearly at a loss. "Right. Sorry. I guess I should've asked where they are."

Stepping closer, I reach past her and pull open the appropriate cabinet. "No problem. I'm also guessing you weren't really coming in here for water."

Her chin tips up so she can meet my gaze since I'm crowding her in the tiny kitchen. I should move back, but being so close to her is intoxicating, and I can't seem to make my feet go anywhere.

She clears her throat. "No. I just ... needed a minute."

"Are you okay? Sorry if everything seems extravagant, it's just ..."

Her hand on my chest makes the air leave my lungs, and I hold my breath, waiting to see how long her willingly touching me will last. Wondering how I can encourage more of this.

"It's wonderful," she whispers. "I'm not upset. I'm just ..." She shakes her head. "I'm not sure what the right words are. It's not bad, though. I promise."

"Good." My voice is little more than a hoarse whisper as I stare down into her face. My eyes catch on her lips and can't seem to move away. They part on an indrawn breath, pink and plump, and that question about if she still wears flavored lip gloss floats into my brain again.

Bending my head slowly, giving her plenty of time to move or turn her head or shove me or something if she doesn't want me to kiss her, I bring my lips to hers. Instead of pushing me away, her fingers flex against my chest, clutching my T-shirt and holding on for dear life as my lips brush against hers.

Not wanting to push my luck, I content myself with just that brief contact, little more than a peck really. But she's not having it. Pushing up on her toes, she claims my mouth. And that's all it takes for me to lose myself to her. My hand comes up to cup the back of her head, and I hold her in place, parting my lips, my tongue seeking hers—

"Timber!" shouts a little voice from mere feet away, followed by a crash.

Tiffany's hand spasms against my chest, and we break apart like we've been shocked. She stares at me, wild eyed, her hand covering her lips. Her eyes never leave mine as she drops her hand and calls, "You alright, Ben?"

"Yeah!" he shouts back.

Smiling, she tilts her head toward the living room. "We should get back out there," she whispers.

Without waiting for my agreement, she slips past me, cheerfully talking to Ben about what he just did like nothing at all happened between us while I stand in the kitchen in complete shock.

I just kissed her.

And she didn't shove me away.

I'm not sure what that means.

CHAPTER TWENTY-TWO

Tiffany

I stomp down any and all feelings for the rest of the visit and do my best to avoid looking at Grayson. Thankfully, he follows my lead and keeps his attention on Ben. When it's time for us to go, I have to fight a strange mix of anticipation, relief, and regret.

Anticipation because I'll finally have an excuse to look at him, and I want to see him look at me again with that unique combination of affection and longing he had on his face right before he kissed me. It's almost like he wants to recapture what maybe could have been had life played out differently years ago. If I'd given him my number. If I'd found him at another party. If I'd actually been able to contact him.

If ...

If Disney fairy tales could actually exist in the real

world.

At the same time, I'll be glad to get out of his presence so I can lock myself in the bathroom at home for a few minutes to relive and process that kiss. But I'm also sad to be leaving. Sad that we won't get another opportunity to try kissing again—which is at least ninety-five percent my fault. I'm quite sure Grayson would happily kiss me some more if we set Ben up with something to distract him and I yanked him into another room.

But that's a terrible idea.

I've already decided that there can't be anything between Grayson and me. We shouldn't have kissed today. We definitely shouldn't consider doing it again.

And yet ...

I haven't been kissed like that in so long. Not at all in like a year. And the last guy I dated had reasonably okay technique, but lacked the indefinable quality that Grayson's short kiss had in spades.

I really have to get out of here.

With our coats on and our things safely tucked in my tote, I finally bring my eyes up to Grayson's and force a smile. "Thanks again for everything. As you can see, Ben loves his jersey and his football. We'll be sure to bring it next time. Maybe the weather will cooperate and you can play again next weekend."

"I'd like that," Grayson says, his voice a low rumble, and maybe it's all in my head, but I feel like there's some kind of double entendre there, like he'd enjoy repeating more than just playing football with Ben.

He steps forward, and his arm goes around my shoulders and pulls me against his chest. I can't help but inhale him, the warm smells of man, clean cotton, and citrus from some body care product. I wish I could stay like this indefinitely, the solid warmth of Grayson holding me, surrounding me, protecting me. Making me feel like I'm not alone in this gig for the first time ever.

Yes, my parents help out a ton, and they're amazing and I couldn't have done this without them. But they're not partners.

Grayson isn't either. Not really. Not like they are to each other.

Tears prickle behind my closed eyelids, and I blink them away quickly, stepping back and looking down to hide the sudden rush of emotion. I'm being ridiculous.

Fortunately, Grayson takes my reaction in stride and just squats down to give Ben a goodbye hug as well.

"Bye, Gray!" Ben's voice is muffled against Grayson's chest, and I wonder if and when Ben will start calling him Dad. Does Grayson want that? Is he going to insist on it at some point?

Though he hasn't really seemed like the type to insist on much so far. Yes, he insisted on getting to see Ben, but I suppose I can't really blame him for that. Otherwise, though, he's been pretty go with the flow. I'm not sure I'd be as accommodating if I were in his shoes.

Another surge of warmth and gratitude fills me. He really is a good guy. And spending more time with him makes it easier to let go of the lingering bad feelings I had toward him.

But be that as it may, Ben still has to be my top priority. Pursuing a relationship with Grayson, especially now when things are still so delicate, seems like a surefire way to screw everything up.

* * *

It's a Wednesday night, and while it's unusual for me to go out on a school night, I decided to make an exception this time. After class, Autumn invited me to hang out with her and her friends tonight. Her roommate is dating a football player, so we're meeting at Crowley's, the local sports bar that's apparently a favorite hangout of the football team.

I'd given her a noncommittal answer as she rushed off to her next class telling me to think about it and text her. But my mom encouraged me to go, saying that I need friends and that it's good for me to go out and have fun.

She's right. I know it. She knows it. Apparently even Autumn knows it. And it's nice to have an excuse to get dressed up and put on makeup and feel good about myself. It's been too long. Between classes and homework and taking care of Ben and being all twisted up in my feelings after that kiss with Grayson over the weekend, I need a night off.

When I get to the bar, Autumn stands and waves at me from the circular corner booth that she and her friends have already claimed. She has her pinky-purple hair flowing over her bare shoulders. Her strapless top looks more suited for summer than early February, but it's pretty warm in here, so maybe she knows something I don't.

I wore a long sleeve bodysuit under my favorite sparkly stretch velvet pants, so hopefully I don't roast to death.

"Oh my gods," Autumn says when she greets me. "You look amazing. Doesn't she look amazing guys?"

She turns to her friends, both couples, for confirmation. The girls give enthusiastic endorsements, "Fucking hot!" shouts the one with long dark hair while the other giggles and shouts, "Yeah!"

Their boyfriends are more reserved, nodding along and murmuring their agreement. Smart men. Don't want to be too appreciative of another woman in front of their girlfriends.

"Thanks." I smile at everyone as I slide into the booth after Autumn and nod as she makes introductions. Piper's the one who said I look fucking hot, and next to her is Ellie, Autumn's roommate, who's still giggling. I'm wondering if they either pregamed, or they've been here for a bit already. Piper's boyfriend Cal has his arm around her, and Ellie's draped all over Simon, the guy on her other side. They're introduced as football players, and I believe it. They're both big and broad and muscular, sorta like Grayson.

Suddenly the mood at the table shifts, and Piper's eyes are fixed on someone behind me.

Turning, I look up to see Grayson looming over the back of the bench, as though just thinking about him conjured him up.

"Hey, guys," he says lightly, loud enough to be heard over the bar noise. "Mind if I join you?"

"What do you want, Gray?" Piper demands, and I whip my head around, wondering what that's about. Did they used to date or something and she hates him? Do I need to add her to my list of reasons not to get involved with Grayson?

Grayson's sigh is audible as he takes the spot next to me, and I have to scoot over to make room for him, causing a ripple effect as the others all have to scoot farther around as well.

Piper glares at him. "That wasn't an invitation to sit down." Her boyfriend's hand tightens on her shoulder, and I'm not entirely sure if it's supposed to be support or trying to rein her in. If these two used to date, he's clearly not threatened, because other than his hand on Piper's shoulder, he appears entirely relaxed by Grayson joining our table uninvited.

For her part, Autumn looks like she's thrilled to pieces by this development. She leans closer to me. "Don't worry about them. Sibling bickering. They'll get over it eventually."

Ah, okay. They're siblings.

"Not anytime soon," mutters Piper, and Grayson sighs again.

"I actually came over to say hi to Tiffany," he tells his

sister, and his leg presses against mine under the table. Without waiting for a response from Piper, he turns to me, giving me a soft smile. "Hey."

My cheeks warm under his affectionate gaze. Which is silly, but I can't help it. "Hey."

Autumn makes a funny squeally noise next to me. When everyone turns to look at her, she shakes her head and waves her hands. "Sorry. It's just ... I know things were, ah, awkward to start. I'm glad you guys are finding your way. I've been pulling for you."

Ellie's hand slaps the table. "*That's* what all that was about?" She points a finger at me. "Them? They're the ones—"

"Yup," Autumn interrupts, glaring at her roommate. "Yes. Now hush." She looks around on either side of her, then looks at Simon. "Why don't you go get drinks. And the rest of us will ... come with you. Yes. Let's all pick out something new to drink. We always only ever get the same things here. It's time for a change." She claps her hands imperiously, like that should be enough to get everyone to follow her orders.

I glance at Grayson and he shrugs, an amused smile tugging at his lips. When he moves to get up, Autumn puts out a quelling hand. "No, no. You two stay here. We'll surprise you." She gives us a look, examining us, then nods. "Yes. I think I know just the thing." To the others, "Come on. Move around. Let's go, let's go."

"I don't understand what's happening right now," Piper mutters as she obediently scoots all the way around the table.

Leaning over, Ellie whispers something I can't catch, but whatever she says seems to mollify Piper. Or maybe it's the way her boyfriend is also following along with this.

But it's pretty clear to me what's happening. Autumn thinks that Grayson and I should be a couple, and she's giving us some time alone. It's not exactly rocket science.

Once they've all wandered toward the bar, Grayson turns to look at me. Even though there's plenty of room for me to scoot over now, I don't. I like the way his thigh feels pressed against mine, the way his shoulder is right there, the way I could just lean into him if I really wanted to.

And I kinda do.

But I won't.

Because I shouldn't. Though for the life of me, I can't remember why right now.

Grayson clears his throat, drawing my attention to his eyes. "So ..."

He lets the word hang, and I raise my eyebrows, silently prompting him to continue.

Adorably, his cheeks turn pink, and he looks down at the table where he fiddles with one of the empty coasters. "We haven't really talked about what happened this weekend. At my place."

I hum, wishing I had a drink already. Because then I could stall for time by taking a sip. But sadly, all I have is my coat to fiddle with, which doesn't help at all. "No. We haven't." I clear my throat. "Is there something specific we need to talk about?"

"We kissed."

"Mmhmm." I still can't bring myself to look at him.

But his fingers trace along my jaw, tipping my face up, and after blinking and looking at his lips and nose, I finally raise my eyes to his.

"I want to do it again," he whispers. "Can I? Please?"

Oh, dear sweet baby Jesus. Has anyone ever asked to kiss me like that? He sounds like he's pleading, like if I say no it will have a serious negative impact on the course of his life.

And the truth is, I want him to kiss me again. Right now. More than I want anything else.

I give the barest nod, and his lips brush mine. Soft and gentle, just like on Saturday. But he doesn't try to pull away or end it too soon like he did then. Instead his fingers trail down to the back of my neck, tipping my head back a little more, giving him full access to brush soft, sweet kisses across my mouth.

And once again, just when we get to the good part, when the tip of his tongue teases the seam of my lips, we're interrupted.

A hand slapping the table makes us jump apart, and we both turn to face a furious Piper. "You have a kid?" She's loud enough that people around us turn to see what the commotion is.

Grayson holds up a hand. "Piper, please."

"I don't care, Gray. I don't care if I'm making a scene.

I will abso-fucking-lutely make a scene when it turns out everyone in the whole goddamn universe seems to know that you have a kid and I don't!"

He sighs, frustrated. "And when was I supposed to tell you, huh? You haven't talked to me in months. You send me to voicemail if I call, and if I'm lucky you'll text a response. You don't want to forgive me? Fine. Don't. But you don't get to butt in to my business and demand to be involved if you're going to freeze me out the rest of the time. That's not the way things work, Piper."

Her cheeks turn red, and I half expect to see steam rising from the top of her head. Cal reaches for her, placing a hand on her back. She reaches back and holds his wrist, but doesn't back down from her confrontation with her brother.

"He's my nephew," she spits, almost too quiet to hear. "I deserve to know."

Grayson rubs a hand over his face like this confrontation is too exhausting to continue. "I really don't want to get into this with you right now, Piper."

"I want to meet him," she demands, arms crossed over her chest now, her chin raised like she's bracing for a fight.

"Piper," Grayson growls.

"What? He's my nephew. I want to meet him." She turns her fiery gaze on me, and I force myself not to flinch. I reeeeally don't want to be in the middle of sibling drama.

"Fuck's sake, Piper. I've barely met him. Mom and

Dad haven't even met him yet. Get in line. You're actually not the most important one in this situation right now. You'll get to meet him when you get to meet him."

She blinks at that, deflating, her arms falling back to her sides. Cal steps up next to her, gathering her against him and whispering something to her. Biting her lip, she nods and lets him steer her away from the table.

Autumn appears, her face apologetic. "I'm so sorry. I didn't know she didn't know. I thought—"

Grayson waves off the rest of her apology. "It's fine. You didn't do anything."

Her gaze bounces back and forth between us, and she takes a step back. "Well, I'll go wait for the drinks. Let you two finish … catching up."

She disappears, and Grayson lets out a weak chuckle, rubbing a hand over his face again. Leaning in, he gives me another quick kiss. "I don't think here and now is the best place for this conversation. You obviously had a night out planned. Is Ben with your parents?"

At my nod, he nods as well, contemplating. "Hey, um, I know it's still new, but if you need someone to watch him, could you ask me? Next time?"

"Yeah," I croak, then clear my throat. "Yeah. I can do that."

With a nod, he stands. "Alright. Cool. I'll see you tomorrow for pickup. Have a good night."

Before I can say anything else, he disappears into the crowd, and I'm not sure if he's leaving altogether or just rejoining whoever he was with before. Either way, I'm left alone in a swirl of conflicting thoughts. He wants to be my first call for childcare. And he wants to kiss me more.

But if we're out kissing, he can't also be watching Ben. But I guess if he's with me, he'd want someone else watching Ben.

Is more kissing even a good idea? My hormones say, *More please*. But my brain and my heart are throwing up caution signs and caution tape and turning my insides into a caution party.

Before anyone can come back, I gather my coat and slip out of the booth. Staying here will definitely not help me come to any useful conclusions.

CHAPTER TWENTY-THREE

Gray

I stand in my living room with my hands on my hips, surveying the simultaneously familiar and unfamiliar room. After seeing Tiffany at Crowley's, I immediately called my mom, because if I'm going to impress her with my parenting abilities, I need to have everything Ben could possibly need, and the only other mom I know and trust is mine. She gave me tips on things to buy for a toddler, then ended the call by ordering me to meet her at Target.

Once there, she pushed a cart in my direction and marched away, leaving me to follow in her wake. She led me to the baby section where she promptly filled the cart with a variety of cups, dishes, utensils, bath toys, regular toys, towels, and a dizzying array of things I never would've guessed a toddler would need.

But what do I know? The last time I spent a significant amount of time around a toddler, I was little more than one myself. It's not like my parents expected me to take care of my little sister when I was in Kindergarten.

Now I'm standing in a sea of pastel and primary colored toys and diminutive furniture. Apparently three-year-olds need tiny couches and chairs too. Regular furniture isn't good enough. Or maybe it's just not good enough for my mother's only grandchild, because when I questioned her, she arched an eyebrow and said, "My job is to design spaces to provide maximum comfort and functionality. I know you don't usually ask my advice and are happy to grab whatever couch you can rescue from a dumpster, but my only grandchild will not be left to molder on whatever eyesore you salvaged from a trash heap."

And then she picked up the shark-faced bean bag chair and balanced it on the shopping cart followed by a flat pack miniature table and chairs set that I spent an hour putting together after I got home. We made a quick detour through the school supplies aisle where she also added paper, crayons, and safety scissors. Between those and the Play-Doh, I should be able to keep him entertained for at least a little while.

"What about coloring books?" I asked as we passed a rack of those.

Mom wrinkled her nose and shook her head. "Blank pages allow for free creative expression. If he asks for one later, you can consider it. But to start with, let's offer him unlimited potential."

She came over, keeping her opinion about my trash heap salvage furniture to herself, and helped me set up and arrange the furniture and toys she bought.

And now I'm looking at it all wondering if maybe I let her go a little overboard. My living room is surprisingly spacious for a cheap apartment, or at least I always thought so when all it had in it was a couch, a coffee table, a TV, and a TV stand. Now it's almost crowded, though Mom did rearrange everything to maximize the space. Well, *I* rearranged everything at my mom's direction. It was just like working for her on one of her jobs, except this time it was my furniture I was moving to ten different spots before she was satisfied.

At least I have a ground floor apartment, so no neighbors to get irritated with me for dragging a couch around at ten pm.

She commandeered a corner of the room for Ben's furniture—the child-sized table and chairs, an easel with a roll of paper at the top that I didn't even see her buy at Target so she must've had it stashed and brought it over, and a small set of shelves holding plastic bins full of the toys and art supplies she selected. The only item of furniture for him not in his corner is the shark chair, which she had me put near my usual spot on the couch. "So he can feel close to you, but have his own space if he wants it," she said.

Which is probably a good idea, because as the seconds tick by, I'm realizing that I have no idea what I'm doing. Tiffany and I agreed this week that I'd watch him on my own soon. Not today, but maybe next weekend. What was I thinking? And where are the adults?

The fact that I'm supposed to be one of the adults in this situation is legitimately terrifying.

There's a tentative knock on the door, and I hear a little voice on the other side.

They're here.

I make one more quick scan of the room—not that I have time to change anything—and pull the door open, finding Tiffany standing on the other side with Ben holding her hand.

He bounces up and down, pulling on her hand, eager to get inside, looking past me at the new additions. "Gray! Gray! You got more stuff!"

I can't help the grin that spreads across my face. This kid is so full of energy and curiosity, it's impossible not to smile in his presence. "Yeah, bud. I thought you could use a few more things. Come on in."

Pulling away from his mom, Ben races inside. Tiffany follows more slowly, looking around the space, her face impassive. Ben is all reaction, though, bouncing from the couch to his chair to the space my mom set up for him in the corner.

He turns to face me, his eyes wide. "Can I sit here?" he asks almost reverently, his hand on the back of one of the chairs at the table.

"Of course," I tell him, infusing as much warmth into my voice as possible. "I got it for you."

"You did?" I can't decide whether his astonishment that I would buy him something like a table and chairs is funny or sad.

"Who else would I get it for?" I ask, crossing to his side to show him the bin full of paper, crayons, stickers, and safety scissors, and then the next one with the puzzles and toys Mom said would be good for a kid his age. "I wasn't sure what all you liked, so I just got a few basics to start with. I hope it's okay." I glance at Tiffany, who's looking around at all the latest additions with an unreadable expression.

Ben pulls out the scissors and gives them a few experimental snips, his tongue caught between his teeth. Then he turns to Tiffany. "Mama! Scissors! Can I cut?"

"The package said they can't cut skin," I put in just to make sure she knows I got him the appropriate kind.

She gives me a grateful smile. "If it's okay with Gray, it's okay with me."

Bouncing on his toes and vibrating with barely restrained excitement, Ben peers up at me. "Can I, Gray? Please please please?"

Laughing, I pull out a few sheets of paper and set it on the blue plastic table. "Knock yourself out."

He sits himself down and starts cutting, his face screwed up in concentration.

Tiffany watches him from her spot next to the couch. "When did you get all this?"

Rubbing the back of my neck, I suddenly feel a little sheepish. Is this too much? Did I let my mom go overboard? "Uh ... honestly?"

She gives me an acerbic look, crossing her arms and cocking her hips. "No. I want you to lie to me."

Chuckling, I drop my hand back to my side. "After I

ran into you the other night. I want him to be comfortable if he's going to spend more time here. So I called my mom for help."

Her eyes widen, and I nod. "Yeah. This is pretty much all her. I thought she was gonna buy out the whole store, or at least the children's section."

Tiffany pulls her lips between her teeth, and I'm not sure if she's stopping herself from laughing or commenting or both.

I make a rolling motion with my hand and grin. "Come on. Spit it out. I know you have something to say."

Turning in a slow circle, she takes in the rest of my apartment, and when she's facing me again, she's biting the inside of her cheek. But her perfect pink lips are pulling up in an irrepressible smile. "No, it's just ..."

I raise an eyebrow, silently inviting her to continue.

She drops her arms and sighs. "It's ... sweet. Even if your mom picked everything out, the fact that you would call her, it's"—she shrugs—"reassuring, I guess. It means you care enough to get it right. But ..." She bites her lip and shakes her head.

"But what?"

She narrows her eyes and glances at me sideways. "Your mom doesn't do all your shopping, does she?"

Laughing, I gesture at the couch. "No. You should've heard her blast my decor choices in this apartment. She's an interior designer, so she has strong opinions about how people set up their homes. The fact that mine only meets minimal functionality standards is a sore point for her. And she likes to bring up the fact that I rejected her help when I moved in, calling my couch a dumpster rescue"—I hold up my hands in reassurance—"it wasn't, by the way. I bought it off Craigslist like any normal college student. But I think I only paid fifty bucks, so it's definitely not the newest or nicest piece of furniture in existence. I'm perfectly capable of taking care of myself without my mom's help. But I don't know anything about little kids ..."

The amusement bleeds out of her face as she nods. "Yeah. I know. Which is why all this," she waves a hand around, indicating all the new additions to the space, "is such a surprise. I was happy with what you had the last time, so it didn't occur to me that you would add to that already, and so ... extravagantly. And now for Ben to discover you have *scissors*, his absolute most favorite thing, he must think he's died and gone to heaven."

A warm glow fills my chest that I got something that he loves. "If there's anything I'm missing that he'd really like, let me know. I'll get it before next time."

She nods, still somber. "Next time ..."

The words hang in the air between us.

She sucks in a breath, her luscious tits pressing against the low scoop neck of her sweater, drawing my eyes involuntarily. I quickly look back at her face, and either she doesn't notice me checking out her tits, or she's choosing to ignore it.

"Are you expecting next time to be just you two?" she asks quietly, just above a whisper. "Without me?"

I open my mouth, hesitating. Glancing at Ben happily cutting at his table, I make my decision and give a nod that's firmer than I really feel. "Yeah." I have to clear my throat to get the hoarseness out of my voice. "Yeah, I think it'd be good for us. He seems pretty happy and comfortable here already, don't you think?"

Looking in his direction, her expression turns wistful. "Yeah," she whispers. "He does."

CHAPTER TWENTY-FOUR

Tiffany

I should be glad that Ben is comfortable at Grayson's place so quickly. I already knew that Grayson wanted to have Ben on his own soon. He's said so from the beginning. But part of me thought, with the kissing maybe ...

Maybe he wouldn't actually want that to be part of the schedule. Maybe he'd be content only getting Ben to himself when I have an appointment or something.

And then there's the tiny, anxious part of me that worries ... what if Ben prefers Grayson over me? What if Grayson tries to take Ben away from me? What if ...?

A multitude of questions swirl in my head, around and around, dizzying me with the implications.

I know that I'm being ridiculous. Mostly. I can't imagine a world where my son would prefer a virtual stranger over me, even if that stranger is his biological father.

But there's no denying the way his face lit up when he saw all the child sized furniture in this otherwise bare bones apartment. There's more of that here than at our house. We have a booster seat for him, and a play table outside on the back patio, but otherwise he sits on the regular furniture like the rest of us.

That chair with the shark face close to the couch is adorable … but I've looked at those kinds of things. Even if we had somewhere to put it, they're expensive.

I guess Grayson's parents do alright if his mom went on an impromptu shopping spree last night without batting an eye. He said she's an interior designer, but I have no idea what his dad does. Does he rely on their money? But if so, why not let his mom buy him nicer furniture?

While "dumpster rescue" might be taking it a bit too far, his couch has definitely seen better days. The steel blue fabric over the piping is nearly worn away on the arms, white cord showing through almost as much as it's covered. Sagging seat cushions and flattened back pillows round out the look.

"I know it's not much to look at." Grayson steps up behind me, following my gaze to his couch. "But it's comfortable as long as you don't sit in the middle. That's a sinkhole."

Chuckling, I turn to face him. "I sat on it last week, remember? I know. Well, I didn't realize about the middle seat. But your mom does have a point that it's not nearly as nice as Ben's new furniture."

He laughs, making a face that reminds me so much of Ben that my heart seems to constrict, painfully squeezing in on itself.

Not that there was really any doubt about Ben's paternity—and if there had been, the DNA test would've fixed that—but seeing expressions that I've always considered uniquely my son's on someone else's face is ... disconcerting to say the least.

I love those expressions. And even though I find Grayson attractive and I like his kisses too much for my own sanity, I'm definitely not in love with him.

Not yet, whispers a voice in my head that I slap away and firmly ignore. I'm not going to fall in love with Grayson.

"So are we ever going to address the elephant in the room?" Grayson murmurs.

I glance at Ben, who's happily reducing the paper Grayson gave him into a pile of confetti, his face screwed up in concentration. Grayson might think he's being smooth, but I'm well aware that little ears pick up more than you realize.

Pursing my lips, I shake my head. "Not right now." I glance meaningfully toward my son. *Our* son. Even though it's been weeks since Grayson showed up, it's still difficult for me to think of him that way.

"I can think of another elephant that needs addressing," I murmur, gratified by Grayson's confused look. "You. The NFL draft. When is that? How long are you going to be out of town? And what happens after?"

A range of expressions crosses his face before settling on wary. He looks down and smooths his hand over the soft fabric of his joggers. "I'll be going to the combines at the end of this month. I'll be gone for about a week, then again at the end of April for the actual draft." He lifts his hands in a shrug. "After that? I'll finish out the semester and then I'll need to find a place to live in whichever city I'll be playing for."

I hum and nod, looking down to pick at a piece of lint on the couch. "And where does that leave us?"

"Us?" he asks.

I nod toward Ben. "Us. Ben and me. In relation to you. How's this going to work once you're gone? You get him all attached and just ..." I spread my hands in front of me, "vanish back into the ether from whence you came? What about Ben?"

His eyebrows crimp together. "What about Ben? I'm not just going to drop you like a sack of rocks and vanish into the ether, like you put it. I'll still be in touch."

"It won't be the same."

He stares at me for a long moment. "No," he says at last. "It won't be."

* * *

Putting in my earrings, I pause a moment to look at my reflection. My hair falls in soft ringlets around my shoulders in a half-up style, my makeup is flawless, and my dangly silver earrings catch the light. I picked out my favorite blue dress with the low V-neck that always makes me feel good.

Will Grayson like it? flits through my head unbidden. I shouldn't be thinking about him or what he might think of my outfit, though, because I'm going on a date with someone else.

Another pang of guilt hits me. Anton had asked me out a couple weeks ago, before Grayson even kissed me the first time. I'd actually forgotten about it until yesterday when Anton caught up to me after our biology class and asked if he could pick me up for our date.

I'd politely declined and said I'd meet him at the restaurant. He'd clearly been disappointed, but it was that or cancel altogether, because I don't like being trapped on a first date like that.

When I'd asked Grayson that afternoon if he'd wanted to do their first overnight on Friday night, i.e. tonight, at first he was thrilled. But when he found out it was so I could go on a date, his attitude soured dramatically.

Not enough that he was anything less than his usual self with Ben when we picked him up from preschool, but his responses to me were short, bordering on curt, and while he still hugged me goodbye—which has become a thing since that first time at his place—it was perfunctory and lacked the usual warmth that makes me look forward to them.

Sighing, I run my hands down my sides and turn away from the mirror, sitting on my bed to put on my knee high boots, then gathering my clutch and heading into the hallway.

Mom meets me, giving me a once over, her expression disgruntled. Still. She was even less happy than Grayson when I told her I had a date tonight and that Ben would be spending the night with Grayson. I'm not sure if it's the date or the overnight visit that she actually objects to.

Sighing, I take Ben's little suitcase from her. "It's just a date, Mom. I'm not planning on marrying the guy."

She gives me a sharp look in response, but doesn't say anything.

"And it's inevitable for Ben to spend the night with Grayson. We've known this was coming for a while. And I believe him. About what happened senior year. He really didn't know about Ben, and now that he does, he's doing his best."

Pursing her lips, Mom shakes her head. "Yes, I know you've said that. But you also said he'll be leaving in just a few months. Where does that leave the two of you then?"

"I don't know, Mom," I say on a sigh. "Pretty much where we started."

"And with a broken-hearted little boy on your hands."

"Plenty of people have to be away from their children for long periods of time for work or because they're deployed in the military or whatever. They survive. We can too." At least that's what I keep telling myself. No, I don't know what that'll look like, and we haven't talked about it since last weekend's unsatisfactory conversation, but we're figuring this out. I've figured out everything since I found out I was pregnant, and I can keep figuring it out even with the new developments.

"It'll be fine, Mom," I say again, heading to the living room to get Ben into his coat so we can go.

Maybe if I tell myself that enough times, it'll actually come true.

CHAPTER TWENTY-FIVE

Gray

Nerves jangling, I scan my apartment to make sure I have everything I need. It'll be my first time having Ben on my own, and it'll be all night. We talked about a sleepover as a possibility the last time they were here, and Ben seemed excited by it. Even though I know Tiffany was less excited, I think her hesitation has more to do with this being the first time she's ever been away from Ben all night.

They're coming over right before dinner, and I made sure to stock the house with his favorites. It's a little weird to stock so much pasta in my pantry since I don't eat it at home very often, but if it means I can feed my son when he's here, I don't mind. I even got some ice cream special for his visit.

After that, we'll play for a while and I'll do as close to

his usual bedtime routine as I can manage. While I'm sure it won't be exactly what he's used to, he's at least already comfortable getting into all the things I have here for him—toys, art supplies, scissors, and even the plastic dishes I bought for him—without my mom's help this time—and stashed in a lower cabinet so he could reach them.

I'm so wound up wanting everything to be perfect, that I jump at the knock on my door, even though I know it's Tiffany and Ben. When I open it, Ben leaps at me, and I quickly crouch to catch him so that he doesn't accidentally head butt my junk. He's come uncomfortably close too many times, so I've gotten quicker at bending down to greet him out of necessity.

Boosting him into my arms, I straighten and take in Tiffany as she sets his tiny backpack and a navy blue roller suitcase covered in colorful dinosaurs inside the door.

Under her open gray wool peacoat, she's wearing a royal blue dress with a plunging neckline that skims over her curves before flaring at her hips and swishing around her thighs just above her knees as she moves. Heeled knee high boots leave only a tiny strip of skin exposed below the hem.

She's going on a date tonight. I'd almost managed to forget, but I can't even pretend to with her dressed like that.

I bite back the growl of jealousy that wants to rise up in my throat. I have no claim on her. And apparently she agreed to go out with this guy before we'd kissed. Which,

I guess at least it wasn't after, but that's small consolation, especially when I want to take her out and show her off, take her dancing so that skirt can flare out, watch the flush travel from her neckline up to her cheeks and then taste it as I peel her dress off.

I ruthlessly cut off that train of thought.

I don't need a semi—or worse—while holding my three-year-old son.

Clearing my throat, I turn away to set Ben in front of his shark chair. "Settle in," I tell him, forcing myself not to ask any questions about Tiffany's date. I don't want to know. And it's none of my business anyway. "I'm gonna finish dinner, and then we can watch a movie and have some popcorn, okay?"

He claps his little hands and scoots back into the chair. "Ice cream too?"

Tiffany moves past me, tucking her dress around her thighs as she crouches in front of Ben with her knees together. She leans in and gives him a hug and a kiss on the cheek. "Be good for Grayson, okay? And Mommy's just a phone call away if you need anything. Sleep good."

He throws his arms around her neck and gives her a big squeeze and a big smacking kiss on her cheek. She holds him for a shade longer than normal, like she's reluctant to let him go. But then she releases him and stands, meeting my eyes briefly as she heads for the door. "You guys have fun tonight. And if he needs me for any reason—*any* reason—call me. Okay?"

"I'm sure we'll be fine," I reassure her, slightly annoyed at the idea that she thinks I might not be able to handle one night with a little kid.

She narrows her eyes and points a finger at me. "I mean it. Call me. No matter what."

I'm tempted to salute, but I'm not sure she'd appreciate it, so instead I say, "Yes, ma'am." That gets me more of her narrow-eyed glare, and I hold up my hands in surrender. "I promise. If he wants you at all, we'll call, okay?"

She looks at me for another long moment before nodding. "Thank you."

* * *

Once Tiffany leaves, we have dinner in the living room, because I might as well make being here as fun as possible, right? Except that Ben trying to eat macaroni noodles in a bean bag chair is actually a terrible idea.

But when I suggest moving to the table, he wails, "Nooooo," like I just suggested that we start murdering puppies.

I manage to convince him to sit on the floor at the coffee table so we can watch *Monsters, Inc*, which is apparently his favorite movie. After we finish our dinner, I pause the movie and make popcorn, having Ben eat his at the coffee table still.

He doesn't last long on the floor by himself, though. The monsters scaring kids is too real to him, I guess, and before I know it, he's burrowing into my side, his plastic bowl tipping, popcorn kernels spilling onto the couch. I scoop them up and deposit them on a napkin on the coffee table before wrapping my arm around him. "It's alright," I reassure him quietly. "I've got you. You're safe."

He whimpers, his little arm wrapping around my middle, more popcorn spilling between us. But right now I don't care. I can clean up popcorn later. He's wanting comfort. From me.

Scooching down, I set my bowl on the cushion on his other side, pulling him closer and up so his head is on my shoulder. Once we get past the scary part, he relaxes, burrowing in again any time something tense happens on screen.

All too soon for my liking, the brief interlude where I'm comfort more than playmate is over. He's bouncing on the couch chanting, "Ice cream! Ice cream! Ice cream!"

Chuckling, I stand. "I did promise ice cream tonight, didn't I?"

He nods, bounding after me into my tiny kitchen. "Pick out a bowl," I tell him, pointing at the cabinet where his dishes are stashed. He comes up with a green one, handing it to me as I pull the carton of ice cream from the freezer. I give him a small scoop, then pull out a bowl for myself, and dish out the same amount. Much as I'd love to dig in and eat the whole carton, that would be both a bad example to my son and a lecture from my coach and nutritionist when they see my food log.

We eat our ice cream at the dining table with Ben in the sleek white booster seat my mom picked out the night of our shopping spree. It has straps, but I don't bother with them, since Ben climbs in and out of his chair pretty competently. After we finish—Ben with chocolate ice cream smeared all around his mouth—I wipe him down, rinse our bowls and declare it time to get ready for bed.

And that's when the problems begin.

First, he crosses his arms and refuses. "No."

"Come on, Ben. We'll do it just like your mom does, okay? She told me everything. I got you covered. Let's go to the bathroom and get started."

"No." No conversation. No reasoning. Just a flat, unequivocal *no.*

Ummm ... I really don't know how to handle this.

Rubbing my hand through my hair, I look at my son, who's staring me down, mutiny in every line of his face, his arms firmly crossed over his little torso. He's heartbreakingly cute, but also infuriating.

I crouch down so we're on the same level and I'm not towering over him. Tentatively, I reach out and rub his knee. When he doesn't object or, I dunno, kick me in the face, I leave my hand there and put on my best stern Dad voice. "Ben. It's eight thirty. Your mom says that's when she starts bedtime with you so you can get to sleep at a reasonable hour. That means it's time to change into pjs and brush teeth."

"No."

Dropping my hand from his leg, I force myself to take a deep breath. I'm really not sure what to do with this kid. Do I scoop him up and take him to the bathroom? I mean, I could, obviously, but what then? Will that suddenly make him cooperative? Somehow I doubt it.

I vaguely remember seeing Tiffany give him certain

choices when it's time to do something, like asking if he wants to put on his shoes first or his jacket first when it's time for them to leave. So I decide to give that a whirl. "Do you want to change into pjs first or brush teeth first?" I ask, striving for that same balance of reasonableness and firmness I've heard his mother use.

Still no dice. "No."

Just no.

"Yes," I tell him, unable to hold it back any more.

"No!" he repeats, louder.

Pressing my lips into a firm line, I force another breath. "Why not?"

I don't really expect an answer, but I get one anyway. "Want Mama," he says in a small voice.

And that's when understanding dawns. It's not that he's necessarily unwilling to get ready for bed. It's that he's unwilling to get ready for bed for *me*.

But Tiffany has a date. It's too early for her to be done, unless it's gone really badly. *Please god, let it have gone badly.*

Which is kind of a shitty thing to think, but I hate the thought of her with anyone else. I'm fully aware that it's stupid to be jealous when we've only kissed twice, and both times were interrupted. And she's made it clear from the beginning that she doesn't want anything to happen between us. Me leaving soon also complicates things, and I had no intention of getting involved in a relationship at this point either.

But dammit, we're already in a relationship, even if it isn't romantic. It could be romantic, though. If she'd let it.

I've always wanted to see what could happen between us if our chemistry were given air to breathe. And spending time with her over the last few weeks has only made me want that more.

But I push those thoughts aside, because none of that matters right now. What matters is that it's bedtime. If I'm going to have overnights, I need to learn how to get Ben ready for bed. Without Tiffany.

Maybe part of the problem is that he doesn't know where he's going to sleep. Maybe if I show him his bed, he'll feel more comfortable.

Holding out my hand to him, I try that tack. "Can I show you something?"

His face brightens, and he places his hand in mine, scooting out of his booster seat and hopping off the chair. I lead him to the bedroom, where I've set up the toddler cot my mom sent over when I mentioned we were planning on an overnight soon. It's blue and covered by a Buzz Lightyear sleeping bag and matching pillow.

At first, his eyes light up and he runs to the cot, shouting, "Buzz!" clearly excited by the sleeping bag and pillow.

But that's where the excitement ends. Because once he climbs on the cot, he gives me a look of intense betrayal. I had no idea a three-year-old was even capable of such depth of feeling.

"What's the matter, bud?" I ask cautiously.

He pats the cot. "Hard. Dis too hard."

"Is it?"

He nods, poking it some more.

Crouching down, I press on it experimentally. I mean, it feels like a cot—canvas stretched tight over a frame—which I guess isn't the most comfortable thing in the world. "Not much like your bed at home, huh?"

He shakes his head emphatically.

I blow out a breath, letting it inflate my cheeks while I contemplate what to do. My options here are limited. If I could pull the cushions off the couch, I could make a bed for him out of those, but they're not the kind that come off. The thought of putting him out on the couch seems wrong.

He's clearly not going to sleep on the cot. I can't, because I'd crush it. I guess that leaves me on the couch and him in my bed ...

Sitting down on the floor, I wrap my arms loosely around my knees and give Ben a level look. "You don't want to sleep on the cot, right?"

"No."

At least that one isn't said in the same tone of defiant refusal as when we were in the kitchen.

"Alright, how about this? We can move your Buzz Lightyear stuff onto the bed. Would that be okay?"

He brightens, sitting up straighter. "Okay!" And he grabs the pillow and sleeping bag, trying to drag them onto the bed. While the sleeping bag is toddler sized, it's too big for him to easily move it from the cot onto the bed that's almost as tall as he is.

"You have to promise not to fall out of the bed, though," I say as I pick up the sleeping bag and spread it out on top of my blankets. The thought of him falling out of bed honestly hadn't occurred to me until just now.

"I promise," he says solemnly.

Can I really believe that, though? Does he roll out of bed at home, ever? And if not, is it because he has rails on the bed or something?

Is there anything here I can use as some kind of bed rail?

I glance around my room, but come up empty. All I have is a dresser, a closet, and some clothes. I could maybe get my quilt from the hall closet. Maybe a towel? Would that work, though? It seems like he could just roll right over it if he were determined to. How determined is a sleeping kid to roll over things?

Pulling out my phone, I contemplate texting Tiffany. Just to ask. She said I should text her if anything comes up, after all. But if I ask, would she be worried? And if so, would that worry be enough to cause her to cut short her date, and cut short my night with Ben, swoop in and take him home?

Do I want her to do that?

I mean, yes to the date part, but no to the rest. I don't want her to think I'm incompetent and can't handle having Ben on my own.

Though if she cut short her date and came here and just stayed ... Part of me thinks that sounds like a pretty great idea.

Okay, I'll be honest. My dick is the part of me that thinks that.

But I'm not usually one to let my little head run the show. We're not going to interrupt Tiffany's date. I'm a grown man. I have Google on my side. I can figure this out.

Leaving Ben to arrange his sleeping bag and pillow to his satisfaction, I head out to the living room and grab Ben's suitcase and backpack. "Let's see what pjs you packed," I say as I set the suitcase on the now-empty cot and unzip it.

"Spiderman!" he shouts, jumping off the bed and running to his suitcase. He pulls out his pjs and brandishes them at me. "See? See? Spiderman!"

"Those are awesome, bud. Let's put them on, okay?"

I guess showing him the bedroom was the right call, because he lets me change him into a Pull-Up and his pjs, and after that he grudgingly consents to let me brush his teeth. Maybe I can do this fatherhood thing after all.

Except after reading him the books Tiffany packed three times each and insisting it's time for lights out, it all goes sideways.

"I want Mommy," he cries between high pitched keening wails, his tears wetting my shirt. No amount of holding, comforting, reassurance, or offers of rereading his books makes any difference. This little guy wants his mom.

Which leaves me only one choice.

CHAPTER TWENTY-SIX

Tiffany

Grayson has good timing, I'll give him that. While my date with Anton is perfectly pleasant, I've been on edge the whole time knowing that I'll be going home and spending the night apart from my son.

I haven't ever been apart from him overnight. This semester is the first time I haven't personally put him to bed every night, since my evening class interferes with that. But it's always my parents picking up the slack.

And tonight? Tonight Grayson will be doing it all. My stomach clenches, wondering how it's going.

Is everything okay? Is Ben happy? Scared? Worried?

I've kept my phone on the table face up so I won't miss a text or call, and I've been so tempted to text just to check in so many times I've lost count. Which has made it difficult to focus on Anton.

He's a junior Computer Science major, and apparently he had a class with Autumn last semester. They even went on a few dates, but nothing really came of it and they somehow remained friends. Though with Autumn, I don't find that especially surprising. She seems like the type who collects people. Everyone sort of falls under her spell, and even if they don't get what they want from her, they're still happy just to have her in their life.

She's even added me to her collection, which apparently includes matchmaking with other members of the collection as well.

By the time the server clears our dinner plates, I'm starting to relax and think maybe everything with Ben and Grayson is fine. That they won't call me. And it's just as she brings out the dessert menu that I get the text.

Grayson: He won't stop crying. All he wants is you.

My heart clenches as I read the text, imagining my sweet little boy crying for me.

I must make some expression that gives me away, because Anton asks, "Everything alright?"

Setting my phone down, I meet his eyes with a regretful smile. "No. I'm so sorry. I'm going to have to cut tonight short. My son ..."

He holds up a hand. "Say no more." He stands along with me, leaning in to kiss me on the cheek. "I had a nice time tonight. I'll take care of the bill. Is it alright if I text you later?"

While he's a perfectly nice guy—as evidenced by this reaction, if I hadn't already figured that out anyway—there are zero sparks between us. Still, I can't quite bring myself to tell him no. "Of course. Thank you for dinner." I give his hand a squeeze, then grab my coat off the back of my chair and head for the door. After shoving my arms in the sleeves, I pull up Grayson's text again and type out my reply.

Me: On my way. Be there in ten.

That might be an overly optimistic estimate given how far Grayson's apartment is from the restaurant here, but I'll do my best to get there as soon as possible. My baby needs me. I won't keep him waiting.

* * *

I throw the car in park almost before I come to a complete stop in front of Grayson's apartment, catching myself in the seatbelt as I stumble out of the car in my haste to get to my son.

I don't think he's hurt. I'm sure Grayson would've told me if that were the case. But he's crying. Grayson said he wouldn't stop crying because all he wants is me. And I don't want my baby crying for any longer than necessary.

My car beeps, signaling that I've locked it as I stride away as fast as my heeled boots can carry me. Once I'm in front of Grayson's door, I hesitate. Do I knock? Do I just go in? Will it be locked? He's expecting me, but maybe he locked the door and hasn't had a chance to unlock it because he's been trying to comfort Ben. *He better be trying to comfort Ben.*

I decide to knock and try the handle at the same time, but it doesn't budge. Seconds later, I hear the distinctive clunk of a deadbolt sliding back, and then the door opens and Grayson's there, filling all the space and taking all the air, my child looking impossibly small curled against his chest, supported by one muscular forearm.

Ben turns his tearstained face my direction, reaching for me with a wail of, "Mamaaaa!"

"Oh, my baby," I say as I take him from Grayson, pulling him close. His arms cinch tight around my neck, and he buries his face in my shoulder, little hiccuping sobs of relief coming from him.

Grayson steps out of the way and gestures me inside with his head. I sink onto the couch in the spot I claim every time we've been here. Instead of going to his spot on the opposite end of the couch, Grayson sits in the middle, sinking down lower than I thought possible on that sagging seat. But he doesn't seem to notice, because his attention is all on Ben.

His big hand covers Ben's little back almost entirely, leaving only a small space for my own hand. And every time I pat between Ben's shoulders—the only real estate available to me—I brush against Grayson's fingers.

But I steadfastly ignore how his skin makes mine

tingle in a way that was distinctly lacking with Anton, because nothing's going to happen between us. I'm here for Ben.

"Shh shh shh," I whisper. "Mommy's here. You're alright. It's alright. I'm here. Mommy's here."

His cries subside to sniffles, and he slides down into my lap. Grayson finally moves his hand away, and I'm able to rub Ben's back all the way up and down like normal. Ben still has his head on my chest and one hand on my shoulder. "Want mama."

"I'm here, sweetie. I'm not going to leave you, okay?"

He nods against me, and I look up to meet Grayson's eyes over Ben's head, not sure what I'm supposed to do now. "Sorry," I whisper. "I know you were looking forward to an overnight—"

With a shake of his head, Grayson cuts me off. "Don't apologize. I texted you, after all. We had a good night, though, didn't we, bud?"

Ben nods again. "We had popcorn and watched a movie."

"Oh yeah?" I shift so I can look at his face easier. "Which movie?"

"*Mossters Inc.*"

"Oooh. That's a good one. Did you like it?"

He rubs his eye with his fist and yawns really big. He's normally asleep by now, so no surprise that he's getting tired. "Yeah," he whispers. "Was kinda scary some, but Gray kept me safe."

Grayson touches his arm. "I'll always keep you safe,

bud," he whispers.

Ben is growing heavier against me, his eyelids staying closed longer with each blink. "I should probably get going if I'm going to get him in the car before he's all the way asleep," I whisper.

But Ben's clearly not out yet, because his eyes pop open. "No!" he protests. "Stay."

"Uhhh ..." I glance from Ben to Grayson, not really sure what the best course of action is here.

Grayson shrugs. "It's fine. I was already planning on sleeping on the couch. He didn't like the toddler cot I have for him. You guys can take my room."

I glance down at my dress. "I don't have anything to wear."

Another shrug. "I can loan you something. Seriously. He needs you. It's no trouble. I swear."

And just like that, another piece of the wall I've been trying to keep up between us breaks off and goes tumbling into the abyss.

Watching him with my son does things to me. And the fact that he's not annoyed by Ben's insistence on me interrupting their first night together and is actively inviting me to stay and offering to make me as comfortable as possible is ... sweet. Considerate. Caring. All the good things you want in a guy, especially when that guy is the father of your child.

Ben settles against me again, his eyes closing.

"Bedroom's this way," Grayson says as he stands, heading into a short hallway.

Standing, I follow him. He goes to his dresser and pulls out a red T-shirt and a pair of black and gray athletic shorts. "They have a drawstring." He flips open the waistband of the shorts to show me before setting the clothes on the foot of the bed.

"Thanks," I whisper, not wanting to disturb Ben. I gently lay him in the center of the bed. "He didn't give you any trouble until bedtime?"

Grayson moves to stand next to me, looking down at Ben. He shakes his head. "No, he was great. The first inkling of trouble was when I said it was time to get ready for bed. He put up a fight about that, but I eventually got him to come around. After reading the stories you packed multiple times and declaring it time for lights out, he became inconsolable." His big shoulders move up and down, and I feel his shrug more than see it. "The only option was to have you come over." He glances down at me. "Sorry if I ruined your date." He doesn't actually sound sorry, though.

I shake my head. "Don't be sorry. You didn't ruin anything. And anyway, Ben's more important than a random first date."

He grunts in response, then moves to his dresser again. "I'll go change and head out to the couch. I'll knock when I'm done in the bathroom."

I watch him walk to the door. "Grayson?"

He turns, one hand on the doorknob. "Yeah?"

"Thanks. For texting me. For taking such good care of him. For"—I gesture at the room—"letting us take over your room for the night."

He gives me a sweet smile that's such an echo of Ben's that my breath catches. "Of course. Don't worry about it. I'm glad you came."

And with that, he leaves, pulling the door softly closed behind him.

He's glad I came?

Because Ben wanted me and he didn't know what else to do? Or for his own reasons?

CHAPTER TWENTY-SEVEN

Gray

Tiffany is in my bed, wearing my clothes. Yeah, she has a three-year-old in there with her and not me, but still. She's here. In my apartment. In my bed.

I turn over, trying in vain to get comfortable on the couch. With the dip in the middle, it's pretty much impossible. I'm going to have to rethink the sleeping arrangements if Ben has overnight visits more often.

Am I going to have to call Tiffany every time we try to have a sleepover?

Is it really that awful if I do?

When she said that I didn't ruin her date, my heart leapt. Which is selfish and dickish, because that likely means it wasn't that great of a date, and I really shouldn't be happy about that.

But knowing she wasn't having a great time goes a

long way toward soothing my jealousy. Jealousy I have no right to feel. I know this. But it makes no difference.

The snick of a door opening has my ears perking up. And when I hear the unmistakable sound of quiet footsteps, I throw off my blanket and stand up. I'm not sleeping anyway, and clearly neither is Tiffany.

I stand in the entrance to the hallway, and Tiffany freezes in the bathroom doorway, little more than a shadow in the dim light. If I didn't know better, I could think she were a ghost conjured by my incessant thoughts of her.

"Sorry," she whispers. "I didn't mean to wake you."

"You didn't. I was awake."

She flicks on the bathroom light, brightness spilling into the hallway. "Sorry," she says again at my flinch. "I feel weird talking to a big, hulking shadow."

A low chuckle rumbles in my chest. "Hulking shadow, huh?"

She shrugs and gives me a half smile. "Well, you're not exactly small."

"No, I'm not."

When she sucks in a breath, I realize that sounded like a double entendre, which wasn't what I was intending. I open my mouth, though I'm not sure if it's to make a denial or apology.

But then she lets out a soft laugh. "No, you aren't," she agrees. Crossing her arms, she leans against the doorframe, scanning me up and down.

I return the scan, noticing that my shirt fits her like a dress, and she doesn't appear to be wearing the shorts I got out for her. Does she have anything on beneath that shirt? If I slid my hand up that smooth expanse of thigh, what would I find at the top?

Shifting my stance to disguise my growing chub, I force my mind away from that train of thought, no matter how much I'd love to stay there. *Later,* I promise myself. After Tiffany's safely tucked in my bed.

"Couch too uncomfortable for sleeping?" she asks. My dick wants me to interpret that as an invitation of some kind, but my brain knows better. This is Tiffany. While she may have thrown caution to the wind and taken me up on my invitation into a bedroom once, that was years ago, when we were both younger and dumber, and there were no children involved.

I grunt. "Something like that."

She glances back toward the bedroom door. "He conked right out as soon as I got him into bed. I lay down with him for a little bit, but I'm too wound up to sleep." Her eyes meet mine. "I should be tired. But I don't go to bed this early normally, so my brain just won't shut off yet."

"Come hang out with me," I say before I can think better of it. "I'm not gonna fall asleep anytime soon either. Crack the door if you want to listen for Ben. We can watch a movie or just talk or whatever."

The way she eyes me with that inscrutable mask in place makes me think she's going to say no. But after a moment she nods. "Alright. Let me go to the bathroom first, and I'll meet you out there."

"Cool." We stare at each other for another beat, and

then move at the same time, like we were released from some spell simultaneously. I step back toward the living room, and she slips into the bathroom, the door closing and cutting off the light, leaving me in darkness.

In the living room, I switch on a lamp and then the light over the stove. Nothing too bright, but enough not to trip over anything, my pulse kicking up in anticipation.

Down boy, I scold myself. We're just going to hang out. Nothing's going to happen. Yeah, you kissed her twice. But she had a date tonight. With another guy. She clearly doesn't want a relationship with you. And you're not supposed to get involved in a relationship now anyway, remember?

But would it be so terrible if I did? I mean, I'll be seeing Tiffany plenty after I leave because of Ben anyway. Wouldn't it be easier—and more enjoyable—if we were together? And better for Ben in the long run? Am I just coming up with reasons to justify letting my dick get its way?

Probably, I acknowledge with a sigh as I sit in my usual spot on the couch, pulling the blanket and pillow out of the way to make room for Tiffany to join me.

The TV adds its bluish glow to the room as I navigate to the home screen so she has her choice of streaming options. I don't even know what kinds of movies she likes. We have a kid together, but I literally know nothing about this woman.

Except the way she tastes, and the way she feels as I sink into her ...

Though it's been so long ago, do I actually remember

that? Or is it just the memory of a memory that's been layered over by so many other encounters and experiences that they're all really just echoes of each other?

Before I can spend more time pondering that question, she emerges and settles on the opposite end of the couch, her legs folded beneath her. As the hem of her T-shirt slides up her thigh, I can't help wondering what she has on underneath the shirt once again.

Setting my jaw, I force myself to focus on the TV and pretend that Tiffany's wearing a jumpsuit or something. Though that's only one piece of clothing, too. Unzip it, and she's naked—assuming she has nothing on beneath.

Good god, I really need to stop thinking about Tiffany naked, wondering what all those luscious curves look like now ...

Clearing my throat, I gesture at the TV. "Any preferences?" God, I sound like a fucking moron, my voice all low and husky, like I'm offering to find a pay-per-view porn or something.

But if Tiffany thinks I sound like I'm propositioning her, she doesn't let on. "I'm fine with whatever," she says softly. "What do you normally watch?"

What *do* I normally watch?

Shrugging, I settle farther into my seat, propping one ankle on the opposite knee. "I dunno. Not much lately, to be honest. Between classes and practice and spending time with you and Ben, I haven't watched much of anything in a while. When I want to veg late at night like this, I usually just put on something I've seen before so I don't have to actually pay attention."

I glance at her in time to catch a quick smile. "That sounds good to me. It's been a long week. Whaddaya got?"

I open Netflix, and flip through the shows I'm most prone to rewatch—*Schitt's Creek*, *Community*, and *New Girl*.

"Oh, let's do *Schitt's Creek*," she says, excitement clear in her voice.

I opt to start over from the very first episode. By the end of the episode, I notice that she's tucked her knees inside her shirt.

Chuckling, I stand. "Want a blanket? I have one right here."

She presses her lips together and wrinkles her nose, half embarrassed and half pleased. "That would be lovely, thank you."

I shake out the quilt my grandma made me for high school graduation that I'd planned to use tonight and spread it over Tiffany.

She pulls it up around her and snuggles into the couch, then she looks at me as I sit back down and holds up a corner. "What about you? Do you want to share?"

My mouth opens, a denial on the tip of my tongue. I don't need a blanket. I'm not cold. But she's offering to share, and I've wanted nothing more than to be closer to her since she got here tonight. I'd be foolish to turn it down.

"Alright," I say after what I hope isn't too long of a pause.

She quirks an eyebrow, and I'm not sure if it's more challenge or invitation. Either way, it's clear the answer is to take the middle seat.

So I lift the blanket and slide over. I mean, what other choice do I have? The couch sinks under me, and my knees come up so that it feels almost like I'm sitting on the floor. But right now, I couldn't care less.

We make it through another episode when Tiffany's stomach growls—loudly.

Holding her stomach, she gives me that pursed lip, wrinkled nose look from before and busts out laughing.

"Getting hungry?" I ask, amusement tinging my voice. I can't help it.

She nods. "I'm sorry. I know you weren't planning on feeding me tonight. I don't mean to impose."

Waving a hand, I fight my way out of the couch so I can stand. "Don't worry about it. I'm sure we can scrounge up something for you—you'll have to choose between my super exciting meal plan options and kid food, though."

"I'm easy," she says. "Just hungry. I was too nervous at dinner to eat much, and that was hours ago now."

The reminder of her date makes my gut clench with jealousy. Grunting in response, I head for the kitchen to see what I have that she might want. She was nervous about her date. Nervous enough that she didn't eat much.

The fact that I get to feed her now makes that a little better. But only a little.

I open the fridge and stare inside without seeing anything. "So was the date worth the nerves?" I ask, trying to sound as casual as possible. She said I didn't ruin it, which could be interpreted as meaning it didn't go well. But I want specifics.

"Hmm?" she asks. "Oh. Um ... not really. I mean, he was nice enough, but we didn't really have chemistry. Still, it's the first real date I've been on in a really long time, so ... nerves."

I grunt again, but force myself to say, "Makes sense."

She laughs, soft and husky in a way that sends all my blood rushing south. "I'm sure you don't have that problem."

Closing the fridge, I turn to look at her. "What problem is that exactly?"

She waves a hand. "Finding dates. Going on dates. Nerves about first dates. Take your pick."

Another grunt. Which prompts another of those low, sexy chuckles. Leaning back against the counter, I cross my arms over my chest and force myself to formulate some kind of intelligent response. "You seem to have the idea that I must be dating lots of women," I say slowly after a moment.

Her head pops up above the couch so she can look at me. "Are you saying you don't date lots of women?"

I rub a hand over my jaw, contemplating the best way to answer that question. I mean, I've been on my share of dates. But not lately. I'm not exactly a one man sex show. "Let's just say that I can count on one hand the number of dates I've been on since I came to Marycliff."

"Ohhhh." She draws it out, like she's coming to some significant conclusion. "So you don't bother with the date part. Just bring 'em home and wham-bam-thank-you-ma'am?"

I start cracking up. I can't help it. Because holy shit, she just said that out loud.

"What's so funny?" she asks when my laughter starts to subside, but that just starts me off again.

When I finally catch my breath and wipe the tears from my eyes with the heels of my hands, I shake my head. "I can't believe you actually said that." I clear my throat and try to stop smiling, but I just can't. "But no. That's not how it is. Like I said earlier, I've been busy. Last semester was football and family drama. This semester it's more football, and I guess more family drama." I let out my own soft chuckle. "This time I'm the one causing the drama, though. Last semester it was all my sister."

"Yeah, I caught onto the fact that there was some kind of conflict between you a couple weeks ago. What's the story there?"

Sighing, I drop my head, not sure how much to tell. "Aren't you hungry? I thought I was supposed to be getting you a snack."

She stands from the couch and walks into the tiny kitchen, so close I could just reach out and pull her against me. Instead I grip the counter behind me, keeping my hands to myself by sheer force of will.

She opens and closes cabinets seemingly at random, checking what's behind each door. "Oh, you have an actual pantry," she says, turning and spotting the little door near the table. "I didn't realize that."

"It's small," I say with a shrug, "but it's a place to keep

food."

Opening the folding door, she peers inside and comes out with one of the Z Bars I keep for Ben. Holding it up, she wiggles it back and forth. "This will do while you tell me that story. If I'm still hungry after, I'll find something else."

With a chuckle, I settle at the kitchen table as she rips open the wrapper. "You're not going to let me get out of detailing my family drama?"

She shakes her head, her mouth already full.

Sighing, I look up at the ceiling, trying to figure out the best place to start and how much of Piper's story I should tell.

I decide to keep it minimal, glossing over the trouble Piper had in California and the reason we both ended up here, spending more time on how her relationship with McAdam drove a giant wedge between us.

Tiffany listens to all of it, making supportive or encouraging noises to show she's listening, but doesn't say anything until it's clear I'm done.

She folds and unfolds the empty Z Bar wrapper in front of her as she contemplates what I've told her. "I'm sorry you and your sister are at odds right now. It sounds like you were close before."

"Yeah." My voice comes out as a rasp. I clear my throat, but the emotion clogging it doesn't go away. "Yeah, we were. But now ..." I turn my hands palms up in a gesture of helplessness.

"Have you apologized?" she asks quietly.

I nod, clearing my throat again. "Yeah. I've tried to,

anyway. She doesn't really seem to want to hear it."

Tiffany tips her head back and forth. "She's not required to forgive you, you know."

Oof. What a gut punch.

"That's ... I dunno. Growing up, we always had to apologize and patch things up."

Tiffany nods. "I get it. Well, not really. I'm an only child raising an only child. I never had a sibling to fight with and patch things up with via parental intervention. But I watched friends go through that, and I can kinda get the impulse now from a parent perspective." She raises her eyes to mine, deep pools of blue that seem to look into my soul. "But you're not little kids anymore. This isn't an argument over whose turn it is to do the dishes. I can see how she would object to the way you treated her." She lets go of the wrapper and spreads her hands. "The best thing you can do is just continue to treat her as an adult— since she is one, after all—and hope she eventually comes around. But it's up to her to forgive you. You can't force it."

I let out another long sigh. "I know. I know you're right. But it still sucks."

She nods sympathetically. "It does."

My eyes wander over her face, taking in the soft affection there, feeling closer to her than ever. It fills me with warmth and ... hope. Maybe tonight hasn't gone according to plan, but maybe—just maybe—it'll turn out even better in the long run.

CHAPTER TWENTY-EIGHT

Tiffany

Grayson's eyes linger on my lips, and I shift, suddenly aware of the intimacy engendered by discussing his troubled relationship with his sister. This isn't what tonight was supposed to be. If I was supposed to go home with anyone, it should've been Anton—not that such a thing was ever in the cards. But still. I wasn't supposed to end up here, wearing only a T-shirt and a thong, sitting in Grayson's kitchen with him looking at me like he's about to declare his undying love.

Or come around the table and kiss me.

While the first would make me intensely uncomfortable, the second ...

Shouldn't happen.

Can't happen.

Is a terrible, terrible idea.

We've already kissed twice now. And I've told myself that it's not something we should pursue because his relationship with Ben is what's most important.

I mean, yeah, sure, I've replayed the memory of those kisses and that night at the party when we made Ben in my head waaaay too many times in the last week or two.

Clearing my throat, I push to my feet and take my empty wrapper to the trash can at the end of the counter. "Well, um, I should probably get some sleep."

"Right. Yeah. Of course." Grayson stands too, shadowing me as I go through the living room and head for the hall. Is he walking me to the bedroom?

He stops in the opening to the hallway, one of his hands reaching out to brush my arm. "Tiffany, I—" He stops, and I know he's staring at me from the shadows, even though I can barely make out his features.

"What is it?" I ask softly, stepping closer.

"I'm glad you came over tonight," he whispers, closing the distance between us. "I know things have been awkward between us, but I … I enjoy talking to you."

Heat blooms on my cheeks, and I'm grateful that he can't see my blush in the darkness. "Thanks," I whisper back.

His fingers trail up my arms. "Can I—"

"Can you what?" I prompt when he doesn't finish the question.

In response, he ducks his head, his breath fanning over my lips, pausing an inch away from making contact. "Tiffany," he whispers again.

And even though I literally just finished telling myself what a bad idea this is, I close the distance between us, and press my lips to his. We can pretend it's the darkness and the conversation or ... or ... temporary insanity.

If him moving closer was a question, my response seems to be the answer he was looking for. His arm snakes around my waist, pulling me against him as his lips move over mine.

From the way his arm feels like a steel band holding me to him, I would expect him to be trying to devour me. But instead, his kiss is almost ... gentle. Soft lips press against mine, exploring the contours of my mouth. Several seconds pass before I can't take it anymore, and I slide my tongue along the seam of his lips.

They part on a ragged gasp, his chest inflating, and his tongue makes a tentative pass over mine.

I press myself against him even more, feeling him hardening against my belly. And to my surprise and dismay, he stops kissing me.

Pulling his head back, he looks down at me, examining whatever he can see in the low light. "Is this okay?" he asks. "Or are you going to run away again and pretend it never happened?"

My mouth opens, but no words come out.

He kisses me again, this time all hunger and heat as his tongue sweeps into my mouth, demanding a response.

And I give it to him, pressing against him, my tongue meeting his stroke for stroke, wrapping my arms around his body and gripping his shirt with both hands

This time he breaks away with a groan. "I can't keep doing this, Tiff. You're fucking killing me."

"Oh. Uh. Okay." I loosen my grip on his shirt, slowly—reluctantly—unwrapping myself from his body.

He lets out another pained groan, his arm tightening around me, not letting me get away. Dropping his forehead against mine, he shakes his head slowly. "Just tell me what you want," he whispers.

"I don't know." My eyes fall closed on the confession, and I move to pull away again. This time he lets me, but wraps his fingers around mine and leads me back to the living room, where he sits in his spot on the couch and pulls me across his lap.

Draping his arms loosely around me, he lets me get comfortable before leveling a serious look at me. "Let me tell you what I want."

"Grayson," I start to protest, but he cuts me off with a shake of his head.

"No, we'll do it this way. I think it'll be easier. First off, I want you to call me Gray. No one calls me Grayson except my mom when she's mad at me. And even she doesn't do that anymore."

Fighting back a smile, I nod. "Okay. I think I can handle that."

He nods as well. "Good. Second, I wanted to explore our chemistry back in high school. That hasn't changed. I really hated that you went out with another guy tonight, even though I know I have no right to be jealous. You haven't promised me anything other than the chance to be part of Ben's life. But ..." His dark eyes examine mine, and he takes a deep breath. "But I'd like to be part of yours too."

Sighing, I look away, torn and unable to bear his unwavering gaze. "For the record, the date tonight was a set up. Not a genuine connection or anything."

He nods. "Good."

A spluttering laugh escapes, and I shake my head. "At least someone's pleased with tonight's outcome."

One of his eyebrows lifts. "You're not?"

I shrug.

He adjusts me on his lap, his hands on my hips pulling me closer, his legs shifting to tip me against his chest. "I could make sure you're *very* pleased with tonight's outcome."

I snigger into his chest, and after a second, feel him laughing with me. "Okay, okay," he says like he's admitting defeat. "That was corny, I admit it. But the offer's genuine."

"I dunno," I whisper, still with my face against his chest.

"What's the hesitation?" His hand skates down my spine, soothing and warm.

I spread my hands across his pecs and address them. "What if … what if we do this. You and me. 'Explore our chemistry,' as you put it. And everything goes sour? What will that mean to your relationship with Ben?"

His hand skates back up my spine, stopping at the base of my skull and massaging the muscles there. When I chance a glance at his face, his brow is furrowed. "Why would it mean anything to my relationship with Ben?"

Pushing myself more upright, I furrow my brow in return. "How could it not? You don't think it would be difficult for us to have to see each other all the time if we couldn't stand each other?"

His sigh sounds half amused and half exasperated. "Well, we've already kind of been there and done that, haven't we? I mean, you couldn't even stand the sight of me at first. Blocked my number. Did everything in your power to avoid me. And we've managed to overcome that and end up here." He rocks his hips up into me, letting me feel the hard ridge of his dick against my outer thigh.

His face softens, and he brushes a stray wisp of hair back from my face. "I can't imagine ever hating you so much that I'd stay away from my son." Then he cracks a grin. "And if we do end up hating each other, then we do whatever angry divorced couples do when they have to share custody. I'm sure we could figure it out if we had to."

He pauses, as though giving me the opportunity to either agree or argue some more, and when I don't, his face softens. "Is that really what this is about? You're afraid we might end up hating each other and it'll negatively affect Ben?"

"I mean … yeah? Is that not enough reason to be cautious? Because in my book it is."

His arms go around me again, and he tips me against his chest once more, holding me for a moment before speaking. "So you're just never going to have any serious relationships? Because what if you date someone, introduce him to Ben, and eventually you might break up?"

I trace a tiny circle on his chest, stupidly content to let him hold me like this, enjoying the warm wall of flesh against my cheek and the comfort of his rumbly voice and his arms around me. More than anything, that's crumbling my resolve to keep my distance from him. He just feels so … good.

"I've never honestly felt regret for accidentally knocking you up," he says softly. "That probably sounds shitty, but it's true. I didn't do it on purpose, and I didn't even know it happened until recently. But if it means that you're too afraid to live your life?" He grunts. "That's just … That's not the way it should be. No matter what, or if, anything happens between us, there's nothing that will make me do less than my best with Ben, okay? And we're adults. If things don't work out with us, we just make sure that we don't let that affect Ben."

I let out a soft chuckle. "You make it all sound so simple and reasonable."

"Isn't it, though? I'm not asking you to marry me. I'm just asking for a chance."

Sitting up straight again, I meet his eyes. "No telling Ben. Not yet. Which means no PDA in front of him."

"I can handle that," he whispers.

CHAPTER TWENTY-NINE

Gray

Pulling Tiffany close, I claim her mouth, tasting her again, the sweet thrill of victory humming through my veins.

I was avoiding relationships this year. Ignoring the girls who'd want more than a single fun night together. And then Tiffany showed up and wrecked all of those good intentions. I'm not even interested in trying to fight my attraction to her anymore. Haven't been for weeks now.

And now that I've finally convinced her to give me a chance, I'm going to do my damnedest to make sure she never has reason to regret it.

My hand glides up her bare leg, sliding under the hem of her T-shirt where I encounter more bare skin. Eventually I find a tiny strip of fabric crossing her hip and let out a groan.

A thong. All she's wearing under this shirt is a thong. A skimpy, stretchy thong that would be just as easy to tear off as it would to move sideways so I can sink into her tight heat.

She rips her mouth from mine. "You don't still keep your condoms in your wallet, do you?"

"What?" The question catches me entirely off guard.

"It's bad for them," she mutters, turning on my lap so she can straddle me. And holy hell, I can feel the heat of her pussy through the thin layers of fabric separating us—her thong and my athletic shorts. A few minor adjustments, and I could be deep, deep inside her.

"What?" I repeat. I have no idea what she's talking about.

"Condoms," she breathes. "In your wallet. It's bad for them. Makes them not work as well. Hence, Ben."

Chuckling, I slide my hands up the smooth column of her back, loving the way she arches and moves against me. "I have some in my bedroom."

She freezes. "Ben's in there."

"Mmhmm." I drag my mouth down her neck, nuzzling the shirt out of the way so I can get to her collarbone. "You saying I should go get one?" She melts under my attention, all soft, sensual woman with vanilla sweet skin. I want to get under this shirt. I want to rip this shirt off her. But I need her to answer the question first.

Her fingers tighten in my hair, pulling my mouth from her skin. When her eyes meet mine, it's not lust or arousal I see there. It's fear.

"Baby," I whisper. "What's going on?"

"I'm scared."

Cupping her face in my hands, I press my lips to hers softly. "Of what?"

Her eyes fall closed, and she shakes her head, her lips pressed tight. I'm about to prompt her again, worry beginning to thread through me, but she finally answers.

"What if it happens again?" she whispers so softly I almost can't hear her. "We used a condom before, and I still got pregnant. What if it happens again?"

My breath leaves me in a whoosh. Fuck. No wonder she's scared.

I open my mouth, wanting to reassure her, but not really knowing what to say. I've never had another condom failure? But how do I even know? I didn't know about Ben for four years. If someone decided not to tell me, it's clearly simple enough to keep the information quiet.

My swirling thoughts coalesce around one key point, though—she won't be alone.

I kiss her again, then pull her against my chest, wrapping her in my arms. "It won't happen again. Even if you did get pregnant, it won't be like before. Number one, you have my phone number." That provokes a reluctant chuckle. "And number two, I won't let you do it all on your own again. I'm here, and I'm not going anywhere."

She goes stiff and still again, pushing up so she can look me in the eyes. "That's not true, though. You *are* going somewhere. You'll be leaving at the end of the school year. Let's not pretend otherwise."

"That's true," I acknowledge slowly. "I will physically be in a different place a lot of the time." I give her a crooked smile. "But you're not prying me out of your life that easily. I plan to visit as often as possible, and fly you guys out to see me when that's possible too." Her eyes soften, so I press my point further, repeating what I already said. "I want to do this with you, Tiffany. For real. This isn't just a one night thing. Not for me. I've wanted you since we were in high school. I've wanted to give us a chance since that first night. That hasn't changed."

If I'd hoped for some kind of declaration of undying love, I don't get it, but I do get her mouth on mine, hot and hungry, her tongue parting my lips. I let her lead for a moment, but soon it's too much and I take over, my hands gripping her ass and pulling her pussy tight against my aching cock, my tongue tangling with hers and sliding into her mouth.

She pulls away from me, and I let out a low growl until I see a swish of fabric and then it's just Tiffany in a thong on my lap.

"Holy fuck," I breathe. Her tits, perfect and round and tipped with hard little berry colored nipples, bob in front of my face. I'm transfixed. Mesmerized. And I need a taste like I need my next breath.

My hands slide up her sides, caressing and cupping her, loving the way she arches into my touch. When I suck one nipple into my mouth, she gasps, so I suck harder, scrubbing the tip with my tongue and giving her the barest hint of teeth.

"Jesus, Gray! Shit!"

Pleased, I move to the other side and give it the same treatment, moving back and forth until she's writhing, rubbing her pussy against the hard ridge of my dick.

Holy shit, I might come in my pants if this goes on for too long. And I never did get a condom.

Reluctantly, I move away from her nipples, leaving a trail of light kisses up over her collarbone until I reach her ear and take the lobe delicately between my teeth. She shivers, letting out another soft gasp, and I can't help smiling at her reaction.

When I start to shift her off my lap, she clings to my shoulders and lets out a whimper of protest.

"I'll be right back," I whisper. "Condom."

"Oh! Right." She scrambles off my legs fast enough to make me chuckle.

Bending over her, I kiss her deeply. "Be ready for me when I get back."

I jog on tiptoes down the hall, pushing the door open slooowwwllly, because I absolutely do not want to risk waking my son. Not when his mother is finally giving me the time of day.

When the door's open wide enough, I slip inside, grateful that the nightlight I bought just for tonight gives me enough light to see by.

Ben is sprawled on one edge of the bed, his arms above his head, his legs wide. One good roll, and he'll topple onto the floor. Do I risk moving him, though?

On the one hand, I don't want him to roll out of bed. He could hurt himself. And depending on the timing, could interrupt my plans, which I also don't want.

But if I move him, will he wake up? Will I ruin my plans before they even get started?

Should I ask Tiffany what she thinks I should do? Or should I just decide and execute and hope for the best?

I've made a name for myself as a quarterback by being willing and able to call a successful audible when needed.

I'm going to move him. His safety's more important than sex. And even if he wakes up, he'll hopefully settle right down.

Decision made, I stand over him for a second, looking down at his soft round face, a surge of affection squeezing my heart. He's such a cute little kid. How could anyone not fall in love with that face?

The only problem is, I'm not really sure how to go about moving him …

"Everything alright?" Tiffany whispers from the open door.

When I look up, I'm disappointed to see she has the shirt back on.

"I thought I told you to be ready and waiting."

She gives me a look that's a mix of amusement and scorn. "I was, but then you were taking forever. I thought you might need backup."

I gesture at Ben. "He looks like he's about to fall off. I was trying to figure out the best way to move him."

Stepping closer, she cracks a grin, her nose wrinkling. "You just kinda have to do it. There isn't really a best way. He's all floppy and loose like this. Just scoop him up and slide him into the middle. He probably won't wake up."

I raise my eyebrows. "Probably won't?"

She shrugs. "The longer we stand here arguing about it in whispers makes it more likely he'll wake up. Just scootch him into the middle and let's go, Kilpatrick."

I have to stifle my chuckle. "Getting bossy, huh?"

"If that's what it takes."

"Yes, ma'am."

She's right, though. He *is* all loose and floppy, and all he does is hum and snuggle back into the pillow when I scoot him into the middle. That done, I slide open the drawer of my bedside table, ultra aware of the scraping sound it makes in the near silent room. Once again, Ben doesn't budge. When I close it, he rolls over, humming and nuzzling again, and we both freeze. But he stays asleep.

Tiffany tiptoes to the door and beckons me. "Come on, Kilpatrick. It's go time."

With one last glance to make sure Ben is still asleep, I hurry after her, pulling the door closed with the handle turned and releasing it slowly. No way am I going to wake him up by making too much noise. Not when paradise is literally moments away.

When I get to the living room, Tiffany is stripping the shirt off again, her back to me, giving me a delectable view of her back stretching and relaxing as she undresses.

And fuck me. She's already lost the thong. Did she have it on when we were talking about Ben?

She did say that she'd been ready and waiting but I had taken too long …

Fuck. She was totally naked under my shirt.

I'm not sure why that's such a turn on, but it really is.

She turns as I'm stripping off my own shirt, her eyes dropping to my waist, her lips parting with anticipation. Slowly I tug my shorts down. I'm freeballing it tonight, since normally I sleep naked. I didn't want any more clothes on than absolutely necessary.

Her eyes widen as my shorts fall to the floor. I step out of them, stroking my cock slowly with my free hand, enjoying the look on her face as she watches me.

"You ready?" I ask, holding up the condom.

Her eyes flick up to mine, then back down to where I'm still slowly stroking myself, using my precum as lube.

"Yeah," she whispers, breathless. "Yeah, I'm ready."

And fuck if that isn't the sweetest thing I've heard in ages.

After rolling on the condom, I sit in my spot on the couch and reach for Tiffany. "Come here. Climb on and ride me."

She takes my outstretched hand, settling one leg next to me on the couch, then fitting her other between me and the arm of the couch. I shift a little, making sure she has enough room. "You good?" I ask as she settles her weight on my thighs.

Nodding, she gives me a shy smile. Placing her hand on my shoulder, I gather her close with my hands at her waist, tipping my head up for a kiss.

She meets me, pressing her lips to mine, sliding farther into my lap until my dick is caught between us. Sliding one hand up to cup her tit, I pinch her nipple, making her gasp into my mouth and move against me.

The friction is nice, but nowhere near enough.

"Come on, baby. I need to be inside you."

"Yesss," she hisses, lifting up on her knees.

I reach between us and hold myself steady for her. With one hand, she lines herself up, and when she sinks down, we both let out soft groans of pleasure.

"Fuck, babe," I hiss as she slides all the way down. "Fuck, you feel so good."

CHAPTER THIRTY

Tiffany

Gray hisses as he stretches me, and I feel so full. More full than I can remember in ... too long.

It's been a long dry spell, to put it mildly, and no one has ever looked at me the way Grayson does. It's intoxicating. He wants me, and he's not shy about letting me know, even while being respectful of my decisions. Wanting to make sure I'm on board and okay before moving to the next step.

And now ... holy shit, I'm glad I decided to take the next step.

I finally sink all the way down, my thighs meeting his, my clit grinding into the lower muscles of his six pack.

He curses softly, flexing under me, driving himself in farther. I make some kind of unintelligible noise, because sweet baby Jesus on a cracker, I'm full to bursting, almost to the point of pain, but riding the line just this side of pleasure.

I sit still, letting my body adjust, sighing as my muscles relax.

Gray's eyes flutter open, and the look on his face is pure adoration. Reaching up, he brushes a wisp of hair back from my face and tucks it behind my ear. "You alright, baby?"

Biting my lip, I nod. "You?"

He lets out a soft, sexy chuckle. "Oh, yeah. I'm feeling really good."

With a coy smile, I give him an experimental squeeze with my inner muscles. "Anything you can think of that might make you feel better?"

Another low chuckle. "You're a fucking tease, aren't you? But you already know that."

I shrug one shoulder. "I'm sure I have no idea what you're talking about."

"I bet you don't," he says, his voice taking on a slightly darker edge. Lifting one of my breasts, he bends his head to take the nipple in his mouth.

Anticipating a repeat from earlier, I'm extra shocked at the quick, sharp pain before he laves my nipple with his tongue, looking up at me from beneath raised brows.

I give him a scowl. "I can't believe you just bit me."

Releasing my nipple, he gives me a dark smile. "Yes, you can. Ride me, baby. You know that's what I want."

"You gonna bite me again if I don't?"

He purses his lips, squinting as he considers his

answers. "You want me to?"

I suck in a breath, a denial on the tip of my tongue, but that short, sharp pain followed by pleasure seemed to send sparks straight to my clit.

His smile turns positively sinful. "Yeah, babe. I'll bite you as often as you want. I'll give you anything you need, got it?"

Nodding dumbly, I start to move, and some part of me deep down inside thinks his promise pertains to a lot more than just sex. But I'm not willing to examine that right now.

He lets me set the pace, and I take my time grinding and swiveling and sliding up and down, just enjoying the feeling of him inside me, the way he watches me, his eyes dark with lust, lids at half mast. His hands rub up and down my thighs, enough pressure to feel almost like a massage. He explores my whole body this way, every part he can reach in this position anyway, his fingertips pressing into my skin, kneading the muscles on my thighs, butt, and back, then moving to the front to caress my breasts, tweaking my nipples before kissing and sucking them sweetly. No biting, at least not for now.

One hand slides down my front, his thumb leading the way down, down, down, until he's between my thighs, resting just above my clit.

My breath hitches as he draws little circles with it, close enough that I can feel it, but not in direct contact, slowly drawing out my pleasure.

"You like that, don't you, baby?" he asks as I lean

back, bracing my hands on his knees so I can move up and down and give him plenty of room to work.

I nod, biting my lip.

"Let me hear you. I want to hear how good I make you feel."

"It feels so good," I whisper. "You make me feel so good."

"That's right. No one makes you feel this good, do they?"

I shake my head.

He lets out a soft growl. "That's right. I know what you need, and I'll make sure to give it to you."

"Yesss," I hiss out softly.

There's no more talking after that, just soft sighs, low growls, and stifled moans of pleasure. His thumb on my clit circles lower, faster, and my hips move to match his pace. Soon I'm panting, so close, so so so close.

"That's it," he whispers. "Yeah, baby. Give it to me. Let me feel you come all over me. Let go."

And I do. My whole body tightens and shudders with the release, a wave starting at my center and working its way out.

Gray's hands go to my hips and he keeps me moving through my orgasm, making it last as he moves my body for me, his hips rising up to meet me. All I can do is hang on and ride the wave as he chases his pleasure. He groans, holding my hips tight to his, grinding up and inside me as he comes, triggering a round of aftershocks that leaves me breathless and boneless.

Breathing hard, he rests his head against the back of the couch, pulling me down to his chest. I listen to the thud of his heart as it begins to slow back to normal, relishing in the feel of his bare skin against mine.

"God, I don't want to move," he says quietly, "but if I don't, we might have a repeat of senior year after all."

He chuckles as I hurriedly climb off him and topple into the hole in the middle of the couch. "Don't hurt yourself," he says, leaning over and placing a kiss on my shoulder before walking off.

I prop myself up to watch that tight, round ass walk away from me, enjoying the divots flexing on the side with each step. Damn, this man is fine.

Looking down, I notice the soft roundness of my belly, the faded stretch marks I can't see in the low light, but I know are there. But Gray didn't seem to notice or mind if he did. In fact, he seemed maybe even more enamored of my body now than he did when I was a skinny little cheerleader.

He's back before I can finish the comparisons between then and now, settling back in his seat and hooking a hand around my ankle. "C'mere. The middle seat is the worst, which means your options are the other end of the couch or my lap. I vote for my lap."

Smirking, I sit up and climb across him, sitting with my back to the arm and my legs across his lap like I was earlier.

He tips my chin up and places a soft kiss on my lips, humming contentedly. "This is nice," he whispers when he ends the kiss.

"It is."

"We should do it again."

I laugh. "What? Now?"

"I mean ..." He flexes his hips under me. "I'll need a few minutes at least, but sure, I could go again tonight if you're up for it. What I meant was another time, though. Another day."

"You want to have sex while Ben is sleeping on another day?"

He grins that sinfully sexy grin. "Another sleepover? I'm good with that if you are. But also ... you could just ... come over by yourself sometime. I'd like to hear you uninhibited. At least once."

For some reason that makes me blush, which only makes him chuckle. "You blushed like that for me the first time we were together."

I cover my cheeks with my hands. "Oh god. I so did. I'd never had a party hookup like that before. I mean, sure, Carter and I had sex at parties, but we were a couple, so it wasn't the same thing. Even with Carter, I was always embarrassed after, because everyone knew what we'd been doing. I think he liked that, though. That I was embarrassed."

When I glance at Gray, he's frowning. "Seriously? He got off on embarrassing you? That's messed up."

Dropping my hands, I lay my head against his shoulder. "Yeah. It is, now that you mention it. I'd actually forgotten about that." I wave a hand. "Anyway.

That's ancient history. I haven't seen Carter since around New Year's senior year. That was when we had him do the DNA test. I knew I was pregnant, and I was pretty sure it wasn't his, but we tested just to be safe. Which left you, of course."

His muscles all jump to attention under me, and when I look up at his face, the muscle in his jaw bulges rhythmically. He lets out a heavy sigh, his hand curling around my thigh and pulling me close. "I'm sorry, Tiff. I wish I'd seen your messages or that my coach hadn't decided he knew better than me what was best. I wish I could've been here for you all along."

I lay a finger over his lips. "I know," I whisper. "I believe you."

He sighs, gripping my hand in his and kissing my fingers, then pulling my hand away and kissing me. "I wondered," he confesses after a moment. "If you actually believed me or not. I can't exactly prove my side of the story."

Taking in a deep breath, I hold it for a moment and consider his statement. "I didn't, really. Not at first." I shake my head slowly. "Like you said, it's easy for you to tell me that, especially if it gets you what you want now. But then, why would you change your mind all of a sudden? If anything, I'd think you'd be even less likely to change your mind now, on the verge of the draft, expecting to sign a huge deal with a pro football team. Why add the complication of taking responsibility for a preschooler on top of that? And obligate yourself to give up some of the big payday you have coming?"

Shrugging, I cuddle into his chest. "It doesn't make sense. You not knowing before is the only explanation that really does. It took a while, though, for me to come to that conclusion. I hated you for years. Letting go of that wasn't easy."

He squeezes me, dropping a kiss on the top of my head. "I'm glad you did."

"Me too."

CHAPTER THIRTY-ONE

Gray

Eventually Tiffany climbs off my lap and, much to my dismay, gets dressed. She gives me one last lingering kiss before heading to my bedroom to sleep with Ben. Part of me wants to join them, but I don't. She doesn't want Ben to know about us yet, and given everything that's happened the last few years, I can't say I blame her, even if I don't particularly like it.

So I pull my own clothes back on and do my best to get comfortable on the couch. Maybe I should just let my mom pick out a better couch for me, especially if I'm going to have Ben and Tiffany over on a regular basis. Too much shitty sleep on a crappy couch will negatively affect my game, too. So it's for my career that I want a new couch.

Right. Exactly. Perfect justification.

The fact that it'd be more comfortable for sex is just a nice bonus. And I definitely won't be mentioning that part to my mom.

I drift to sleep with the memory of Tiffany pressed against me and wake up with a raging hard-on. It's too early for Tiffany and Ben to be awake, though. It's earlier than I prefer to wake up too, especially on the weekend. But between the sunken cushion and my aching dick, there's no way I'm going back to sleep.

And while Ben might've slept like the dead last night, that doesn't mean he'll do the same now that it's seven in the morning. So sneaking in to wake up Tiffany and see if she's up for another round is too risky.

Which leaves going for a run. And since it's the weekend, it'll be a short one, my heavy training taking place during the week when the coaches are around and the facilities are fully open.

Pulling on sweats that I got out last night, I head outside, shivering in the cold February air. My breath comes out in billowing puffs that'll only get bigger once I start breathing harder. Frost lines the rail on the stairs leading to the apartment above mine and makes all the car windows opaque.

Earbuds in, I walk to the back entrance to the apartment complex to get my blood pumping, then start an easy jog through the neighborhood. It feels good to move, and as usual, my mind starts to wander, processing through all the current puzzles and problems.

Before today I've been circling back to Ben and Tiffany pretty regularly, wondering things like: Is Ben warming up to me? Will he ever call me dad on his own or will I need to ask him to? Is Tiffany warming up to me? If not, why did she let me kiss her? And why kiss me back? But she refuses to discuss those kisses, and what does that mean?

But after last night, all I can think about is the way she felt against me, around me, and how soon can we do it again? I haven't even begun to get my fill of her.

As thrilled as I am about last night, I'm still not convinced she won't run away again, though, so I cut my jog short, circling back. I don't want her to scamper off while I'm gone and then pretend last night never happened.

Although if Ben's up, I won't be able to kiss her …

Damn. It hasn't even been twelve hours, and I'm already chafing at the restrictions.

Still. It's worth it—*she's* worth it—if in the end I get them both. And that's my new goal. I've got the NFL all but in the bag as long as I keep up with my training, which I will definitely do. I've been trying to figure out what should be next for me. And now I know.

I've managed to convince Tiffany to give me a chance. Now I just need to convince her to give me forever.

* * *

When I get back to the apartment, I find Tiffany back in her dress from last night sitting at the kitchen table with Ben and giggling over breakfast.

Ben straightens as soon as I come through the door.

"Gray!" he yells, with the unmatched exuberance only a little kid can muster, then scrambles out of his chair and hurls himself at me. "Mama wanted to leave before you got back, but I said no no no, we hafta see Gray."

"Oh really?" I scoop Ben up for a hug and look at Tiffany, who at least has the grace to blush and look away, brushing imaginary crumbs together on the table.

"We have things to do today, is all. I wasn't trying to avoid you," she says.

"I see." When she meets my eyes, I know that I've effectively communicated my disbelief. Setting Ben back on the ground, I pat his back and direct him back toward his seat. "Finish your breakfast, bud. Your mom and I are going to get your things together, alright?"

Ben scrambles into his seat, and Tiffany eyes me warily, but eventually stands and follows me to the bedroom.

Once there, I close the door behind her. When I turn to face her again, she's transformed from the chagrined girl in the kitchen back to the fiery ballbuster who tried to serve my nuts to me when I approached her after class about getting time with Ben.

She points at the door and hisses, "He's not that far away. We don't have time for a repeat of last night right now."

Crossing my arms over my chest, I tamp down the urge to laugh. "Oh, I know that, sweetheart. That's not what this is, though I have to admit if it were on the table, I certainly wouldn't be upset."

She narrows her eyes and lifts her chin. "What is it

then?"

I spread my arms. "You were going to leave before I got back?"

Her chin dips a little, and her cheeks grow pink again. "I already said that we have things to do today. It has nothing to do with you."

"Doesn't it, though? This is your MO, Tiff. We hooked up in high school, and you ran off immediately after. I looked for you. That night, I looked for you. I stayed until almost everyone had gone home, hoping you hadn't left already, that you'd been closeted away with your friends or something and would come out, giggly and drunk, and I could get your number and give you a ride home. But you left immediately, didn't you?"

She opens her mouth, but no words come. And I'm not interested in waiting for her to figure out what to say anyway.

"And here we are again. Every time we've kissed, you've avoided me for days after. What is it? Am I that bad of a kisser? Is that it? I'm so terrible in bed that you can't stand to even be near me? But you're ... what? Too nice to just tell me the truth?"

"No!" Her protest is too immediate, too instinctive to be a lie. Not that I thought that was the case. I know it's not me. Number one, I'm a fantastic kisser. And number two, I've made sure she's gotten what she needed from me both times we've had sex. I'm not saying I'm some kind of sex god or anything, but I make sure she's satisfied at the very least.

No, she's been running scared since that very first

night. But I'm not going to let her get away with it anymore. Not without telling me to my face, anyway.

"Then what's the problem, Tiff?" I ask softly.

Her mouth opens again, and again, she can't seem to find the words. Then all the fight goes out of her. Her shoulders slump, and her arms fall to her sides for a moment before she brings her hands to her face.

"I don't know, Gray," she says at last. "I don't know why I'm like this with you. And it's only ever with you that I've acted this way."

That has my eyebrows climbing my forehead, and I step closer to wrap her in my arms. After a moment, she tangles her fingers in my sweatshirt and clings to me. I press a kiss to her forehead. "Am I really that scary?"

"No. Yes. I don't know." She straightens, and I let her put space between us, but don't back up.

She shakes her head and turns to look at the door. "You make me feel too much. You always have. And it's … dangerous."

"Why?" She makes me feel everything too, but I'm not running away from it. I'm trying to figure out how I can get more.

When she looks at me, her eyes look like shattered glass. "Because you're always leaving. Don't you see? In high school, I'd just gotten out of a nearly four year long relationship. In *high school*. That's still the longest relationship I've ever had. And there you were, the quarterback for our biggest rivals who just trounced our team's hope of making it to state, all swagger and sex and sweeping me off my feet, telling me you'll help me get revenge on my ex as often as I want when I'd literally just decided that I didn't want a boyfriend before college."

She pauses, taking a deep breath and turning to face me, her shoulders square. "And *then*. I get pregnant. Because of *you*. And you *left* me."

I open my mouth to protest, but she holds up a hand, forestalling me. "And I know. I know. You didn't know. I never was able to tell you. But *I* didn't know you didn't know. *I* was told you denied even meeting me. That you didn't remember our night together." She lets out a choked laugh, and for the first time I realize that she's on the verge of tears. "The night that very literally changed the entire course of my life."

"And now," she continues after sucking in a ragged breath. "And now, here you are, wanting to be involved with Ben—which is fine, it is, good even—but you're not just content with Ben. You want *me*." She layers her hands over her chest. "And you're not just satisfied with some kisses or a night together, no. You want *everything*. And I ... I don't know if I can do that. Not after the last few years. Not after everything I've been through on my own."

I open my mouth to say something, though I don't have any idea what, but she keeps going, shaking her head. "You're leaving," she whispers. "You're leaving in a few months, and where does that leave me? Where does that leave Ben? Where does that leave *us*? You want me to just ... what? Be a normal twenty-two-year-old? Just go along with whatever you want? I was going to go to college. I was going to cheer in college, get my degree in finance to make enough money so I could try my luck at cheering professionally. I *loved* that sport. It was everything to me. And I gave it all up when I got pregnant. Changed my plans entirely. Switched to accounting so I can get a job as soon as I have my degree. And now you want me to just give up my own dreams, my own goals? Again?"

"No." I reach for her, pulling her against my chest once more. "God, no. I want everything for you. I just want ... I guess I just want us to be together while we both get everything we want."

"How?" she asks, her voice plaintive. "How is that even possible?"

I don't answer. I can't. I don't know how it's possible. I just squeeze her tighter and hope, somehow, we can figure it out. Because I know that I don't want to do any of it without her.

CHAPTER THIRTY-TWO

Tiffany

My outburst of doubts and fears doesn't seem to do anything to deter Gray from pursuing me. And while I'm still worried about the future—a concern he hasn't really addressed—I'm also glad that he's not so easily deterred.

I've always been a lot. Too much for some people to handle. That was Carter's problem with me, the reason he said he cheated. I was too much—too driven, too committed, too focused. And my other fizzled relationships all ended for much the same reason—a young single mom with goals and a plan and who puts her kid first is too much.

Some part of me keeps waiting for Gray to decide the same thing. That this—me, Ben, us, our whole life—is just too much for him to want to deal with. So the fact that he hasn't given up is ... something. I'm not sure what exactly yet. I just know that it makes me want to see what might happen next.

After our sleepover, he starts texting more regularly, calling at Ben's bedtime to tell his son goodnight, and asking me to call him back once Ben's asleep. I'm pretty sure I'm keeping him up later than normal, but he hasn't complained. And he's an adult. If he needs to get off the phone sooner, he can say so.

In so many ways I feel like I'm in high school again, talking to the boy I like on the phone as often as possible, trying to keep exactly how often from my parents.

Their reactions are mixed. My mom is mostly happy for me. "I've always only wanted you to be happy," she told me one night after walking in to find me smiling at Gray's latest text. "If he makes you happy, then I'm happy for you."

Dad isn't so easy to appease, though. He doesn't really trust Gray. Not after what happened four years ago, and the fact that I believe Gray doesn't really matter.

We've largely avoided the subject, because I have too much going on to want to fight with my dad on top of everything else, so I'm not sure if his hangup is that he doesn't believe Gray or if he's worried he'll abandon us again.

If it's the former, I'm not sure how to convince him of Gray's truthfulness. I wanted nothing to do with him when he first showed up again. Even if he approached me out of some latent sense of guilt, he had an easy out from my rejection of his overtures. Plus, with him poised to make it big as an NFL player, he had every reason to stay away unless he genuinely cares about doing the right thing.

Of course that's another potential sticking point in my relationship with him—is he only wanting to be with me out of some old fashioned sense of making things right? You get a girl pregnant, so you should marry her automatically?

Because fuck that nonsense. I have no interest in being with someone who only wants me out of obligation.

He hasn't said or done anything to make me think that's his motivating factor, but …

The worry still likes to rear its head whenever I let my guard down. And my dad grousing about how much time Ben and I spend with Gray doesn't help.

So it's with a certain amount of trepidation that I wait for Gray to come pick me up for an actual date the next Friday evening. Mom and Dad are watching Ben for us, and he told me to dress up because he's taking me to a nice restaurant.

The fact that we've had sex twice now and have a kid together before our first date makes it all feel a little ridiculous, but even so, nerves swirl in my belly as I get ready. I opt for a turquoise wrap dress that makes my cleavage pop and pair it with my favorite charcoal ankle booties. Ben plays on my bed as I finish putting on my jewelry in my bedroom, singing to himself while he goes through the quiet book my mom made for him last year, unzipping the mama lady bug to get out the babies inside and play with them, counting them under his breath. I watch him in the mirror, smiling to myself.

When the doorbell rings, he pops up, his quiet book forgotten. "Gray's here, Mama!" he shouts, running out of the room.

Chuckling, I pick up my clutch and follow him more slowly, knowing that my parents will beat me to the door no matter what. My dad's been sitting in the living room pretending to read his newspaper all evening just waiting for this moment.

I rolled my eyes at his antics, but no power on heaven or earth will stop him from trying to scare Gray into treating me right. Not that Gray needs that kind of fear put into him. He's the one who sought us out, after all. But reminding Dad of that fact did nothing but make him grunt and turn on the TV, his clear sign that he doesn't want to discuss the matter further.

When I get to the entryway, Gray stands just inside the door, my parents ranged opposite him while he holds Ben in his arms. My mom looks almost starry eyed at the view of this young, handsome football player holding an adorable child.

My dad on the other hand ...

He's not so easily impressed.

He stands there, arms crossed, glaring at Grayson holding Ben, and I can't help but smile.

Gray looks up and catches my eyes, his smile going from polite to delighted to mischievous in a matter of seconds. Oh man. I'm in trouble. If he's sticking around and I'm getting a preview of what Ben will grow up to be like, that streak of mischief runs wide and deep.

He passes Ben off to my mom, ignoring Ben's indignant squawk of protest, and comes straight for me, that smile firmly in place. "Hey," he says to me, voice low. And I know without any shade of doubt that if it weren't for my ban on kissing in front of Ben, he'd absolutely have locked lips with me already.

"Hey," I return, my own smile curving my lips.

He looks me up and down, then reaches for my hand and spins me. "You look beautiful."

Dad harrumphs, but Mom smacks his arm. "Be nice," she loud whispers. "Let's all say goodbye and let these two get out of here, okay?"

Tearing my attention from Gray, I give my dad a hug and a kiss on the cheek. "Everything's alright," I whisper to him. "I can handle myself. I promise."

His stern expression softens as he looks down at me, finally uncrossing his arms to return my hug. "Be safe. And if you need anything, we're only a phone call away."

"I know." Turning to my mom, I take Ben from her, and he winds himself around me like I've never left him alone with my parents before, instead of it being a regular occurrence.

"I wanna come too," he pouts.

I pat his back and give him a squeeze. "I know. But we're going to a boring grownup restaurant to talk about boring grownup things. I promise you'll have more fun here with Gramma and Grampa."

His pouty lower lip and baleful glare tells me he doesn't believe a word of it, but my mom reaches for him and whispers, "We'll make cookies, okay?"

That does the trick, because he releases me instantly, his face all smiles now. "Chocolate chip?"

"Whatever kind you want," she promises.

He claps his hands. "Chocolate chip!"

Leaning in, Mom gives me a quick hug. "Have fun," she calls over her shoulder as she lets Ben drag her to the kitchen.

I retrieve my coat from the front closet under my dad's watchful glare. Gray takes it from me and holds it out for me to put on. As I'm adjusting my hair and doing up the buttons, he slides his hands in the pockets of a nice black wool coat I've never seen before. Charcoal gray slacks cover his legs, and he has on sleek black loafers. I've never actually seen him dressed up before.

He looks yummy.

Dad makes a disgusted snort. "Get on out of here before I puke from watching you make eyes at each other."

Raising my eyebrows, I turn to him. "You're the one who decided to stay and watch."

Gray stifles a laugh next to me, trying to turn it into a cough and fooling exactly no one.

Shooting him one last glare, Dad turns and walks into the living room, casting glances at us over his shoulder.

"We should go," I whisper to Gray, and he snickers but holds the door open for me.

Once we're outside, I collapse against the porch railing, uncaring that it's cold enough to see my breath. "Oh my god. I feel like I'm in high school again with my parents inspecting my date. I'm so sorry about that. He'll eventually get over it. I hope." The last time he acted anything remotely like that about a guy was when Carter and I started dating. But that was understandable, since I was only fourteen.

Now, though? Now it just seems ridiculous.

Grinning, Gray reaches for me, pulling me close and settling his arms around me. "I don't mind. It's kinda funny, in a way."

I shake my head and return his grin. "I'm glad you think so." My smile fades. "He doesn't really believe you. That you didn't know. He's still mad about the way everything went down."

Bending his head, Gray kisses my lips softly. Once, twice, and then he straightens, the warmth in his eyes driving away the chill in the air. "I can't blame him, I guess. You didn't believe me at first, either. And it's not like he's had the chance to get to know me the way you have." He glances at the front door. "Give him time. He'll come around."

But that's the thing, I think but don't say. *We don't actually have time.* Not much, anyway. Nowhere near enough. Soon he'll go to the combines, then just over a month later, it'll be the draft. Graduation is a few weeks after. And then …

Everything after that is a big question mark. We have a couple of months. Even if Dad comes around during that time, what good will it do?

"Hey." Gray's fingers touch my chin, tipping my face up to his. "We'll figure it out, okay? Whatever it is that's making you look worried, I promise we'll find a way to figure it out. Together."

I press up on my toes and brush a kiss on his mouth, then force a smile and nod. "Okay."

He seems to accept my response, stepping back and taking my hand in his to lead me to his car in the driveway. It's not until I climb in the open door he holds for me that I let my smile slip.

I wish I could borrow some of his confidence. Because even though things between us working out for the long term sounds ideal, I don't see how it's possible.

CHAPTER THIRTY-THREE

Gray

Since this is not only our first date, but also since regular dates aren't necessarily an easy option for us, I decided to go all out tonight. We have reservations at The Waterway, a high-end restaurant downtown. I've never been, but my parents go there for special occasions—anniversaries, milestone celebrations, things like that. It seemed fitting for tonight.

I want to spoil Tiffany. To show her that she's important to me, and that even though things between us haven't gone according to any kind of normal schedule, I don't want anyone else.

Not that there's been anyone else in quite a while. I wasn't supposed to get involved with anyone. But I've always been the kind of guy who goes all in, and if things are going to work out between Tiffany and me, I can't see a better way of accomplishing that. Her drive and dedication to pursuing her goals fits right alongside my own, even if her goals are different. She's smart, funny, and so sexy. I wish I could spend even more time with her, but our schedules make that difficult.

I know she still has big reservations about us. And my goal between now and graduation is to lay as many of her doubts to rest as possible, even though I haven't figured out a way around the biggest one—how to make anything work between us when she still has two years left of her degree and I'll be leaving after graduation.

As the hostess leads us to our seat, I hold her hand, enjoying the way she looks around, taking in the sleek bar in black and dark wood, the tables covered in white tablecloths, and the warm, low lighting as we wind our way to a table near the back.

"Oh my god," she leans in and whispers over the top of her menu after the hostess leaves. "I wasn't expecting anything this fancy."

Smiling at her, I shrug. "You deserve something fancy."

She presses her pretty pink lips together and examines my face, her eyes briefly tracking down to my chest. I left off my suit jacket, but I'm wearing the tailored shirt my mom insisted I'd need for the draft and have on the vest that comes with the suit. I opted for no tie and left the top button undone, cuffing my sleeves at the elbow.

It seems to be the right choice, because ever since I took off my coat, Tiffany's eyes keep roaming my upper body.

My lips quirk in a grin as her gaze lingers for a moment before returning to my face. "Thank you," she says at last.

"You're welcome."

Fortunately any awkwardness she might feel about the fanciness of the restaurant is short lived, and after we decide on what we want, we settle into the kind of easy conversation we've had more and more of as we've spent time together.

Originally the plan was for me to get Ben on my own more, but now? Now I want them both with me. All the time. Well, at least as much as reasonably possible.

The image of the two of them living with me pops into my head, and try as I might, I can't shake it. Throughout dinner, even as I keep up my end of the conversation, I can't help imagining doing this with her and then picking up Ben and going home all together.

Not my apartment, though. It's too small for all of us. We'd need at least a two bedroom. And since I'll be leaving shortly after graduation to an as of yet unknown location, moving now would be dumb.

Doesn't mean I don't want to, though.

Giving up the NFL at this point would be foolish. I know this. I don't think my parents would let me get away with it—though I am an adult and I suppose they couldn't actually stop me if I made up my mind.

Thing is, though, I don't want to. I love football. Playing professionally has been my dream for as long as I can remember. Nothing and no one has ever made me reconsider that.

Until now …

If that were the only way for Tiffany and I to be together, would I do it?

But then what would I do? Yeah, I'll have a degree in psychology, but I'd have to keep going to school to really be able to do anything with it. That was always a fallback idea, not the main plan.

Maybe I need to consider the fallback. Especially if losing Tiffany when I've just gotten her again is the consequence of pursuing Plan A. Would she ever forgive me for leaving again? Would she be willing to give long distance a try? Would she even consider coming with me?

After what she said last weekend about giving up everything for me again, I don't even want to ask. But I worry I'll regret my choices forever if I don't at least bring it up as a possibility.

Not tonight, though. Tonight is supposed to be all about enjoying ourselves.

Which is why I nod when the waitress offers the dessert menu.

Tiffany regards me with raised eyebrows. "Dessert? You're going way off plan tonight, aren't you?"

I shrug. "I worked it so I can eat whatever I want tonight." I give her my most mischievous smirk, accompanied by a lascivious wink in case my double entendre wasn't clear.

She snickers, covering her mouth with her hand, but I don't miss the way her cheeks turn pink. "Oh, really? And what exactly are you wanting to *eat*?"

My smirk pulls wider, and I glance at the dessert

menu before meeting her eyes. "I feel like something creamy."

She bites the inside of her cheek, then taps the menu. "They have a creme brûlée." Her voice is all husky, and I can tell she's trying hard to keep up with the pretense we're talking about dessert and not me going down on her.

"Sounds delicious," I tell her, my eyes never leaving her. "That might take the edge off my craving to start with. But I'll have to finish my dessert once we get home."

Reaching out, I caress the space between her first and second fingers, and she shivers at the contact, her eyes almost navy when they meet mine again.

I order the creme brûlée when the waitress returns, managing not to let on that my dick already wants to bust out of my pants. Good thing my coat goes down to mid thigh. Because I don't think my hard on is going anywhere until after I get Tiffany home and satisfy us both.

* * *

The little minx teases me all through dessert, scooping up bites and lapping them slowly off her spoon, staring at me with a coy smile on her face the entire time, moaning with pleasure with each mouthful.

When I narrow my eyes at her, she just giggles. "You're asking for it," I growl.

Her eyes widen, and she makes an O with her mouth, holding her hand in front of it in a pin-up girl look of surprise. "What?" She lays her hand on her chest. "Moi? Asking for it?" Setting her spoon down, she lays her forearms on the table and leans closer, the deep V of her dress gaping to give me an even deeper view of her cleavage. "What exactly am I asking for?"

I scoop up the last of the dessert in one huge bite and shove it in my mouth, then raise my hand for the waitress's attention, my eyes never leaving Tiffany's. Her lips curl up in a Cheshire smile.

It seems like it takes ages for the waitress to run my credit card and come back, though I'm sure it's only a couple of minutes. I overtip to make it easy to calculate and scrawl my signature, stuffing my card back in my wallet and pulling my coat off my chair so I can hide my dick while putting it on.

Tiffany, of course, stands more slowly, drawing her coat off the back of her chair, the satin lining making a swishing sound. Glowering at her, I hold out my hand for her coat, then hold it open for her. She rewards me with a beautiful smile of thanks.

And I kiss her. Hard. Fierce. Uncaring that we're in a restaurant and people can see how much I want to devour her.

When I pull away, her smile is gone, her lips parted as she pants with arousal, her eyes glassy with lust.

"Let's go," I mutter softly in her ear.

Swallowing hard, she nods, threading her hand into the crook of my elbow as I hurry us out the door. I'm more thankful than ever that I found a parking spot close by, because if I don't get home and inside this woman soon,

I might die.

As soon as we're both in the car, she leans in close, her fingers creeping over my thigh. I suck in a breath. "Jesus, Tiff. Careful or I might crash the car before we get back to my apartment."

She chuckles, low and sexy. "Do you want me to stop touching you?"

I swallow hard. "No," I croak. "Just don't move, okay?"

"Okay," she breathes.

But she's a dirty, dirty liar, because as soon as we stop at a stoplight, her fingers slide higher, so close to my dick that I'm in pain from the anticipation of her touching me. I might pass out from lack of blood flow to my brain.

I growl her name, and she looks up at me, eyes wide and innocent. "We're stopped."

When I narrow my eyes, her innocent look turns back into that sexy teasing one she wore all through dessert.

"You're the worst," I tell her.

She just laughs. "You say that now, but I'm pretty sure you won't later."

At the next stoplight I hold my breath, wondering if she'll move into the crease of my thigh, and if she does, will she actually rub against my dick?

Do I want her to?

I mean, hell yes, obviously I do. But also I'm driving so maybe it's not the best idea.

To my disappointment and relief, all she does is draw tiny tickly circles on the inside of my thigh. When I flex my quad under her hand, she gives me a squeeze in return and then goes back to the circles until the light turns green.

Between the restaurant and the drive, I'm not sure I'll have the control to do everything I want once we're in my apartment. But damn if I'm not going to give it my best shot.

Her hand leaves my thigh as soon as I put my car in park, and she's out the door before mine's even open, waiting for me at the front of the car.

After all the teasing she's put me through, I take my sweet time, getting out slowly even though drawing it out is as much torture for me as it is for her.

She's practically bouncing with impatience and anticipation, and I raise my eyebrows and smirk at her as I stroll to the front of the car and offer her my elbow.

She scowls at me as she threads her arm through mine. "I thought you were in a hurry."

"Payback's a bitch."

She laughs as we walk to my front door, and she releases my arm so I can unlock it.

Once we're inside, though, all bets are off. Coats fall to the floor, and I push her up against the door, hooking one leg up over my hip as my mouth crashes into hers.

She wraps her hands around my neck and hangs on, using her grip to pull herself closer to me, her hips tilting to rub against whatever part of me she can reach.

I find the hem of her dress and slide my fingers up her leg, relishing the feel of her satin soft skin under my fingers.

I move higher, higher, higher, expecting to find a thin

layer of fabric, but I reach her waist and there's nothing.

Nothing.

I tear my mouth from hers with a curse. "Jesus, Tiff, you mean to tell me you weren't wearing panties all through dinner?"

That coy, sexy smile is back on her face as she shakes her head.

"Fuuuuuuck."

She pulls my mouth back to hers, but I don't stay there long. Instead I slither down her body, dropping kisses along her neck, collarbone, and cleavage, nipping at her belly through the fabric of her dress and sink to my knees.

Smoothing her dress up her thigh, I push the fabric into her hand. "Hold this."

She takes it from me, bemused uncertainty on her face. But when I move her leg over my shoulder, grip her ass, spread her open with my fingers, and sink my tongue in her sweet, wet pussy, any uncertainty about my intentions has to be wiped away.

With a gasp, she tilts her hips toward me, giving me better access, feeding me her pussy.

And dear lord, I don't know if I'll ever get my fill of this woman. Sweet and tangy and so wet for me, so naughty, and I fucking love it.

I take my time tracing every inch of her soft flesh, dipping in and out of her opening, then lapping at her like she did her spoon in the restaurant. Exploring, enjoying, savoring. Listening to her sounds and waiting for the things that make her muscles jump or clench or go lax to figure out what will take her to the edge when I'm ready to send her there.

After taking my time teasing all around her pussy but never directly on her clit, I make my way back there and suck it between my lips. She jumps, her whole body stiffening like she got zapped by a live wire. I ease off a little and let her get her bearings, then move my hand so my thumb rests just at the base of her opening, circling her clit slowly with the tip of my tongue.

She rocks into my mouth, silently begging for more, but I keep up what I'm doing until she's actually begging.

"Oh god, Gray, please please please."

And with her asking so politely, how can I do anything other than give her what she wants?

I suck her clit into my mouth again, scrubbing my tongue over it just like I did her nipples last week, sinking two fingers into her at the same time. She immediately clenches around my fingers, and I'm not sure if it's on purpose or involuntary at first, but then her hands tighten in my hair so I can't move, and I know she's close.

Fucking her with my fingers, I keep going with my mouth until she's rubbing her pussy against me, crying, "Yes, fuck, *ngh, fuck!*"

She comes on my face with a wordless cry, her pussy spasming around my fingers, and I can't fucking wait to get inside her and make her do it again.

I bring her down with slow strokes deep inside and soft laps of my tongue until she's pushing me away instead of trying to pull me closer.

Releasing her leg, I sit back on my heels, grinning up at her as her dress falls between us, covering where my hands still hold her hips to make sure she's steady before I let go.

"Holy shit," she breathes, panting against the door.

Standing, I kiss her, and she doesn't shy away from kissing me back.

When I pull back, her eyes flutter open, and that wicked smile I've come to look forward to curls her lips. Her palm goes flat on my chest, and she gives me a little push.

"My turn."

CHAPTER THIRTY-FOUR

Tiffany

Gray lets me push him into the living room, his expression going from surprised to pleased. "Your turn?"

I bite my lip and nod, giving him a little shove so he sits down on the couch. Right in the middle. Except he doesn't sink in.

Blinking away the haze of lust clouding my vision, I actually look at it for a second. It's light blue like I'm used to, but a few shades lighter and it's not threadbare. "You got a new couch."

He chuckles, running a hand over the smooth upholstery. "I did. After sleeping on the old one last weekend, I decided it was time."

"That's a terrible color to choose when you have a preschooler coming over regularly."

He grins. "It has stain shield. Now, are you really going to lecture me on my choice of couch colors right now? I thought you had something else in mind."

With a laugh, I shake my head and climb into his lap. "You're right," I say, giving my voice a dark edge. "I have other plans after all."

His hands settle on my waist, which is fine for now, especially since he's just resting them there and not trying to control my movements. I stay high on my knees and thread my hands through his hair, tugging his head back. His eyes practically glow with arousal, and I'm extra aware that I've gotten off already and he hasn't. And he was already hard before we left the restaurant. I saw the tent in his pants that he tried to conceal while he put his coat on. And felt the way his pants were stretched tight near his crotch on the drive over.

But instead of torturing him by rubbing against him through our clothes, I torture him by kissing him deeply and not rubbing against him at all.

He tastes like me, like sex and sin and decadence, and his dirty line about wanting something creamy for dessert goes through my head.

Ending the kiss, I scoot back and drag my fingernails down his chest. "I like this," I tell him, rubbing the silken fabric of his gray vest.

"I know," he says, his voice gravelly. "I could tell. You couldn't stop ogling me at dinner."

My lips quirk in a half smile, and I meet his eyes. "Well, it was mutual. You could barely keep your eyes off my boobs all night."

As though to prove my point, he looks at them again, his hands sliding up to cup them, his thumbs finding my nipples with scary accuracy considering I'm wearing a bra with enough padding to disguise them. But not so much that I can't feel him working them.

"You like when I pay attention to your tits," he whispers, and I can't deny it because we both know it's true.

But he's distracting me, and we can't have that.

I circle his wrists with my fingers and pull them away, placing them behind his head. "These stay here."

He raises his eyebrows in response, but doesn't protest.

With a nod, I return my attention to his vest, circling the top button with my finger a few times before undoing it. I undo the rest more quickly, then start on his shirt.

"If this were a movie, I'd just rip your shirt open and send the buttons flying," I murmur as I work my way down.

He chuckles, the movement making it slightly more difficult to work the buttons. "If this were a movie, we'd be in bed already, and your bra would stay on while you're on top. I think I like it better in real life."

I glance up at his eyes. "You don't want my bra to stay on?"

He raises one eyebrow. "Do you?"

No, but I'm not giving him the satisfaction of that answer. Not yet, anyway. I refocus on his shirt, pulling the tails out and spreading the fabric.

"If you let me move my hands, I can take it off," he suggests.

Cocking my head to the side, I let out a thoughtful hum as though I'm considering his suggestion. Ha. I knew he wouldn't be able to take his shirt off without moving his hands when I put them there. Having him half clothed like this is part of the experience. Like I wouldn't have planned this already? I'd shake my head and tsk, but I don't want to give away just how much I've thought this through.

"Nah," I say lightly, rubbing my hands over his bare chest. "This works for me for now."

He grunts, his eyes falling closed as I caress his torso, his abs popping as I move lower.

Since he called me a tease earlier, I might as well live up to the accusation. I slide my hands over his waistband and down his thighs, pulling his pants tight over his erection, but never actually touching it. I scratch my fingernails slowly up and down his thighs a few times until his muscles jump and twitch every time I get anywhere even close to his cock.

Smiling to myself, I meet his eyes as I finally slide all the way up and stroke him through his clothes.

"Jesus Christ," he mutters when I finally touch him. "You're fucking killing me, Tiff."

I give him my most wicked smile. "Good."

Reaching up, I pop the button on his pants and slowly lower the zipper, rubbing my hand down his cock as I do it. He hisses, and I love having this kind of power over him. Especially after the way he took his time working me over. Slow starts are good for foreplay, but when half our foreplay took place before we even got here, I didn't need that much of a warm up before I was ready to go. Even so, he seemed to be down there as much for his own enjoyment as mine. So I'm going to do the same thing.

The royal blue cotton of his boxer briefs pokes out from his open fly, and I rub him again, circling and tugging him slowly.

He shifts his hips and groans. "Please, Tiff," he begs.

And oh, wow. I don't think I've ever made a man beg before. I have to admit, I definitely see the appeal.

But he didn't make me beg for long, so I won't do that to him either.

Pulling his waistband out and down, I free him. He's so big and hot and hard, my fingers not quite touching when I circle him even without the barrier of his clothes.

He hisses and groans and pushes himself into my hand, and when I look up at him, his eyes are fixed on where I'm touching him.

"Fuck, Tiff. Fuck fuck fuck."

I'm going to take that as encouragement. Flipping my hair so it's all over one shoulder, I lower my mouth until I'm nearly close enough to kiss his weeping slit.

"Jesus," he breathes.

I meet his eyes, extend my tongue, and swirl it around.

You'd think I'd electrocuted him with the way he

jumps at that first contact. I pull back and wait for him to settle before licking him again. This time he stiffens, but holds himself in check.

I spend some time just lapping at him like I did the spoonfuls of creme brûlée, slowly licking all around the crown, teasing just underneath with the tip of my tongue—he really seems to like that—picking up hits of salt every time I go over the top of the broad head.

When I open my mouth and suck him in, he seems to lose all control. His hands come down, one gathering my hair, the other planting on the couch next to him, and his hips thrust up as he pushes himself into my mouth almost too deep. I pull back enough to keep from gagging, but keep him in my mouth.

"Fuck, Tiff. Sorry. Jesus. Don't stop. Please don't stop."

I don't. Holding him steady with one hand so that he can't go too deep should he get carried away again, I bob up and down slowly, sucking and swirling my tongue at the top of each stroke.

When I glance up at him, he has his head pressed into the back of the couch, his eyes closed, and the tendons in his neck stand out in sharp relief.

After a moment he gasps and lifts his head. "Jesus, Tiff, if you don't stop right now I'm gonna blow my load in your mouth."

I lift my head, sucking on the way up so he leaves my mouth with a pop. "And the problem with that is …?"

He chuckles weakly. "I want to fuck your sweet little

pussy. Come here and let me get ahold of myself for a second, and then I want inside you."

I give him a little pout, but do as he asks, taking his hand and letting him guide me up onto the couch with him.

He reaches for the tie at my side, and with one swift tug, opens my dress, spreading the fabric the same way I did to him. His eyes roam my nearly naked body, only my bra and the dress hanging from my shoulders standing between me and full nudity.

"I still can't believe you went commando," he whispers.

My grin fades quickly as he begins worshipping my body. He slides my dress from my shoulders, reaching behind me and unhooking my bra, pulling it all away to leave me completely naked for him.

He peppers kisses down my neck, scraping his teeth along my shoulder, then finding his way to his favorite place—my boobs. Not that I have any objection. I love the way he lavishes attention there, acting like he could spend hours just feasting on me.

Lying back on the couch, I reach above me, my fingers scrabbling against the fabric, trying to find purchase, an anchor to hold in the storm he creates in my body. As he sucks on one nipple, the fingers of his free hand trace down my side, over my thigh, back up the inside, and he does what I did to him, always bypassing my center, coming close, but never touching where I'm beginning to need him again.

On what feels like the thousandth pass, I lift my hips, hoping he'll take the hint and touch me, slide his fingers inside me, rub circles around my clit, *something*. And once again, he traces a line at the join of my thigh, so close to my pussy it ripples the skin, but never quite where I need him.

"Gray," I say on a broken whisper. "Gray, please."

He lifts his head and smirks at me. "I love the way you say that."

And then he's touching me, his fingers spearing inside me in one hard thrust, his thumb rubbing my clit.

I cry out, lifting my hips, though I'm not sure if it's to demand more or to try to escape the sudden intensity of his touch.

"That what you need, baby?"

I can't even form the words to respond.

"Yeah, I know," he whispers. "I need it too."

Reaching for him, I bring his face to mine, and he groans into my mouth as his tongue tangles with mine. Then he's rising up over me, my hands trailing down his torso as he yanks his shirt off and shoves his pants down. He fishes a condom out of his pocket—but not from his wallet—rips open the package and rolls it on in one swift motion.

He settles between my spread thighs, propping himself up with his arm on the back of the couch and rubbing the head of his dick all over my needy pussy. "I was gonna do this in the bed," he says, his eyes never leaving what he's doing to me.

"Next time."

He lines himself up and sinks inside me. "Fucking right there's gonna be a next time." He pulls almost all the way out and drives into me again. "And a time after that. And a time after that."

Leaning down, he kisses me, pumping into me slowly but fiercely, like he's using each thrust to drive home his point. "I'm not gonna be done with you for a long time," he mutters against my mouth. "Maybe ever."

CHAPTER THIRTY-FIVE

Gray

"It'll be okay, I promise," I whisper to Tiffany for probably the fiftieth time since I picked her up for dinner with my parents. I give her hand a squeeze before knocking on my parents' front door and letting us in. "Mom? Dad? We're here," I call as I push it open.

Tiffany's heels clack on the entryway tile as she follows me in, Ben clutched in her arms.

"Mama, I want down!" he whispers emphatically.

"Just a minute, Benny. Let's see what we're doing first."

Turning back to her, I reach for him, and she gives me a grateful smile as he lunges into my arms. Even with me, he still squirms, though I think it's less than with his mom.

My parents file out of the kitchen, all smiles, and

Tiffany steps up next to me, a nervous smile on her face.

"We're so happy you could make it tonight," Mom says, ever the gracious hostess. She holds out her hands to Tiffany. "It's so nice to meet you at last. I'm Melissa and this is Christopher. Gray's told us so much about you."

Tiffany shoots me a glance, eyebrows raised. "All good things, I hope."

Mom lets out a tinkling laugh, but doesn't actually confirm or deny anything. Turning to me, she kisses my cheek and then gives Ben all her attention. She's been holding off, controlling herself and being polite to Tiffany first, but the only reason we're really here is because she's been dying to meet Ben from day one. And since the combines are next week, now seemed like the best time. Especially since I think my mother might murder me if I tried to make her wait another two weeks for me to get back and catch up on all the school I'll miss while I'm gone.

My professors are understanding for the most part. I have one prof for Organizational Psychology who tried to act like the absence wouldn't be excused, so I had to go through the whole process of getting a note from my coach, and when that wasn't enough, going to the Dean of the College of Arts and Sciences to get her to play ball. She's still pissed, and I know the extra work she's been giving me already is her version of punishment, but she can't actually penalize my grade for missing her class next week.

"Hi, Benjamin," Mom says to him in that overly bright voice adults reserve for young children. She clasps her hands together, absolutely enamored with him.

For his part, Ben has gone still, no longer squirming to get down as he stares at my mom, his index finger planted on his bottom lip. I can't blame him. I'd probably stare if there were a strange woman who greeted me by my full name and seemed uncomfortably happy to see me too.

"Do you know who I am?" she asks.

He shakes his head solemnly.

Tears fill her eyes as she says, "I'm your Grandma M."

Ben's brows pull together in confusion.

I boost him in my arms and turn him more toward me. "Remember how we told you that I'm your dad?"

He meets my eyes and nods. "Well, this is my mom, and that's my dad." I nod my head at my dad. "That means they're your grandparents."

The furrow between Ben's brows grows deeper. "Gramma and Grampa are at home."

I nod. "That's right. These are your other grandparents."

He still seems dubious, but doesn't argue with me. I know my mom wants nothing more than to hold him, but he's not being particularly gregarious at the moment, so she's just going to have to wait.

I become vaguely aware that Tiffany is talking to my dad, but it sounds like they're mostly exchanging pleasantries, and she's filling him in on things like her major and her plans after graduation.

Except that makes my gut clench, because she won't graduate for another couple of years. And she sounds very much like she intends to stay here for that time. Which, I mean, I kinda know. And we haven't discussed anything else. But I want her and Ben to come with me. I'd sorta hoped she would soften on that point on her own if we spent enough time together. Which is dumb. Why would she if she doesn't know I want her to come with me? But feelings aren't always rational.

My dad meets my eyes over Ben's head, his eyebrows raised, and I know he's wondering the same thing we all are. What happens when I leave?

Mom says something about dinner, and that seems to be Ben's cue to start squirming again. I put him down, as grateful to be relieved of a squirmy kid as I'm sure the squirmy kid is for his freedom.

My mom holds out her hand and says, "You ready to eat, Ben? I have a special spot next to your mom and dad just for you. And you can meet my daughter. She's really excited to meet you too."

"She is?" Tentatively, he places his hand in hers, and my mom gives me a look that says she's already smitten with him. And I can't blame her at all. I had basically the same reaction when I met him. I mean, how could you not?

Dad follows them, and Tiffany steps close to me, letting out a long, slow breath. I wrap my hand around hers between us and give it a squeeze. "Doing alright?"

She gives me a quick smile that's meant to be reassuring but doesn't quite hit the mark. "I'm fine. Everything's fine. It's just a lot." She looks all around the house, which is much grander than her parents', and I'm guessing she feels a bit out of her element.

"They're normal people," I whisper. "And they're happy you're here. You brought Ben, so that makes you on par with an angel."

She lets out a soft chuckle. "I'm not so sure about that, but thanks anyway."

"Well, I'm glad you're here at least."

That earns me a genuine smile, and unfortunately I have to release her hand because we're in the dining room, and we're supposed to be keeping our relationship on the down low. Even though my parents already know we're exploring the possibility of a relationship. I mean, they don't know all the details, but they know I'm interested in her as more than just a co-parent and ancient history hookup.

But Ben's not supposed to know anything, and while I don't know that he would understand the significance of hand holding, I know Tiffany doesn't want us to even do that in front of him.

Of course my sister doesn't miss a thing, and when I meet her eyes as I take the seat across from her, she raises her eyebrows and darts her gaze between Tiffany and me. I shoot her a glare that I hope will settle her down, but my track record with Piper lately hasn't exactly been great.

But all she does is turn to Tiffany and smile. "It's so great to see you again. How've you been?"

"Oh!" Mom says, pausing mid-step as she heads to the kitchen to grab something. "I forgot that you mentioned you knew Tiffany, Piper."

"We have some friends in common."

"I have a class with Autumn," Tiffany chimes in.

"And Autumn is friends with Dani," Piper finishes. "My roommate," she adds for Tiffany's benefit.

Mom nods and continues bustling around, making sure everyone has everything they could possibly want or need. I give McAdam a nod of greeting, and he nods back, his posture relaxed and his arm propped on the back of Piper's chair.

With Tiffany here, I understand why Piper insists on bringing him all the time. At first I thought it was mostly to needle me, but it's comforting having someone at your side who's not mired in the family history and expectations and is just there as a support.

Though to be fair, Tiffany's here for more reasons than that. Which is why she's been so nervous. She's worried they're going to judge her and hate her and blame her for keeping Ben away for so long, despite my reassurances that I was the one who never extended my mom's standing invitation to Thursday dinners.

Even though I've enjoyed living in our little bubble the last six weeks or so, I've known it couldn't last. And with the combines in a few days and the draft a little over a month later, things are going to be changing fast around here. Although at least once the combines are over I can relax a little with my training schedule. Which means I'll be able to spend more time with Tiffany and Ben. And maybe I can convince her that coming with me won't necessarily mean giving up everything yet again. Maybe I can convince her that it'll mean trading up.

At least I hope so.

CHAPTER THIRTY-SIX

Tiffany

Piper's familiar face does more to calm me than any of Gray's reassurances. It's not that I don't believe him, it's that he's not the one on trial here. But maybe if Piper's on my side, it won't be so bad.

And from her welcoming smile, I'm going to count her as an ally. Plus, she's obviously excited to finally meet Ben.

For his part, Ben is thrilled with all the attention he's getting. Any time attention drifts away from him and conversation centers on anyone else, he says something goofy and draws it all back to him.

It's perfect, though, as far as I'm concerned. Everyone thinks he's the most adorable thing they've ever seen. Even Piper's boyfriend can't help smiling at my super cute kid. It's nice to know I'm not the only one who thinks he's charming.

It makes me wonder what Grayson was like when he was Ben's age, though.

At the next lull in conversation, I decide to ask.

Melissa stops for a second, her fork hovering above her risotto as she contemplates what Gray was like as a child. Then she looks at Ben. "He wasn't nearly as outgoing as your little guy here, for all they look almost identical. Did you see the picture in the living room when you came in? I swear, they look like they could be the same child." Shaking her head in disbelief, she returns her attention to me. "He could, of course, be a charmer when he wanted to with that smile of his. He still does it, as I'm sure you know, and uses it to his advantage. Always has. Whenever I would tell him no while he was growing up, he'd try out that smile to see if he could get me to change my mind."

"Did it work?" I ask.

"Sometimes," Gray puts in. "Often enough to make it worth the effort."

Melissa gives me a conspiratorial grin. "You're a mother. You know how it is. Sometimes it's just too hard to say no to that face, isn't it?"

Chuckling, I nod.

Asking about Gray as a kid seems to be the trick to get them all on my side, though. Not that they were necessarily against me, but the polite friendliness they greeted me with turns into genuine warmth the longer they tell stories. Even Gray's dad seems to have decided I'm okay. Not that he was rude to me before or anything, but there was an unmistakable chill coming off him where I was concerned.

And if there were any doubt that I'd struck all the right notes, Piper makes sure I know the truth before we leave. After using the upstairs bathroom, I open the door to find her waiting for me.

She grabs my arms and pulls me close. "You. Were. Brilliant," she loud whispers. "And asking about Gray as a kid? Genius. I'll be using that trick the next time I visit Cal's parents. Not that I need to impress them, really, but it's always nice to get in good with your boyfriend's parents, right?"

"Uh, right."

Her grin pulls wider. "I'm so glad you two are together."

My cheeks heat, and I look away, grateful that she's released her hold on me. "Oh, um …"

"Right, right," she interrupts my stammering. "I get it. No worries. It's still new or whatever." She leans in closer. "For what it's worth? I've never seen Gray act like this with anyone else. Ever. He's absolutely smitten."

With that, she slips into the bathroom, and I walk back downstairs mildly dazed from the encounter.

Gray's smitten? With me?

I mean, I know he likes me. Obviously.

But some part of me has still been wondering if he's pursuing me to make it easier to get access to Ben.

If Piper's to be believed, though, maybe his feelings for me are separate from Ben. And he has mentioned that he's wanted to pursue a relationship with me since back in high school. Would he still have wanted to if Ben didn't exist, though?

That's the question. And regardless of what Piper thinks, I don't actually know the answer. And I don't know that Gray does either.

* * *

By the time we get back to Gray's apartment, Ben's already asleep. I carefully remove him from his car seat and carry him inside. Gray holds all the doors open for me and gets a Pull-Up and pajamas out of Ben's suitcase. The poor little guy barely twitches as I wrestle him out of his dress clothes and into the Pull-Up and his favorite pajamas with cartoon sharks eating pizzas all over them.

When I finish, Gray stands next to me and gazes at our adorable child asleep in his bed. "How is he even cuter when he sleeps?" he asks, his voice full of wonder.

"I don't know," I whisper back. "But he really is. This is my favorite time of day."

Gray chuckles softly beside me, burying his face in my hair to stifle his laughter. "I can understand that."

Wrapping my fingers around his, I tug him behind me out of the room and wait as he closes the door quietly behind us. We walk to the living room hand in hand and sink into his fancy new couch by silent agreement.

He twists a strand of hair around his fingers. "I like having you here," he says, his voice barely above a whisper.

I give him a smile. "I like being here too."

His eyes meet mine, and his lips part like he wants to say something, but then he closes his mouth and swallows. "Are you hungry or anything? Thirsty?"

Shaking my head, I bend and remove my shoes. "No. I'm still full from dinner. Did your mom cook all that?"

He nods. "Yeah. She went all out tonight since we were having special guests for Thursday dinner."

"Oh, man. She's an amazing cook."

He gives me that boyish grin we were discussing at dinner. "She really is. It's a blessing and a curse."

A bark of laughter escapes, and I cover my mouth to muffle it. "Seriously? A curse?"

He shrugs, his smile going lopsided. "She always wants to feed me too many carbs and all the desserts. No matter how many times I tell her that I need to follow my meal plan, she scoffs and insists that I'm a growing boy and I need plenty of calories. And of course the calories she provides me are far superior to any I could cook for myself or whatever the team nutritionist has recommended."

I laugh some more. "I can totally see that from her."

His gaze softens as he continues to fiddle with my hair. "You were a hit tonight."

I scoff. "I think you mean Ben was a hit tonight."

"Him too." His smile is crooked and a little wistful as he meets my eyes. "But you charmed them as much as he did. You're where he gets that from. He might have my smile, but he has your charm."

Ducking my head to hide my pinkening cheeks, I can't suppress the smile his words bring to my face.

"Thanks."

His warm breath fans over my ear, and then his soft lips find the skin just below it. "I mean it," he whispers. "You're utterly intoxicating."

I turn to face him, wanting to return the compliment, but his lips capture mine, and all I can do is sink into his kiss and the feel of his hands on my body.

At times like this when he's worshiping my body, it's easy to believe that he wants me for myself. That he would want me regardless of the fact we have a child together. That even if I hadn't gotten pregnant years ago after our party hookup, if our paths crossed like they did this year, he would've pursued me.

Part of me wants to believe it. The part that wishes Disney fairy tales could come true.

But the more cautious part of me, the part that ached at his supposed rejection … that part can't quite believe it. And no amount of orgasms or pretty words will bring her on board.

CHAPTER THIRTY-SEVEN

Gray

"So that's what it takes to distract you, huh?" McAdam says with a grin as he tosses me the football so I can take my turn to throw routes with Martinez.

I give him a quizzical look.

He rolls his hand like I should obviously know what he's referring to. "Your kid? And his mom? Last night?" He tsks and crosses his arms. "If I'd known about her, I would've hunted her down to introduce you to your kid last semester. Maybe then I could've started after all."

Cracking a grin, I toss the ball with Martinez a few times to warm my arm back up. "Nah, man. You still couldn't have pulled it off." After catching the ball, I give Martinez the nod to run his route, watching him before firing off a beautiful pass. Turning to McAdam, I quirk an eyebrow. "See? Tiffany and Ben showing up isn't messing with my head."

He laughs, and as much as I can't quite believe he'd bring up how he tried to throw me off my game and take the starting quarterback spot back last semester like it's a funny joke, on the other hand ... it's nice to be able to laugh about it. To treat it like a joke and get along, if only for Piper's sake, rather than hang onto it forever.

Plus, I can't entirely blame the guy. He started last year and had every reason to expect to start his senior year too. Only the university retired the last coach and brought in Coach Reese who brought me along too.

I mean, for sure trying to use my sister against me is super fucked up, but at least he's admitted as much and apologized for it, even if he won't leave her alone. And if I somehow convinced him to dump her, I'd be on Piper's shit list forever, so there's that. Plus I'd have to beat his ass for hurting my sister. It's much nicer getting along.

"I dunno, man," he continues. "When they first showed up?" He shakes his head. "I was watching you. Your performance took a hit. Even Coach Miles was talking about it. He and Coach Reese were worried if you'd be able to get your head back in the game in time for combines and wondered how much of a hit you'd take in the draft if you couldn't."

I catch the ball Martinez returns to me and turn to face McAdam. "The fuck?"

He shrugs, unrepentant. "You didn't know that?"

Pointing the ball at him, I narrow my eyes. "You still trying to fuck with me? Trying to get in my head so you look better in the combines next week?"

He cracks a grin, which seems like a yes, but shakes his head. "Nah, man. I'm confident in my skills. Yours too. You'll be fine. Plus, that was just a blip, and it could've happened to anyone. Hell, Simon had a few blips too, and he didn't have any baby mama drama."

Simon Hindley perks up from where he's running drills nearby, stopping with his hands on his hips, his breath coming hard. "Shut up, Cal," is all he says before returning to what he was doing.

McAdam meets my eyes, and we both laugh.

With another shake of my head, I signal Martinez to run. This time the pass goes a little high, making Martinez have to jump for it. The guy's got an amazing vertical jump, so it's no problem. But I shouldn't be making him use it.

"Quarterbacks!" barks Coach Miles. "Quit gossiping and focus on your passing game!"

"Yessir!" McAdam and I respond in unison.

McAdam grins at me. "There's gonna be plenty of trash talk at the combines. If you can ignore me blabbing about whatever's going on with you and Tiffany, you can ignore anything. I'm just trying to help, man."

Chuckling, I shake my head. This guy.

Martinez runs his route again, and this pass drops right into his hands.

"There you go," McAdam says. "That's the way you do it." We watch Martinez jog back toward us, and I think maybe McAdam will finally take Hindley's advice and shut up. But instead he asks, "So what's going on with you two? It seems like it might be something, but also she shies away from you whenever you look like you might want to touch her."

A low growl escapes me, and he holds up his hand. "I'm just curious, man," he says like that's some kind of acceptable defense. "We all saw you making out at Crowley's that night. You weren't exactly hiding it. She not sure she wants to put up with your sorry ass?"

I turn to him, eyebrows raised. "My sorry ass? Pretty sure I was the starter, and I'm the one tapped as a likely first round pick. Not you. Whose ass is sorry now?"

He laughs in response. "I won't argue about that. But I notice you're not actually answering the question."

Getting the ball back, I adjust my grip on it, watch Martinez, then launch it for a nice long pass. "It's complicated," I say at last.

McAdam just nods.

"McAdam!" Coach Miles shouts from his spot off to the side. "I thought I told you to quit gabbing. Kilpatrick doesn't need you distracting him again."

"Sorry, Coach!" McAdam shouts back, but he gives me a knowing look before stepping away. "I know we're not actually friends. But if you need one who's dealt with complicated relationships ..."

I snort. "What? You?"

He looks shocked. "Nah. Hindley. He's your guy for that shit."

Hindley stops and looks at us once more. "Cal. Leave Kilpatrick alone before I kick your ass."

And with that, McAdam jogs over to the next set of drills Coach Miles has lined up for us, cackling all the way.

He might've played it off like he wasn't actually offering, but I'm not stupid and can recognize an olive branch when it's offered.

I'm not necessarily going to take him up on it, but it's nice to know it's an option.

* * *

"I'm going to miss seeing you guys next week," I tell Tiffany that night as we have dinner at my place. Even though she and Ben stayed the night last night after dinner with my parents, I'm campaigning for them to stay the night again tonight. Or maybe tomorrow. And maybe I can convince her to let me sleep in the bedroom with them.

I'd be a good boy and keep my shorts on and my hands to myself. I tried last night after we had sex on the couch, but she'd just pressed her lips together, shaken her head, and said, "It's not a good idea."

Ben perks up. "Why?"

"Remember, Benny Boo?" Tiffany answers. "Gray has to go out of town next week, so it'll just be me picking you up from preschool."

Ben clearly doesn't remember, though, because his face crumples. "You're not?" The look he gives me is nothing short of accusatory.

"It's just for one week," I try to reassure him, though it'll actually be a little more than that. The combines start on Tuesday and go through the next Monday, so I'll be flying out the day before and won't return until the following Tuesday. It'll be a long week, made longer by the fact that I'll miss Tiffany and Ben like crazy.

My reassurance doesn't work at all, because tears fill his eyes, and he lets out a high pitched keening sound as he covers his face with his hands. "I don't want you to go," he wails.

"Oh, Benny," Tiffany says in the voice she reserves only for an upset Ben. She moves to his side and pulls him into her arms, boosting him up so she can hold him and rub his back as he clings to her and cries.

I give her a helpless look. This isn't the reaction I was expecting. I know he likes hanging out with me, but I didn't think he'd be this devastated by me being gone for a week.

"Who's going to swing me?" he cries, sniffing into Tiffany's hair.

She pats his back and makes shushing noises. "It'll be alright. He'll come back and then we'll swing you every day, okay?"

For some reason, that makes him cry even harder.

Needing to do something, even if I don't know what, I stand and move around to where they are, placing my hand on Ben's back. He lunges for me, and I catch him so he doesn't topple out of Tiffany's arms. He practically climbs me like a tree, wrapping his arms around my neck and clinging to me with surprising strength.

"It's okay," I tell him. "I've got you. I'm not leaving for a few more days, okay?"

He buries his face in my neck and cries.

"What do I do?" I mouth to Tiffany.

She gives an exaggerated shrug of helplessness. "This. He's sad. Just comfort him," she whispers back.

I move us to the couch and sit down. He cuddles into my lap, crying against my chest with a kind of broken-hearted despair I'm not sure I've ever witnessed before.

"Why do you hafta go?" he asks between hiccuping sobs.

I pull him close and rub his back. "I'm trying to get a job for after I graduate, so I have to go to this place so they can decide who hires me."

"What's grad-ju-late?"

I can't help smiling at his pronunciation. "It's what you do when you get done with school."

He looks at Tiffany, who's settled on the couch next to us. "Are you gonna grad-ju-late, Mama?"

"Not this year," she says, "but eventually."

For some reason she meets my eyes when she says that, as though she's issuing a challenge. But I just nod in response, because of course she's going to graduate. I'm just hoping she'll maybe consider switching to an online program or transferring or something so they'll come with me. Especially if me leaving causes this kind of upset for Ben. I'm only going to be gone for a week, and he's acting like I'm never coming back.

What'll he do when that's actually happening? I mean, yeah, I'll come back for visits no matter what. My parents live here, for one thing. Even if Tiffany and Ben came with me, we'd come back for visits. And if they're still here, I'll definitely visit as often as possible.

But once I know where I'm going, when I move, it'll be permanent, not just a weeklong trip.

All the more reason to convince Tiffany that I'm serious and that I want her to come with me somehow.

But when I meet her eyes over Ben's head, the question reverberates through me like a gong.

How?

CHAPTER THIRTY-EIGHT

Tiffany

It takes a while for Ben to calm down, but eventually he does. And his clinging to Gray has me agreeing to stay the night again when he asks, even though I know I'm making a mistake.

I should put a stop to these overnight visits once and for all. In such a short amount of time, my son has gotten so attached to Gray that the prospect of one week without him has reduced Ben to a worn out sobbing mess in need of an early bedtime.

I knew he'd get too attached. And I knew it would turn into a problem.

Is it really only Ben who's too attached? a voice whispers in the back of my mind.

I try to ignore it, but that question plagues me all through getting Ben ready for bed and singing him to sleep with Gray sitting on the other side of the bed holding his hand, staying and watching him sleep for far longer than necessary.

When we eventually tiptoe out to the living room, Gray reaches for me. And just as I know that staying the night here is a mistake, I know letting him kiss me, letting him make love to me—because there's no mistaking that's what we're doing—is the wrong choice.

It'll only serve to make everything between us so much harder, so much worse, when the time comes for him to leave. If we're already this attached after less than two months, how much more attached will we be by mid-May? How much more devastated will Ben be when Gray moves to wherever he ends up going?

And what about me?

As much as I want to ignore that voice prodding at me that Ben's not the only one who's grown attached to Gray, I know I'll miss him while he's gone. The difference is that I know that a week isn't really that long. To Ben, a week sounds like an eternity. Which, I suppose when you've only been alive a few years, a week is a much higher percentage of time.

Still, will that week feel like an eternity to me once it's started?

Maybe.

And what will happen when weeks apart is the norm? When weeks turn into months with no plans to see each other? When he's a hot, professional athlete with his pick of women? Those guys date models and actresses, and I'm just a frumpy twenty-two-year-old sophomore who never managed to lose all her baby weight. Sure, I'm the mother of his child, but will he really care once he's distracted by the grind and glamour of life in the NFL?

How can I compete with that?

The reality is that I can't.

So it seems like the prudent choice to cut ties now before it's too late.

Except it might already be too late. And when he kisses me like I hold the secret to life and touches me like he's been tasked with mapping a sacred artifact with his bare hands, how can I say no?

"Tiffany," he whispers against my skin, his lips finding my nipple and sucking deep. "Baby. I need you so bad."

I whimper and writhe as he tongues one nipple and then the other, his fingers already sliding between my spread thighs.

"Yessss," I hiss, arching into his hands and mouth. "Please."

"I've got you," he tells me, just like always. And he says it like he means it forever. Like he'll always have me, always give me what I need.

Squeezing my eyes shut tight, I push that thought away and instead focus on right now. This moment. Because this moment is what we have, and I don't know how many more of these moments we'll get, and I won't ruin this one by thinking about what will happen next.

What has to happen next.

He lifts up and rolls on a condom before lowering himself over me again. Claiming my mouth, he slides inside me, owning me in a way no one ever has before. And I doubt anyone ever will again.

It takes everything in me to fight back the tears that threaten to fall. I wrap my arms around him, gasping, grateful that it's easily interpreted as passion, and lose myself in the feel of his skin under my hands, his lips on my neck, and the smooth, easy rhythm of his cock moving in and out of my body.

I raise my hips to meet his, sliding my hands down his back, and he picks up the pace at my encouragement.

"Open your eyes," he whispers as he raises his head.

And I can't help but do as he asks, letting him see into me as he drives me to the edge and watches me shatter.

Except it's too much, and I turn away and close my eyes at the last moment just before my orgasm overtakes me. He kisses me, deep and slow even as his hips pound into mine in the short, jerky rhythm that means he's about to come.

I hold him against me as he shudders through his orgasm, grateful for the sweet cover of the kiss. Because how can I show him what I'm feeling when I'm not ready to face it yet myself?

* * *

Despite seeing Gray every day before he leaves, including skipping class to drive him to the airport on Monday morning, Ben is despondent the rest of the day.

"Can we call him?" he keeps asking every five minutes or less the whole drive home and the rest of the morning until I finally get a break for my afternoon class.

I'd considered skipping the whole day, but I need something to keep me busy. Something to distract me from all the feelings swirling around that I don't know what to do with. And snapping at Ben for asking the same question a million times won't make anything better either. Gray said he'd let me know when he gets there and gets settled. He won't be able to have a video chat with Ben before then, no matter how many times Ben asks.

When class is over, I check my phone to find a few texts from my mom with pics of Ben playing and a video of him telling me he wants to call Gray as soon as I get home. But I haven't heard from Gray yet, so …

I guess we could make a video for him like Mom did for me and text that to him. It's better than nothing, at least.

But I'm not ready to go home yet, so I make my way to the campus coffee shop for something to do. I can bring Ben a hot chocolate and a croissant or something to cheer him up. And have an excuse to stall on going home for a little bit longer.

After paying for my order, I turn to find Autumn waving at me from a corner table. When she beckons me over, I figure I can spend a few minutes hanging out with her until my order is ready. I shouldn't stay longer than that, though.

With her is Piper, Ellie, and another girl I don't know.

Autumn beams at me. "Tiffany, this is Dani." She indicates the girl with her dark hair in a ponytail wearing a black hoodie bearing the silhouette of a weightlifter holding a barbell above his head. "Dani, this is Tiffany."

Her face lights up with recognition. "Oh! Hi. You're Tiffany. Nice to meet you."

Wary, I offer a polite smile. "Hiiii. Nice to meet you too."

"Sorry," Piper chimes in. "Dani's my roommate. She heard about dinner last week. She's not trying to be creepy. She just knows you're dating my brother and have the most adorable kid I've ever met."

"Oh, um—"

"Wait," Piper interrupts, sitting up straighter in her chair. "You are dating him, right? I mean, I saw you guys holding hands. And you kissed that night at Crowley's. And I mean he brought you to family dinner. He wouldn't do that if you weren't together. Would he?" On the last question she looks around the table for support, but only receives a bunch of shrugs.

"I'd think you'd be the best one to answer that question," Ellie puts in.

"Ugh. Fine. You're right." Piper returns her attention to me, spinning her paper cup in one hand and leaning her chin on the other. "So. Please share with the class."

My mouth opens, but I don't even know how to answer that question. Are we dating? I mean, we went on *a* singular date and we have sex fairly regularly. Is that dating? I don't really even know what that means.

"Aww, look at her. She's not even sure." Ellie leans over and pats my arm. "I get it. Things between Simon and me started off all hush-hush, and I don't know what I'd have said if someone asked me that question to my face like that."

Autumn cackles. "I know what *I* would've said."

Ellie shoots her a glare. "Well, yeah, but no one's asking you. Anyway," she looks at me again. "Ignore her. My point is, you don't have to answer Piper's nosy questions just because she's putting you on the spot."

"Who're you calling nosy?" Piper gasps. "You're the one who was all up in mine and Cal's business when we were first together."

Mouth dropping open, Ellie straightens, her palm hitting the table. "I was not!"

"Suuuure. You just *happened* to need to get your textbook and what was it? Lip gloss? The night that Cal and I went out the first time. You weren't curious at all who your brother needed the house to himself for?"

The redness in Ellie's cheeks gives her away. "I mean, of course I was curious. Who wouldn't be? But I really did forget my textbook and lip gloss that night. That wasn't a lie."

"Mmhmm. Sure. If you say so."

Something about their banter is relaxing, and I feel like I can finally drop my guard a little bit as a smile takes over my face. Dani leans closer to me. "They're like this all the time. If their attention ever gets to be too much for you, just find a reason to make them argue and you'll be home free."

"Thanks for the tip," I whisper back.

She tips her cup toward me. "Anytime. But also, they're going to keep asking until you tell them what they want to know."

"Noted."

Fortunately, I'm saved by the barista calling my name.

"Alright, ladies, it was nice seeing you all."

"Wait," Ellie interrupts. "You're not leaving already? You just got here. Sit and chat with us a while. We're here commiserating about our boyfriends being away—well, Piper and I are. Autumn and Dani are along for moral support."

"We don't have boyfriends," Dani puts in.

"I have plenty of male companions," Autumn says airily. "Just no single one I've committed to."

"Dani also has plenty of male companions," Piper chimes in. "She just doesn't sleep with any of them."

"Piper," Dani hisses, her cheeks turning pink under her tan.

Piper turns to her, wide eyed. "What? It's true. You don't. You're just friends with like every single football player."

Dani shrugs. "Not *every* single football player. I'm not friends with your brother. Or Simon." She gestures toward me. "Or Kilpatrick."

"I said every *single* football player."

Dani's cheeks get pinker, but she just rolls her eyes and drinks her coffee.

"I really do have to get home," I tell them before this can devolve further. "I appreciate the invite though. Maybe next time."

As I get my coffee, my thoughts swirl even more. Gray and I have never clarified what we really are to each other. He asked me to give him a chance. But a chance to do what, exactly? A chance to be a good dad? A good boyfriend? Something else?

But now he's gone for a week, so I can't ask him that. And even if he were here, he's still leaving in just over two months.

Does it even matter anyway?

CHAPTER THIRTY-NINE

Gray

After an exhausting week, I'm grateful for the familiar sight of the Spokane Airport when I finally get home. The last week was physically, psychologically, and emotionally grueling. Between the drills, the staging for the media and all the primetime talking heads that want to weigh in on your skills and abilities and chances of getting picked to the individual teams evaluating your every move ... I'm just glad it's over.

Plus, things with Tiffany have been weird ever since I left. I thought everything was fine when I boarded the plane. We'd spent the weekend together like we were a little family, and I honestly couldn't get enough. And I spent half my travel time to the combines thinking about how I could convince her and Ben to move in with me. I know he hated the cot, but maybe if we got a little trundle bed or something? We could all sleep in the bedroom together. It would only be for a couple of months, and then I could get us a bigger place and he could have his own room once I know where I'm headed.

But she's barely texted me the whole time I've been gone, and then only in response to me reaching out first. Not once did she text me first.

It hasn't been sitting right with me all week, but given everything else going on, I haven't had the time or energy to really think much about it until my flights home. I've had nothing but time to think the whole way home. Hindley, McAdam, Martinez, and I traveled together, and we were full of energy on the way over. But on the way home, we were all holed up in our seats, headphones on, each lost in our own worlds.

At this point, what happens next is out of our hands. The teams will decide what they decide, and we'll have to wait until April to find out what that will be. In the meantime, it's time to catch up on the classes we missed while we were gone and get our ducks in a row for graduation.

And for me to figure out what's going on with Tiffany.

Have I made a mistake holding off on asking her to come with me? I was trying to give her time to get used to the idea of us as a possibility, but maybe she needs to know that *I* see a future for us together before she can allow herself to think beyond me graduating. I've done my best to show her that she already owns my heart. But maybe I made a mistake by not telling her.

She and Ben wait for me near the baggage claim. When they spot me, Ben's face lights up, and she sets him down so he can run for me. I crouch down and open my arms, catching him easily and standing.

He wraps his arms around my neck and squeezes me tight. "Gray! Gray! You're here! You're here! I'm so happy to see you! I missed you so much!"

I can't help laughing at his enthusiasm. "I missed you, and I'm happy to see you too, bud."

"Mommy and Grampa watched you play on the TV!"

"Oh yeah?" I hold him away so I can see his face. "What about you? Did you watch me?"

He scrunches up his face. "Just a little. It was kinda boring."

Laughing again, I carry him back to Tiffany. I know better than to expect a kiss or even a hug, not with Ben here, but I'd hoped for something more than the tight smile she gives me. "Hey. How was your flight?"

I shrug. "Fine. Boring."

She nods, ducking her head and tucking hair behind her ear. "That's good. Flights aren't supposed to be exciting, right?"

"Right. Exciting travel is usually bad."

She nods again. "Exactly. So boring is good."

"Uh-huh."

Wow. I think this might be the worst conversation we've ever had. Maybe the worst in recorded history.

What the fuck is going on?

I want so badly to ask that question, but I can't. Not with Ben still in my arms. Not in the middle of a busy airport. I wouldn't get any kind of answer. But when will I have the chance to ask that? And even if I get her alone, will she actually tell me anything?

We move toward the baggage claim with my flight number above it, and Tiffany walks next to me with her arms crossed over her body. She hasn't been this closed off with me since ... ever. Even when she hated me. Even when she was leaving parties to get away from me and blocking my number and trying to ditch me when I waited for her after class. She gave me fire and sass and anger, but never this blank wall of nothing.

"How'd the combines go?" she asks as we stand around waiting for the suitcases to start tumbling down the conveyor belt.

"Good. I think." I shrug. Ben starts squirming in my arms, so I set him down.

"Stay right here," she admonishes him.

He holds onto one of my hands and starts walking in circles around me, switching from hand to hand as he goes around. Tiffany watches this, a tiny smile curving her lips. It's the first genuine smile I've seen from her since I got off the plane.

But when she catches me watching her, it fades immediately.

And I growl. I can't help it. It just comes out.

Her eyes jump to mine, surprised.

I clear my throat and stare at the baggage claim, but there's nothing yet.

"You felt good about how you did, though?" she presses. And I'm not sure if it's genuine curiosity or just that she can't think of anything else to say.

"Yeah. Pretty good. I mean, there were days that weren't as good, but that's part of the gig. Passes that go wide or high when you know you have better aim than that. But the nonstop programming and meetings and media attention on top of the actual physical part adds a layer of stress that's different from playing the game."

She nods. "Makes sense."

After that, conversation stalls out and we stand in silence, Ben still running in circles around me as we wait for my suitcase. It's a relief when it finally comes because it frees us from this agonizing prison of politeness and stilted conversation.

Things were so easy between us … and now?

I don't know what happened while I was gone. But as soon as Ben's distracted or asleep, I mean to find out.

* * *

Tiffany drives me back to my apartment, and for a moment, I'm not sure if she and Ben are going to come inside. She turns off the car and just sits there for a moment staring out the windshield.

I sit in silence as well, not sure if I should ask her to come in. I want her to. I would've wanted her to before, just to spend time together. But I especially want her to come in now that she's acting weird, and I want to figure out what's going on.

Ben's the one who asks, saving me the awkwardness and embarrassment. Though, to be fair, it's more demand than ask. "Go in, Mom! Let's go!"

With an indulgent chuckle, she removes the key from the ignition, and that unfreezes all of us enough to get out of the car. She pops the trunk for me to get my backpack and suitcase out while she goes to the back and unstraps Ben from his carseat.

He chatters and runs ahead to the door to my apartment while Tiffany and I walk more slowly, her with her arms crossed again, both of us trapped in our own worlds.

Once we're inside, Ben climbs onto the couch, jumps off, runs around the living room, chattering the whole time and telling me about all the things he did while I was gone.

God, I've missed this kid. I got bits and pieces over FaceTime while I was away, but between the three hour time difference and his inability to stay on a call for long, getting more than a few minutes at a time was basically impossible. And despite making multiple suggestions that Tiffany could call me without him, she never did. I tried once after I knew Ben would be in bed, but she told me how tired she was and chastised me for staying up too late when I needed to be rested and focused for the combines. Which was a good point, but by then I didn't even care. I just wanted to talk to her.

Apparently that had been all me, though, because she didn't seem too interested in talking to me.

Which again makes me want to know—what happened?

Did she meet someone?

That seems unlikely. Not that she couldn't, obviously, but just because it seems like it takes her so long to get comfortable with people. The odds of her falling madly in love with someone in less than a week? Virtually nonexistent.

So did Piper find her and tell her how shit I am?

That one's not outside the realm of possibility. I mean, I wouldn't think my sister would screw me over like that, but if she's still mad enough ... Or it might even be that she was just talking and everything that happened last semester that she got mad at me for came out and that made Tiffany turn cool toward me.

Which would be super shitty, especially since I've talked a little about what happened with her and she knows that I feel bad, that I've tried to apologize, and that I'm working on repairing my relationship with my sister. Shouldn't that count for something?

Or ...?

Maybe it's something else altogether.

Dragging my luggage into my bedroom, I get into my backpack and pull out the plush football I got for Ben. When I bring it out to the living room and toss it to him, he squeals with delight. "Is it for me? Can I keep it?"

"Yeah, bud," I tell him with a smile. "I got it for you. To make up for not getting to see you this week and pick you up from preschool."

He pauses his near constant motion. "I was sad you weren't there to swing me."

"I'll swing you tomorrow, I promise."

"Okay!" And he's off again. Running, jumping,

zooming, a real life perpetual motion machine.

"He really missed you," Tiffany says quietly watching him bounce off the walls.

"I missed him too." I chance a look in her direction, but she's still watching him. Her profile seems remote and ... sad. "Was he the only one?"

She turns her face to me, her eyes filling with tears. And then she stands abruptly and leaves the room.

Ben, thankfully, doesn't notice. "I'll be right back," I tell him. "I got you construction paper if you want to cut."

"Okay!" he shouts, heading for his table in the corner. I watch while he rifles through the bins and comes out with a handful of colorful paper and his favorite green-handled scissors. Then he heads back to the bin, his face scrunched. His expression smooths into one of delight when he pulls out the hole puncher I got for him. "Can I use this?" he asks with wonder.

"Of course. Anything in those bins is for you."

Once he's absorbed in cutting and punching holes in paper—which will leave a big confetti mess once he's done—I follow Tiffany down the hall. At first I thought maybe she'd be in the bathroom, but the door is open and the light is off. Instead, I find her in my bedroom, sitting on the bed with her arms wrapped around herself and staring at my suitcase.

She looks so lost and lonely sitting there, looking like she's waiting for someone to collect her and take her away forever to a place she doesn't want to go.

"Tiff," I say just above a whisper.

Her head jerks up at the sound of my voice, and she

pastes on the falsest smile I've ever seen. She swipes her hands over her cheeks like she's been crying. "Hey," she says, her voice hoarse. She clears her throat. "Hey. Sorry. I just needed a minute."

I want nothing more than to pull her into my arms and reassure her that everything will be okay. But I don't think that would be the right thing to do, even if I don't know why.

"What's wrong?" I ask softly, stationing myself against the wall next to the door. Maybe if I give her space, she'll tell me.

She flops her hands into her lap and sighs. "Nothing. Everything. I don't know." Fresh tears track down her cheeks, and I can't maintain my distance.

Sitting next to her on the bed, I put my arm behind her, giving her the option of leaning into me if she wants to. When she doesn't immediately seek comfort from me, I force down the bubble of disappointment that wells up inside me.

"Talk to me," I whisper. "Please. Things have been weird between us since I left. I know me being away was hard for Ben, but I didn't expect you to freeze me out."

She sucks in a ragged breath and wraps her arms tighter around herself. "And that's the problem. You were only gone for a week and it was already torture. How much worse is it going to be when you move for good? When all we get is a few days here and there and video chats punctuating long periods of time apart."

"Okay," I say slowly, trying to understand what she's getting at.

Eyes full of tears meet mine. "Don't you get it? I can't keep doing this. I can't get more and more attached only to have my heart ripped out in a couple of months. I can't."

I blink at her, feeling really dumb right now. Because all those words together like that don't make any sense to me. "What are you saying?"

She shakes her head and looks away. "I won't keep you from Ben." She sucks in a breath. "But I need to keep my distance."

CHAPTER FORTY

Tiffany

Saying those words might be the hardest thing I've ever done. Harder than telling my parents I was pregnant. Harder than approaching Carter for a paternity test. Harder than trying to track down Grayson years ago and failing.

Because the thing is, I don't really want to stop seeing Gray. If I'm being honest with myself—and I try to be—I'm already falling for him. The last week was so hard. Barely talking to him, not knowing what to say, not being sure where we stand … I wanted to have The Talk. The define-the-relationship talk. But over the phone while he's gone isn't the right time. Right before he left wasn't the right time—I didn't want to be responsible for any more distraction than I already was. And then after a few days, the more I thought about it, the more I realized how hard it would be, the more this seemed like not only the best option, but really the only option.

When I look at Gray, though, I start to doubt myself. Even more when all he does is stare at me, baffled, and ask, "Why?"

He's so close, and it's so tempting to just lean into him. I know he wants me to, that when he sat next to me it was what he was offering. And I want so badly to take him up on the offer, because nothing has felt better than being in his arms these last couple of weeks.

But isn't that just prolonging the inevitable? And will only make the withdrawal worse for becoming so addicted?

Instead of leaning into him, I stand, clutching my arms like I'm trying to give myself a hug.

"Tiffany," he says, his voice tortured. "Please. I don't understand. Where is this coming from?"

Turning to face him, I throw my arms wide. "Me. It's coming from me. From watching Ben mourn your absence. From feeling it so deeply myself. And that's after only a few weeks! What are we going to do when you move?"

"Come with me." He says it so quickly, so seriously, and so simply, that it's stunning.

All I can do is stare at him, my mouth hanging open. "What?"

He stands, closing the distance between us. "Come with me," he repeats. "You think I want to be apart from you? I loved having you guys stay here with me before I left, and I spent the entire trip to the combines trying to figure out a way to convince you to move in with me." He gestures at one corner. "We could get a little trundle bed or something for Ben that we could put over there. We'd all be in the same room, but it would just be until after graduation. If you really hate that idea, I can ask if there's a two bedroom available, or we can find a vacation rental for a couple of months or something. There are options. I just want you guys with me."

Now it's my turn to stare, gape mouthed and confused. "What?"

He sucks in a breath, then gathers my hands in his. "I don't know why it's so hard to believe that I want you. I've wanted you for a long time. I've finally got you—and Ben—I don't want to give you up again. Come with me. Even if you don't want to move in with me now, even if you don't want to live with me right away when we move, I don't care. I'll find a place for you and Ben, and I'll have my own place. Maybe we can live next door to each other for a while, or in the same building or whatever. Just say you'll come with me."

I stare at his fingers pressing into mine for a long moment and force myself to close my mouth, my brain rewinding and picking through his words, trying to figure out what he's saying and how best to respond.

Is he really asking me to move in with him? To move with him to wherever he ends up?

Yes. Yes, actually, he is.

"What?" I whisper again.

Instead of repeating himself, he bends his head and kisses me. First it's just the press of his lips to mine, but when I don't pull away, he deepens the kiss, his tongue sliding between my lips. And I respond. I can't help myself. His body calls to mine, and it seems it always has. Maybe it always will.

I hope it always will.

Does that mean I want to move with him?

It's tempting, but there are other considerations.

What about school? What about Ben? He'll miss his grandparents more than he missed Gray. Can I really do that to him? And can I really postpone getting my degree yet again? I guess at least this time I have an actual choice. But …

Tearing myself away from him, I take a big step back and shake my head. "I don't know, Gray—"

"Don't say no," he pleads, interrupting me. "Think about it. I can see that you weren't expecting me to say any of that. So just … just think about it before you decide. I'm not expecting an answer right away. But don't freeze me out. Please, Tiff."

"Mommy mommy mommy!" comes from the hall. My eyes fall closed, and I'm not sure if I'm relieved at the interruption and the out it provides or not.

"Just think about it," Gray repeats. "Please."

I nod quickly, suck in a deep breath, wipe my fingers under my eyes, and put on a smile before opening the door. "I'm right here, Ben. What do you need?"

"I've been cutting!" he announces proudly. "Come see!" Grabbing my hand, he pulls me behind him, and I don't resist or look over my shoulder even though I can feel Gray's eyes burning a hole in my back.

We stay at Gray's for another hour or so, both of us interacting with Ben more than each other. But the entire time, Gray's words loop through my head. *Come with me. Move in with me. I just want you with me.*

Is it really that simple?

* * *

Ben and I eventually leave without me giving Gray an answer. Because of course my first instinct is to tell him no.

I mean, how can I do what he's asking? How can I uproot us, leave the only home Ben has ever known and my entire support system on a whim? Yes, Gray is Ben's father, but ... so what? Us going with him was never the plan. The plan was for him to visit, maybe we go out there some, and he can stay longer in the off season.

But that was before Gray kissed me and asked for a chance. Before we started ... whatever it is we're doing. Having sex while Ben sleeps in the next room, for the most part. Plus that one really sweet date.

If you go with him you could have more of those dates.

And Ben would have his own room. In a nice place. And Gray would be making enough money that we could afford to hire a babysitter for nights out.

He even offered to get me a place of my own if I'm not ready to move in with him yet. I mean ... the only thing that would sweeten the deal is offering to move my parents out too.

They'd never go for that ... I don't think. Maybe when

they retire, though.

But it's just a lot and so soon. Even if I go ahead and admit that Gray and I are together, it's only been like a month since he first kissed me. A month! That's not enough time to decide to move in with someone, much less move to some as yet unknown location in some other city. That's crazy. Isn't it?

My parents leave me to my spinning thoughts after Ben and I get home, though I can tell they notice, because they keep exchanging looks. And my distraction follows me into the next day, making it difficult to focus on class. I keep missing whole slides in my World History class, so my notes are a mess. All I can do is hope the information is in the textbook, because Dr. Henderson is notoriously unsympathetic to people who miss information because they're distracted.

Afterward, I bump into Autumn on the sidewalk. She gives me a wide grin at first. "Hey!" Then she almost does a double take, squinting as she examines me closely. "Yeah. You need to talk. Come on. Let's get a coffee or something." Grabbing my arm, she starts towing me to the door.

I let out a laugh, but go along with her. "Don't you have class?"

She shakes her head. "Not right now. I have time."

"Okay, but I can't get a coffee. I have to pick up my son from preschool."

"Oh, right. Fine. I'll walk with you. But you'll have to make it snappy."

The early March sunshine filters through the still bare

tree branches as we walk, and I fill her in on everything between Gray and me, starting with when he kissed me the first time since reappearing and ending with the invitation to move in with him here and join him wherever he ends up.

By the time we get to that point, we're next to a building that blocks my view of where I typically meet Gray so we can pick up Ben together. I'm sure he's there waiting for me already.

Autumn studies my face as she mulls over everything I've told her. "What do you want to do?" she asks at last.

I collapse in on myself, my shoulders slumping, my spine curving. "I don't know. If I knew that, I wouldn't be here spilling all these details to you."

She grins. "Yeah, you still would. You'd just be more settled about it. But I dunno. I think you have a good idea of what you want. If he were staying, would you want to be with Gray?"

"Yes." The answer pops out, clear and immediate.

She nods. "Okay. Good. So ... why not move with him? You'd get to be with him, and it seems like you want that."

"But what about school? And what about Ben?"

"What about Ben?" she repeats, sounding utterly reasonable. "You'd be giving him regular access to his father, which is important for a child. And you'd make new friends and find a new preschool. Probably the other players' wives and girlfriends could give you recommendations. I'm sure Gray won't be the only one with a preschooler, no matter where he ends up."

She makes it sound so simple. I open my mouth to say something else, but she continues before I can.

"And what about school? Is Gray asking you to drop out?"

I shrug. "He didn't actually say that. He didn't mention school at all. He talked about living arrangements, and then Ben came in demanding attention, and we haven't talked really at all since then."

She gives me an exasperated look. "Then don't make assumptions. You said he was basically willing to bend over backward to give you the living arrangements you want. You think he'd object to you finishing your degree?"

"But I'd be leaving. I couldn't keep going to Marycliff."

"Yeah, and? Number one, that's not necessarily true. You should look at what else you have to take and talk to your advisor. You might be able to finish online. And if not, transfer. If that's the only thing holding you back, there are solutions to that problem. And hey, if it doesn't work out, if you end up hating Gray and never want to see him again, you can always move back home with your parents, right?"

"I guess," I say slowly.

She nods, like everything's solved. "Well, there you go. I think you just solved your own problem."

Wait. Did I? Could it really be that easy?

It couldn't.

Could it?

CHAPTER FORTY-ONE

Gray

I check my phone, wondering what's keeping Tiffany. She usually beats me to our meeting spot, and she's always been super anal about being on time to pick up Ben. And for good reason. So that's why her being late—for her—is so surprising.

Is everything alright? She wouldn't ditch me ... would she?

Pulling out my phone, I'm about to call her when she comes around the corner of the building, all smiles.

She looks dazzling, lit up in the early spring sunshine, her hair glinting gold as it bounces around her shoulders. She has it down today, which is unusual for a school day. I like her hair any way she wants to wear it, but I really love it when she wears it down.

I return her smile, unsure why I'm getting it after how

we left things yesterday, but unwilling to question it for fear of making it disappear. "Hey. I was starting to get worried about you."

Shaking her head, her smile somehow gets wider. "Sorry. I was talking to Autumn for a minute. But you're right. We better hurry up and get Ben. You're free this afternoon, though, right? Because we need to talk."

Oh god. Every man knows that those are ominous words. "Um, yeah. Since the combines are over, I don't have drills this afternoon. I have some homework to catch up on, but I can do that later."

"Good. Okay. I can't come over right after we pick up Ben. I mean, I could, but he'd be with me, so it just seems easier to wait until after my dad gets home, because I'd rather not discuss things in front of Ben."

Uh-oh. That seems ... not good for me.

Swallowing hard, I nod. "Sure," I croak, then clear my throat. "That sounds good."

She gives me a quizzical look as I pull the door open for her. "You feeling alright?"

I force a smile. "Yup. Sure. Great."

Just a man preparing to have his heart ripped out. No biggie.

I let the familiar routine of picking Ben up from preschool take over, helping him get his jacket and backpack while Tiffany talks to his teacher and signs him out. As promised, we swing him out to her car, and once she buckles him in she turns to me, that same smile from before on her face.

And I'm super confused, because last night she would barely look at me. A tiny flare of hope sparks inside me, but I wall it off so it can't expand any farther. I invited her to come with me last night and she was about to tell me no. I know she was. What are the odds she would've changed her mind in less than twenty-four hours?

"I'll text you when I'm headed over, okay?" She checks the time on her phone. "It should be about an hour."

"I wanna go see Gray too!" Ben shouts from his seat.

"Not right now, Benny," she says in her soothing voice. "You get to hang out with Grampa."

"I always with Grampa! Want Gray!"

She holds up a finger to me and ducks her head into the car. "Mommy and Gray need to talk about grownup stuff. You'll have more fun with Grampa. But maybe after we can do something with Gray, okay?"

He crosses his arms as best he can with his harness on and gives her the same glare she's given me so often. "Fine."

I have to stifle a laugh, and when she straightens, Tiffany rolls her eyes and grins, good-natured exasperation on her face.

I'm not sure if her promise to do something with me after our conversation means our conversation will be positive or not. I guess I get a whole hour all to myself to wonder.

"Alright, see you soon," she says before climbing into her car.

Like I've done since that very first time, I stand off to the side and wave at Ben as they drive away.

Let the torture begin.

* * *

I'm just as nervous as the first time Tiffany was coming over. I've been pacing for the last fifteen minutes. Before that I went for a run because I knew there was no way I'd be able to just sit in my apartment and wait. The run and the shower after took up most of the hour, but then I guess her dad didn't get home as early as she was expecting, because it's been more like an hour and fifteen minutes.

When she finally knocks on my door, I practically rip the thing off its hinges. I probably look like a crazy man.

The look she gives me is a mix of pity and amusement. "Oh, Gray. It's okay. Calm down."

That doesn't help me at all.

"Well?" I demand, not even waiting for her to close the door behind her, much less take off her jacket or put down her bag.

She does all of those things, though, without saying a word. She barely even spares me a glance. Then she takes my hand and leads me to my couch. I follow her directions and sit, but what really catches me off guard is when she cups my jaw in her hands, bends at the waist, and kisses me.

My fingers tighten on her wrists, as though that can

hold her in place. Bind her to me. Make her say yes.

Wait, is she going to say yes?

When she pulls away, I let her without protest, though I don't let go of her wrists.

She slides onto the couch next to me, pulling her hands back so that they rest in mine. "I've been thinking a lot about what you said yesterday."

"Which part?" I sound like I haven't had a drink of water in days, my throat parched and my voice hoarse.

"All of it." She takes a deep breath and meets my eyes, her mouth open like she's about to speak, but no words come for a long moment. Finally she gives me a crooked smile. "Sorry. This is harder than I expected."

"It's okay," I tell her, wanting to reassure her. "Whatever it is, just tell me so I know. I think the waiting is harder than knowing at this point."

Her smile turns sardonic. "You're the one who told me to think about it."

I huff a half laugh. "I guess you're right. So what did you think about?"

She shakes her head. "Everything. All the possibilities. And on my own, I couldn't come up with an answer. All I could see were the downsides."

"But?" I prompt when her pause drags on for way too long. Of course way too long might've only been like two seconds. But I'm dying here.

She smiles again, this time all amusement at my impatience. "But Autumn pulled me aside earlier and asked me a very important question that I wasn't really considering."

"What question was that?" My voice is still full of gravel, and no amount of throat clearing appears to make any difference.

"What do I want?"

I blink, waiting.

Her blue eyes examine my face, and her smile breaks free again. "And the answer is that I want you. I kept thinking it was crazy, moving in together and moving halfway across the country when we really haven't known each other very long. But I know that you're a good dad. I know that you care about me and you care about Ben, and ever since you showed up again, you've done everything possible to take care of us, even when I was determined not to let you. Maybe it *is* crazy, and maybe it *is* early, but ..."

She pauses, her eyes meeting mine, her fingers digging into my palms. "I love you, Gray. So yes, we'll move with you when you go. There are a lot of logistics we'll have to figure out, and I want to finish my degree regardless—"

"Of course," I break in, mind reeling. Did she really just say she loves me? She did. She really did. "Of course. I would never ask you to drop out. I know that's important to you, and I don't want to take anything away from you. I want to give you everything."

Pulling my hands from hers, I guide her into my lap, relief swamping me as everything she just said takes root in my brain. I kiss her, hard and fast. "I love you too. You and Ben. I missed you so much while I was gone, and when you wouldn't talk to me, I thought I might go crazy."

She lets out a burbly laugh, tears filling her eyes. "I'm sorry. I was trying not to be a distraction, and it sounds like you're telling me I was a big one."

Cupping her cheeks, I bring her lips to mine for a brief kiss. "You're my favorite distraction," I tell her before kissing her again.

She wraps her arms around my neck, opening for me and sliding her tongue against mine. I don't know if it's because she just agreed to move with me and our relationship suddenly became less ambiguous or what, but somehow she tastes sweeter. Better. Having her in my arms feels right in a way that nothing else ever has. Not even football, and that's the place I've always felt most myself.

Clamping my hands on her ass, I scoot to the edge of the couch. Startled, Tiffany ends the kiss and looks down at me. I give her a quick smile. "Hold on, baby. We're gonna do this right this time. I'm taking you to my bedroom."

With a laugh, she wraps her legs around my waist, her arms holding tighter to my neck as I stand. Holding her like this pulls her tight against my already hard cock, and from the way she sucks in her breath, I know she feels it too. She squeezes my hips with her thighs, rubbing herself on me in tiny movements.

"Fuck, baby," I mutter as I carry her to my bed,

"you're determined to kill me, aren't you?"

"That would be self-defeating," she whispers, then sinks her teeth into my earlobe. And holy shit. I've never had a girl do that to me before. It's erotic in a way I never would've expected, sending heat and goosebumps racing down my spine. All I can do is groan my response and help her rub herself against me.

I can't decide whether to lay her on the bed, or sit on it myself. But when she realizes we've reached the bedroom, she makes the decision for me, unwrapping her legs from my hips and reaching for the floor.

Almost regretfully, I set her on her feet. She drags her hands over my shoulders and down my chest, then slides them back up under my T-shirt. "Arms up," she whispers. Obediently, I raise my arms and let her drag the fabric up, bending to help her pull my shirt off. She rubs her hands over my bare skin, lightly scratching with her nails, admiration and lust stamped on her face.

So many of our encounters have been quiet and quick, the possibility of Ben waking up always hanging over us. We haven't had as much time to explore each other as either of us would like, it seems. As difficult as it is not to just rip off our clothes and sink inside her, I keep my hands at my sides and let her survey my chest at her leisure.

My abs tighten, my breath sucking in as she moves lower, her fingers sifting through the fine hair over my belly button that leads to my waistband.

With a wicked smile on her lips, she hooks her fingers

into my joggers and slides them down. Following their path, she sinks to her knees, and my cock jumps when her breath fans over the tip.

Oh fuuuuck.

I think this just might be the best day of my life.

CHAPTER FORTY-TWO

Tiffany

Gray's soft groan tells me how much he's loving this sweet version of torture. When I slide my hands up his thighs, he sighs. I take my time touching him, watching him, enjoying the feel of firm muscle under skin covered by soft, dark hair.

He's impossibly sexy with his defined chest and abs, trim hips, that V—god, that V—and these powerful thighs. His ass is a sight to behold as well, but I can't see it at the moment. Somehow I feel like making him turn around would be weird, so I don't. Not now, anyway.

Instead, I bring my focus to the proud, hard length that keeps twitching with anticipation if I even so much as breathe on it.

Sliding my hands back up his thighs, I cup his balls with one hand, eliciting another moan, and circle his dick with my other hand. I rub my thumb along the vein on the underside, enjoying the surge of blood I feel there as he grows even harder in my hand. A bead of precum leaks from the tip, and I lick it off, a salty, tasty treat just for me.

I've given blowjobs before to other guys, but I've never enjoyed them as much as I have with Gray. With other guys it was something expected or a kind of transaction—you go down on me, I go down on you—but with Gray it's so much better. He clearly loves it, but doesn't feel entitled to it. And it's that lack of entitlement that makes it such a turn on. That plus the fact that he's letting me take my time and look and feel and touch as much as I want without demanding that I hurry up and get on with it, though his body language makes it abundantly clear that he would like it if I did.

Lifting his cock, I trace my tongue along the underside. His thighs tremble and his balls tighten in my hand just from that. Oh dear. I'm going to have to go slow unless I want him to finish in my mouth. And while I have no doubt he'd make sure I got off too, I think we both want him inside me before he blows.

I make another pass with my tongue before opening my mouth and sucking the crown inside, swirling my tongue over it as well.

He hisses, and his hand cups my cheek. No grabbing, no hair pulling, just a gentle touch designed to communicate appreciation and affection—no, love.

He loves me. He said so. And I love him. And I want to take my time and show him just how much.

I give him the most leisurely blow job I can manage, enjoying his hot, heavy length on my tongue, the way it feels moving between my lips. The entire experience is an exercise in sensuality.

At last, with a groan, he reaches for me. "Please, Tiff. You're killing me. I can't take any more. I need to taste you."

What woman in her right mind could say no to that?

I let him pull me to my feet as he kicks his pants the rest of the way off, raising my arms for him when he lifts my shirt. When I reach behind me to unhook my bra, he gives me a look of censure that has me grinning and dropping my hands.

"This is my job," he grumbles as he undoes my bra and pulls it from my body, his eyes immediately going to my boobs.

He's a boob man to the core. I'd find it kinda funny, except he's so intent and so worshipful, that instead of being funny, it tips the line into feeling somehow sacred. Like *I* am something sacred and beautiful that should be adored, and he is both supplicant and priest.

He bends to give each nipple an open mouth kiss, and when he straightens, he rubs his thumbs over them, making my already hard nipples even harder. And then he smiles at his handiwork, his eyes flicking to mine before he pushes my leggings down my thighs. With one hand on my sternum, he gives me a gentle shove so I fall back on the bed, where he makes quick work of removing the rest of my clothes.

Kneeling before me, he places my legs over his

shoulders. I prop myself up on my elbows, needing to watch this. With his eyes locked on mine, he nuzzles his way up my thighs to my center, rubbing his face all over me before spreading me open with his thumbs.

"So pretty and pink," he murmurs, more like he's talking to himself, and then he licks me from opening to clit with the flat of his tongue.

It's electric after so much teasing, and my whole body jolts.

Lifting his head, he meets my eyes with a shameless grin. Then he does the same thing again.

I relax into the feeling of his mouth on me, surrendering to the fact that he's giving me the same treatment I gave him—slow, leisurely oral focused more on sensation than any specific goal.

And if the sounds he's making are anything to go by, I think he's enjoying this as much as I am.

At a certain point, and I'm not sure what causes the change, he goes from leisurely and sensual to more focused, using the point of his tongue and paying more attention to my clit. When he slides two fingers inside me, I instinctively tighten on them, and he grunts his encouragement. "Yeah, that's it. Let me feel that hot little pussy squeeze my fingers. Pretty soon they're gonna squeeze like that around my cock."

His words combined with the overload of sensation has me scrabbling on the bed for purchase. First I'm grabbing my own hair, cursing as he pumps his fingers in and out of me, curling them up to find that spot deep inside that never fails to send me over the edge, and then

I'm hanging onto the blankets like they'll keep me anchored to the earth when all he's trying to do is send me into the stratosphere.

He redoubles his efforts, like he knows I'll go flying with just another little push, and I do. I come hard, my body curling up involuntarily, a scream of pleasure ripped from my lungs.

He stays between my legs, bringing me down gently, one of his hands sliding up the bed to reach for mine. When I give it to him, he twines our fingers together and holds on like I'm his only anchor in a raging storm.

When my muscles finally go lax, he lets my thighs slip from his shoulders and releases my hand to climb up over me, taking my mouth with a deep, languid kiss that mimics how he started with my pussy.

After a moment he ends the kiss and reaches for a condom. "You ready?" he asks, holding it up between two fingers.

At my nod, he opens the packet and rolls on the condom, kneeling between my spread thighs and rubbing his broad head all over me. I moan at the sensation, and then he slides just the tip inside me. In and out and in and out over and over until I'm glaring at him.

With a soft chuckle, he lowers himself to his elbows, kissing me again as he drives himself all the way inside me.

"Yesss." He kisses me again, starting off slow and easy. But it doesn't stay that way long.

Soon he's reaching between us and strumming his fingers over my clit. "I need you to get there, baby," he whispers. "I need to feel you coming around me. I need you with me. Always."

The double meaning is clear, and I cling to him, squeezing around him voluntarily to increase the sensation until we both come with loud cries of pleasure.

Waves of bliss crash over me, and I surrender to their pull, letting them toss me around and break me into pieces, knowing that when Gray finishes putting me back together, I won't be quite the same. And I'm really okay with that.

Gray has crashed into my life and upended it for a second time. But this time I get a choice. I get to be an active participant instead of reacting after the fact.

And I wouldn't have it any other way.

His heavy weight presses me into the bed, anchoring me back to earth, and I wrap my arms around him, kissing whatever part of his face and neck I can reach.

He turns his head, kissing me deeply before separating his body from mine. After dealing with the condom, he lifts the blankets and we climb in together, actually cuddling in bed for the first time ever, my back tight against his chest, his legs curled behind mine, and his arms wrapped across my chest.

He kisses behind my ear. "I love you."

Turning my head, I give him a smile. "I love you too."

CHAPTER FORTY-THREE

Tiffany

For the first time in my life, I'm willingly sitting down to watch the NFL draft. My dad watches it every year, being a coach and die-hard football fan, it's no surprise. And while I don't mind watching games, the draft is typically as interesting to me as watching paint dry.

But this year everything's different. The next who knows how many years will be determined by the results of this draft. I guess, arguably, the rest of my life will be determined today. Because whoever drafts him will affect how much playing time he gets, and if he gets traded in the future and where, and …

That's too much to worry about right now. After more than a month of uncertainty about anything other than that we'd be together, finding out where we'll be headed will be a huge relief.

While Gray's ideas about Ben and I moving into his apartment were workable, I decided it would be best if we didn't officially move in together until we're wherever we end up. That way Ben gets plenty of time with his grandparents while we're still here and also so we don't have to deal with the stress and routine upheaval of moving twice in such a short period of time. Plus, there wouldn't be room for all Ben's toys at Gray's place.

That doesn't mean we haven't been spending plenty of time at Gray's, and we've been spending the night every weekend. Gray got the trundle he suggested for Ben, that way he doesn't have to sleep on the couch every time we come over. And since we're going to be moving in together, I lifted the no PDA in front of Ben rule, much to Gray's delight.

Mine too, if I'm being honest. And even my dad has come around to the idea of Gray and me together. He grumbled something once about Gray at least being man enough to do the right thing, and since then he's been, if not warm, at least not openly hostile.

Mom, for her part, is thrilled that we're giving things a shot since she thinks we're adorable together, even if she is sad that we'll be moving away. I think she's also secretly relieved that she won't have to spend so much time babysitting, even if she'll miss all the time she gets to spend with her grandson. Fortunately for her, we'll be visiting plenty.

We've also become fixtures at Gray's family's Thursday night dinners, and I've gotten to know Piper a lot better. Since her parents are with Gray at the draft, I invited her and Ellie over to watch with me since both their boyfriends are there too.

"Oh my god, are they ever going to stop talking?" Ellie grouses beside me. "I don't care about all the stats of every player from here to New Jersey!" She rolls her hand. "Get on with it!"

My dad chuckles from his recliner and shakes his head. "This is how it goes. The talking heads have to earn their pay."

Ellie rolls her eyes dramatically. "Why? Do we really need all this speculation and nonsense? It's not like they really know who's going to get picked by which team. And we'll all find out the answer in just a few minutes if they would stop talking long enough for things to get started."

"I think they're talking to fill the time before things get started," Piper points out reasonably. "I doubt the sportscasters are delaying anything."

Piper's reasonableness doesn't seem to mollify Ellie any, but she subsides into grumpy grumbling to herself instead of complaining out loud.

Piper glances around to make sure no little ears are listening, then leans close with one hand in front of her mouth and loudly whispers, "Don't mind Ellie. She's just grumpy about Simon being gone. Not enough Vitamin D, if you know what I mean."

Ellie gasps, looking at Piper with wide eyes full of betrayal. She slaps Piper's arm. "Shut up! And it's not like you're in any better shape."

Studying her fingernails, Piper shrugs. "I seem to be holding up better than you."

With a snort, Ellie shakes her head. "Please. Just this morning you were whining about how much you miss Cal and how you're looking forward to seeing him on TV so you can at least get a glimpse of him. At least when I'm complaining to you, it's not about your brother!"

They both glance at me, and I hold up my hands. "I promise I'm not going to complain about missing Gray in front of my dad."

Their eyes grow wide and they dart glances at my dad, who's covering his mouth with his hand, obviously to hide his smile at their antics, and keeping his eyes studiously focused on the TV. He points the remote at it and turns up the volume way too loud.

"Hey!" Mom yells from the kitchen, where she's putting together more snacks. "Too loud!" You'd think we were having a movie night or a Super Bowl party the way she's making food for everyone. But that's Mom. If people are over, we must have snacks.

Dad obediently turns the volume back down. A little.

"Sorry, Dad," I tell him. "We'll stop. Right?" I glare meaningfully at Piper and Ellie, who nod sheepishly.

"Sorry," they both mumble. I guess my dad blends into the background so well that they just forgot he was here.

Soon the draft gets underway. At last. Though, much to Ellie's annoyance, there's still plenty of talking from the sportscasters between every pick and while the latest choice holds up his jersey with the coaches from his new team.

With each pick, we all get a little more antsy. Gray was predicted to be a first round pick, but so far, his name hasn't been called. Each time a team takes the podium, I hold my breath. And each time, let it out in disappointment.

Piper grabs my hand at one point, and even Ben seems to sense that something momentous is happening, because he climbs into my lap, watching the TV with his finger in his mouth, not squirming or asking a million questions, which is entirely unlike him.

I give him a squeeze with my free hand and kiss his forehead. He lifts his face to me and wraps his arms around my neck, giving me a smacking kiss on the cheek.

"Love ya, Benny," I tell him.

"Love you too, Mama," he says in his sweet little voice.

And then I hear it. His name announced by the man standing at the podium. "Grayson Kilpatrick."

"Wait! Who picked him?"

"Florida!" Piper screams next to me.

Gray stands and hugs his parents, and the screen shows Melissa with tears in her eyes as she watches her son walk to the front of the room and take his place behind the podium. He gives a quick thank you speech he wrote ahead of time, puts on the hat, holds up a jersey with the team representatives, and poses for pictures while the sportscasters discuss his stats again and how they think he'll do for Florida.

"Oh my god," I breathe. "We're moving to Florida."

Piper screams next to me, grabbing my arm with both hands. "Oh my god! You're moving to Florida!"

Laughing, I reach over and hug her, letting Ben wriggle out of my lap now that it's over.

Then Ellie's at my side, hugging me with tears in her eyes. "I'm so jealous," she says, giving me a little shove after moving away. "Regardless of where Simon ends up, I won't be there with him."

"Aww, Ellie. It'll be alright," Piper says, moving to give her a hug. "I'll help you plan out how to graduate early. We'll commiserate together, okay?"

Ellie lets out a spluttering laugh. "Easy for you to say. You've been working on graduating early the whole time. I took over a year to decide my major!"

"Yeah, but you got lots of gen eds out of the way *and* you knew all along what you wanted your major to be so you took the right prereqs. It's not like you're behind. We just need to speed a few things up. We can do it. I promise."

Ellie doesn't quite look convinced by Piper's positive, can-do attitude, but doesn't argue more.

"Or you can do like me and finish online or transfer," I put in. Because I understand the tension between wanting to stay and finish and also wanting to be with your person. This way I get to finish *and* be with my person.

Piper wrinkles her nose. "I already have one transfer on the books. I'm not sure another one will work in my favor. It's easier to just do my best to graduate early. Besides, even if I moved with him, I'd be alone more often than not during the season. He'll be traveling for games a ton. And I'd just be kicking around and studying alone anyway."

"That's a good point," Ellie grumbles, even if she sounds like she wishes it weren't true. She turns sad eyes on me. "I'm sad you won't be here to be part of our sad club next year. But I'm happy you get to do what you want. I'm just jealous."

"You girls are missing the rest of the draft," Dad points out, and while he sounds placid about it, like he couldn't care less if they paid attention or not, I know he wishes we'd hush or go somewhere else.

Smiling, I say, "Sorry, Dad. We'll be quiet now."

Ellie mimes zipping her mouth shut and settles back in her spot on the floor. Piper chuckles, but also quiets down and resumes her seat, grabbing a handful of popcorn from the bowl on the table.

I pick up my phone and shoot Gray a text.

Me: Congratulations!! I can't believe we're going to Florida!

It's several hours before I hear back from him, which isn't a surprise. He had to get through the rest of the show and then deal with all the rest of the hoops there with his new agent and the Florida staff. Plus, his parents planned to take him out for dinner to celebrate.

He calls after Ben is in bed, and I'm in my room reading, waiting because I knew he would call eventually. "Hey, baby," he says when I answer. "Sorry for calling so late. It's been nuts here."

"I'm so proud of you," I tell him, smiling wide.

"Thank you." I can hear the smile in his voice. "It all feels so surreal. I can't believe it's really happening."

"Well, believe it, baby. You're getting everything you ever dreamed of."

"And more."

EPILOGUE

Autumn

I don't know if it's the approaching full moon or the fact that it's the weekend before finals, but I'm feeling extra restless tonight.

Maybe it's that I'm finishing up my second year at Marycliff University, and I still don't feel like I have a better handle on where I want my life to head than I did when I first got here.

Sure, the last two years I've been more focused on having fun than finding a purpose, but now at the ripe old age of twenty, that's wearing thin.

It doesn't help that my closest friends have all settled into serious relationships, even if they are about to become long distance. Ellie, my roommate since last year, is in a relationship with the newest left tackle for the Georgia Rebels—and we'll just gloss right on over the overtly racist undertones of such a team mascot. I guess the fact that teams are finally moving on from using Native American imagery as mascots is a step in the right direction. We can't expect them to give up their links to the Confederacy at the same time.

Regardless of my feelings on his team's mascot, I'm happy for Simon. I really am. He's been good for Ellie, grounding her and at the same time pushing her to be the best version of herself. And really, isn't that what we all hope to get out of a relationship?

Which brings me to Piper, who I'll be sharing a house with next year. Ellie and I are partnering up with Piper and Dani to rent a house together. We found an awesome old four bedroom with old growth trees and a big garden not too far from campus. Simon and Cal, Piper's boyfriend and Ellie's older brother, have promised to help us move before they leave for training camp.

Piper and Cal got together last fall too, though their relationship was a lot more contentious to start with. Still, though, they ended up being just what the other needed.

Dani doesn't have a boyfriend, but she seems content being single.

And me?

Well, I've gathered something of a reputation as a man eater.

And it's not that I use and discard men like that. I don't. At least that's not my intention. But I haven't found anyone who I feel connected to in a way that feels good long term.

Meeting someone new, engaging in the flirtation,

exploring our chemistry, all of that's fun. But I'm not wanting to just have a relationship for the sake of having a relationship. And jealousy of what my friends have and wanting that too actually makes me less likely to settle down.

So I drift through a room full of hot athletes at yet another party put on by the football team. Between Ellie and Piper dating nearly-former Marycliff football players and Dani's connection to Eli Foster and the other players she works out with, we all get invited to these kinds of parties.

I smile and flirt with a few of the guys I recognize. But I already slept with Riley, and while he's cute, I'm not interested in a repeat. And he and Andrew are friends, which could get dicey, especially if Riley's still interested, and he obviously is.

Drifting away, I head to the kitchen to refill my drink.

And that's where I find Jackson leaning against the wall. A cute girl in a crop top and a short denim skirt is talking to him, obviously flirting her little heart out. She drags her fingertips across her chest, flips her hair, touches his arm, smiling at him the whole time.

Poor thing. Jackson either isn't interested or is really oblivious. I never have managed to figure out which it is.

Eventually she gives up and wanders off, leaving Jackson alone.

Fresh drink in hand, I sidle up next to him and prop up the wall as well. I have to know what makes this guy tick. I've been coming to these parties all year now, and never once have I seen Jackson look like he's hooked up with someone. And I've literally seen nearly every guy here hook up, including participating in several of said hookups myself. "You know she was flirting with you, right?" I've learned over the last semester in theatre class that the direct approach works best with Jackson.

"What?" He jerks in surprise, his head whipping around to face me. "What are you talking about? No she wasn't. She was just being friendly."

I snort into my cup. "Jackson, when a girl is being that friendly, it means she wants you to take her into a bedroom and screw her brains out."

Goddess bless him, his ears and cheeks turn a delightful shade of pink.

I peer into his cup. "What're you drinking?"

"Just water," he mumbles.

I spy the slice of lime floating around in it. "Pretending it's a G and T?"

He nods.

I clink my plastic cup of water against his. "I'm hitting the water too. Hydration is important."

We stand there in companionable silence for a few minutes as I wait for his embarrassment to fade so I can address him ignoring every single signal that chick was sending once more. "So," I start.

Eyeing me suspiciously, he sips his water. "What?" he demands after a moment.

I grin. Good. He *can* take charge. That's important. "Are you gay?"

He sprays water everywhere. Wiping his face with the back of his hand, he glares at me. "Why in the world would you ask that?"

Shrugging, I lean back against the wall, watching the party through the opening to the living room. "You had no idea that girl was flirting with you. Though, to be fair, the gay guys I know would absolutely be aware a girl was flirting. They just wouldn't encourage it. Which you also didn't. I'm just trying to figure out why." I turn to face him fully, resting my shoulder against the wall. "So fill me in? What's the deal? Plenty of girls have thrown themselves at you over the last year I've been hanging around. I've never once seen you take anyone up on the offer. You not into girls? Or maybe you're not into anyone? I had a friend in high school who was asexual. Are you asexual?"

His cheeks color again, and he covers his eyes with one broad hand. "Oh my god. No. I'm not gay, and I'm not asexual. Can you please stop?"

Straightening, I nod. "Yes, I can. I'm sorry, Jackson. I'm not trying to embarrass you. But if you're not either of those things, and you really don't understand when a girl is interested in you ..." I shrug. "I can help, you know. If you want."

He snorts, clearly torn between mortification and amusement. "Like what? Some kind of love tutor?"

I shrug again. "If that's what you want to call it, sure. I'll be your love tutor. You have my number, so just let me know if you decide you're tired of missing out on what everyone around you is doing. Whenever you're ready." On impulse, I go up on tiptoe and kiss him on the cheek.

He goes stock still, stunned by my brazen kissing I guess.

"Sorry," I say again. It seems I'm forever apologizing to this boy. I pat him on the chest and leave, wondering if he'll take me up on my offer.

It'd be fun teaching him what flirting looks like. How to flirt. Maybe he'd need help with kissing too. We had that stage kiss in theatre class a couple months ago and he didn't seem hopeless, but if he lacks confidence, having someone build up his ego could be good. I'd happily do that for him. And maybe that would give me the direction I'm craving. At least for a little while …

Acknowledgements

As always, there are people to thank that helped bring this book to life!

To Deb, my long-suffering editor who listened to me complain about how hard of a time I was having with this book until I finally had the light bulb moment that made it all work.

To Leslie for always challenging me to think carefully about my word choices and doesn't complain about getting random memes from me on a semi regular basis. I can't believe it's been over six years that we've been helping each other!

To all my friends and family who stood by me through the writing of this book. You know what was happening, and know that I appreciate you so, so much.

To my Book Junkies and Book Club members who've been excited for this book all along. Your excitement and encouragement buoy me when things get difficult.

To Grey's Promotions, who've done an amazing job with every release I've worked with them on. Thanks for squeezing me in on a shorter timeline than normal since I was a bit behind with this one on everything. You're the best!

To all the bloggers, bookstagrammers, and reviewers who signed up for ARCs. Thanks so much for taking your time and energy to help promote this slice of my imagination! I hope you enjoyed visiting and getting to know the characters and come back for another trip to Marycliff University!

And as always, a special thanks to you, dear reader. Your reviews and comments and the time you spend reading my words make it a joy to bring you new stories.

Thank you!

Jerica MacMillan has been reading romance since she stumbled into the paperback section of the library as a middle schooler. And it's been an ongoing love affair ever since!

You can frequently find her sipping coffee out of snarky mugs while dreaming up stories and trying to bring them to life on the page. Join her Book Club at www.jericamacmillan.com/book-club and get a free book!

Marycliff Football
Off Limits
Trick Play
Unrivaled
The Love Playbook

Players of Marycliff University
Summer Fling
Close Quarters
Always You
Unsaid Things
Coping Skills
False Assumptions
A Very Marycliff Christmas

Cataclysm
Anything You Need
Shouldn't Want You
Everything I Want
Just For Now
Anyone But You

Songs and Sonatas Series
Double Exposition
Development
Recapitulation
Broken Chords
Counterpoint and Harmony
Overtones
Reverb
The Arrangement